"I know you never wanted to see me again. But what either of us wants doesn't matter a damn right now."

Gently Cord shifted the tiny figure in his arms.

"Whose—whose child is she?" Julia forced the question out from between lips that felt as if they'd been frozen.

"She's mine."

Above her, his low voice delivered the information she hadn't wanted to hear. Julia felt as if the ground beneath her was slipping away, letting her slide back into the void she'd so recently escaped.

She raised her head and looked at Cord. "Where's her mother?"

One corner of Cord's mouth hitched up in that wry half smile she'd never quite forgotten, but his obsidian eyes held no hint of humor. "I said she was my child, Julia." He tightened his grip on the girl clasped to his chest. "I should have said she's ours."

Dear Reader,

Welcome to another month of hot—in every sense of the word—reading, books just made to match the weather. I hardly even have to mention Suzanne Brockmann and her TALL, DARK & DANGEROUS miniseries, because you all know that this author and these books are utterly irresistible. *Taylor's Temptation* features the latest of her to-die-for Navy SEALs, so rush right down to your bookstore and pick up your own copy, because this book is going to be flying off shelves everywhere.

To add to the excitement this month, we're introducing a new six-book continuity called FIRSTBORN SONS. Award-winning writer Paula Detmer Riggs kicks things off with *Born a Hero*. Learn how these six heroes share a legacy of protecting the weak and standing up for what's right—and watch as all six find women who belong in their arms and their lives.

Don't miss the rest of our wonderful books, either: *The Seduction of Goody Two-Shoes,* by award-winning Kathleen Creighton; *Out of Nowhere,* by one of our launch authors, Beverly Bird; *Protector with a Past,* by Harper Allen; and *Twice Upon a Time,* by Jennifer Wagner.

Finally, check out the back pages for information on our "Silhouette Makes You A Star" contest. Someone's going to win—why not you?

Enjoy!

Leslie J. Wainger
Executive Senior Editor

Please address questions and book requests to:
Silhouette Reader Service
U.S.: 3010 Walden Ave., P.O. Box 1325, Buffalo, NY 14269
Canadian: P.O. Box 609, Fort Erie, Ont. L2A 5X3

Protector
with a Past
HARPER ALLEN

Silhouette®

INTIMATE MOMENTS™

Published by Silhouette Books

America's Publisher of Contemporary Romance

To David Brennan, the big brother I never really got to know.

I would like to thank the following people for their invaluable and generous help in researching various details in this book: Ruth McDiarmid, Keith Fleury, Dan Taylor and P.K., who asked to remain anonymous.

 SILHOUETTE BOOKS

ISBN 0-373-27161-1

PROTECTOR WITH A PAST

Copyright © 2001 by Sandra Hill

Visit Silhouette at www.eHarlequin.com

Printed in U.S.A.

Books by Harper Allen

Silhouette Intimate Moments

Protector with a Past #1091

Harlequin Intrigue

The Man That Got Away #468
Twice Tempted #547
Woman Most Wanted #599

HARPER ALLEN

lives in the country in the middle of a hundred acres of maple trees with her husband, Wayne, six cats, four dogs—and a very nervous cockatiel at the bottom of the food chain. For excitement she and Wayne drive to the nearest village and buy jumbo bags of pet food. She believes in love at first sight because it happened to her.

SILHOUETTE MAKES YOU A STAR!
Feel like a star with Silhouette.
Look for the exciting details of our new contest
inside all of these fabulous Silhouette novels:

Chapter 1

Julia's scream echoed in her ears as she jerked bolt upright in the dark, her eyes wide open, her heart crashing painfully against her ribs and the last shreds of the nightmare still fogging her mind.

Dear God—the child! Save the child!

She snapped the small bedside lamp on with an automatic gesture and her frozen gaze rested uncomprehendingly on the familiar room around her. Then she felt a cold nose nudging worriedly against her tightly clenched fist and she came back to reality with shuddering abruptness. King whined and nudged her again, his eyes fixed on her.

"Same old, same old, boy," she said shakily. Her voice sounded raspy and hoarse and she realized that she was speaking too loudly. She lowered her tone, feeling foolish. "Both of us should be used to this by now."

Reassured by the sound of her words, the German shepherd beat his tail briefly against the wide pine planks of the floor and stood up expectantly. She smiled tiredly at him. "Yeah, you know the routine—hot milk for me, a dog biscuit for you. Let me get my slippers on."

The sheets, wet with sweat and tangled around her legs like a hasty shroud, bore mute witness to her recent terror but Julia resolutely shut her mind to it. Like she'd said, she should be used to it by now, she thought grimly, peeling the sheets from her legs with distaste and reaching for the old chenille robe draped over a nearby chair. She shoved her feet impatiently into a pair of scuffs that, like the robe, had seen better days. She'd been having the nightmare for almost two years now, ever since—

She stood up and yanked the belt of the robe tightly around her waist. Pushing the damp tendrils of hair from her forehead with a trembling hand, she took a deep breath and deliberately let her gaze dwell on the comforting and homely objects around her. The dog stood beside her quietly, recognizing this as part of the ritual they always went through.

The desk where she'd written her most private girlhood diary entries stood against the wall. A single round stone sat on one corner of the varnished maple surface, and almost unconsciously she reached over and picked it up, holding it tightly in her hand. It felt as silky and cool as lake water against her palm as she looked around the rest of the room, her breathing slowing to a steadier rate.

Earlier in the day she'd crammed a handful of yellow and purple pansies into a jelly glass, and now the warm pool of light from the lamp cast a velvety glow on them. On the wall just above the bedside table was an antique framed lithograph of two children walking hand in hand across a rickety bridge over a chasm; behind them an angel with flowing golden hair watched out for their safety. It had hung there for as long as she could remember. The photograph beside it had been there for years, too. It showed a skinny little boy in swimming trunks, standing on a dock and proudly holding up a trout as big as his arm.

She swayed slightly. King leaned his body solidly against her leg, his attention focused on her.

The overstuffed chair by the bed was covered in a faded maroon fabric, and there was a lump in the back where a spring had worked its way loose, but she'd read *Gone With the Wind* for the first time sitting in that chair. Besides, if she replaced it she'd have to throw out the small, drum-shaped maroon leather hassock that went with it so well, and she knew she'd never be able to do that.

She'd taken that hassock out of Davey's room soon after it had happened, tugging it down the hallway with all her five-year-old might, just to have something of him close by in that frightening and confusing time. It still had the tiny rip in it from when one of his fishhooks had torn through the leather and he'd made her promise not to tell on him.

The stone was pressing into the bones of her hand, and she relaxed her grip on it slightly. The small bookcase by the easy chair, the dark green braided rug by the bed that King slept on, the leaf-patterned curtains at the window—everything was comfortingly familiar. They hadn't changed since she was a child, and their very shabbiness was part of what she'd come back here for, two years ago.

Time stood still in this forgotten corner of upstate New York. If she got in her Jeep and drove down the rutted dirt road to town, if she took the turning just past Mason's Corners that led to the highway, she knew that she'd find the rest of the world was spinning as erratically and as violently as she remembered. But she wasn't going to take that drive, Julia thought with bleak determination. The outside world had come close to crushing her once, and only this sanctuary had kept her from self-destructing completely.

She was safe here. She wouldn't allow anything to upset the fragile equilibrium she'd finally achieved. And if the nightmares were the price she had to pay, then she'd just have to deal with them one night at a time.

She slipped the stone into her robe pocket and dropped her hand onto King's head. "No television, no newspapers, no phone. Just you and me and the lake and the woods, buddy. And that's the way we're going to keep it." She absently ruffled the spot at the back of his ear that he never could quite reach himself, and he heaved a sigh of pure contentment. As she left the room he padded like a silent bodyguard behind her.

The electric clock on the kitchen wall showed almost three-thirty. In another hour she could walk down to the dock and wait for the sun to rise. Instead of reaching for a saucepan to heat milk in, Julia filled the battered tin percolator with cold water from the kitchen tap and spooned coffee grounds into the metal basket that sat inside. She switched on the stove burner and almost fell over King as she turned to sit down at the kitchen table. The brown eyes looking up at her held a hint of reproach.

"Oh—right." She no longer worried that she sounded crazy, talking to him as if he could understand every word she said— if anything, having him as a companion had probably helped her stay sane. Besides, she wasn't absolutely sure he didn't understand English. "One late-night snack, coming up." She opened the cupboard over the counter and pulled down the bag of Milk-Bones, and as she did her glance fell on the tall, square-sided bottle pushed to the back, half-hidden behind the bags of rice and macaroni. For a moment its contents caught the light and shone liquidly gold.

"Like a gentleman," she said, holding out the biscuit. King obliged, taking the treat from her with almost ludicrous daintiness and then settling down in the corner by the door to the screened-in back porch to crunch it enthusiastically with his strong white teeth. She folded the bag closed again, put it back on the shelf and started to shut the cupboard door. Then she stopped.

She kept it there to prove to herself that she could leave it alone. Being afraid to even look at it gave it the very power over her that she was trying to deny. She raised herself on her tiptoes, reached past the bag of rice and grasped the bottle by its neck.

It was full. She'd bought it two winters ago, on one of her infrequent trips to town, and the owner of the liquor store had rung her purchase up quizzically, obviously expecting her to be back later in the week. At the time Julia was half-convinced that his cynical guess would turn out to be right. She'd unpacked her groceries when she'd gotten home, and after she'd put everything else away she'd sat down and pulled the bottle out of its brown paper bag. She'd set it in the middle of the kitchen table—for some reason, she remembered, it had been vitally important that it sat in the exact right spot—and she'd stared at it.

Later that afternoon it had begun to snow, and the wind had whistled off the frozen lake in steadily increasing gusts. King had dozed fitfully at her feet, whining uneasily in his sleep, and she had continued to sit there, staring at the bottle and knowing that all she had to do was reach out her hand, unscrew the cap and pour herself that first drink to blunt the razor-like memories that were crowding in.

Outside, the sun had put on a brief, bloody display before sinking below the horizon, and then the shadows had deepened and strengthened into night. With total darkness had come the ghosts, as they always did, but this time she had been facing them alone. She'd been aware of them, just at the corner of her vision, grouped around her silently.

She'd known who they were and what they wanted. They wanted her to remember, but remembering would be fatal. Keeping her gaze fixed on the bottle in the exact middle of her kitchen table, she had fought two battles that night—one against a false ally and one against enemies who had never meant her any harm.

When morning had come, a thin gray light edging the far side of the lake, she'd still been sitting there but the bottle was unopened.

And all the ghosts except one had faded away.

He was with her now. He'd always be with her, she thought wearily. It had been his name that she'd screamed out in her nightmare, him that she'd been calling for, and it was his ghost that she'd never been strong enough to push away completely. Sometimes she thought that if she whirled around as fast as she could, she'd catch him standing behind her, that straight black hair falling into one dark eye the way it used to, that wryly devastating smile hitching up the corner of his mouth. Sometimes just before she fell asleep she was sure she could almost hear his voice—husky and incongruously soft for such a big man, as if he'd never found a need to raise it—calling her name.

Those nights were the worst.

The percolator began to rattle and looking over at the stove, Julia saw coffee splashing up like a miniature fountain inside the glass knob of the lid. She slid the pot off the element. He was gone. She had made sure of that herself, had left him no reason to stay with her. It had been deliberate on her part, and it had worked. He was gone, and she knew that after their last confrontation he would never come back. He was probably married by now, she thought, pouring coffee into an ironware mug. She closed her eyes and took a sip. He'd been the marrying kind. He'd wanted a family of his own.

The coffee that had been boiling only seconds ago flooded her mouth with scalding heat, and she put the mug down hastily, feeling the prickle of tears behind her eyelids in reaction. He'd be married, and his wife would be strong and uncomplicated, able to take whatever life threw at her without flinching. Julia wondered what she would look like. He'd moved to California the last she'd heard, and she imagined his wife to be tall and blond and lightly tanned, with smooth tennis player's muscles in her arms and the clear blue eyes of someone who'd grown up beside the Pacific. He wouldn't have chosen anyone who bore the slightest resemblance to the woman who'd ripped his world apart, so she definitely wouldn't be fragile-looking and brown-haired, with shadowed hazel eyes. Her mouth wouldn't look a little too wide for her face, and she'd probably be able to wear a low-cut dress without feeling like her collarbones were the most prominent feature exposed.

By the door King got slowly to his feet, his ears pricked forward alertly, but Julia was lost in thought.

They'd have children. It felt as if she'd taken a dull knife and twisted it in her heart, but she forced herself to go on. They'd have the children she'd vowed she'd never have herself, and whatever their mother looked like, the children would be smaller versions of him. Somewhere on the other side of the continent the Seneca heritage that had manifested itself so strongly in him would give his offspring high cheekbones and eyes so brown they almost looked black. His children would be beautiful.

They could have been hers.

She could hear the wind sifting through the topmost branches of the maples that surrounded the house, and somewhere in the woods an owl must have fallen from the blackness onto its prey, because the silence of the night was split with a faraway, high-pitched cry that was choked off abruptly. She flinched. Then she set her shoulders with fatigued determination. It was still well before dawn, but suddenly she knew she couldn't stay inside a moment longer. Tonight had been one of the bad ones. She was edging perilously close to the abyss, and it had taken her too long to climb out the last time to risk falling in again.

She picked up the bottle briskly and started to put it back in the cupboard. Behind her, King whined strangely, and his nails scrabbled at the screen door in excitement.

"In a minute, boy." She glanced over her shoulder and saw the figure standing on the other side of the screen.

It was just as she'd always thought—if she turned around fast enough he'd be there, watching her. But in her imagination he'd always been alone.

He was holding a small child to his chest. Tiny arms were twined around his neck in a desperate grip. He wasn't smiling and he looked as if he hadn't slept for days, and Julia knew with icy certainty that he wasn't a hallucination.

He was real. He'd come back. He'd brought a *child* with him.

The bottle fell from her nerveless fingers and smashed into pieces on the kitchen floor.

"What are you doing here?"

Her whisper was cracked and harsh. The sharp fumes of the whiskey overpowered the smell of coffee in the kitchen, but she hardly noticed. King pressed his nose against the screen and wagged his tail furiously.

"He remembers me. Let me in, Julia."

His words were spoken softly, and he made no move to un-latch the screen door and walk in uninvited. She didn't have to do it, she thought swiftly, meeting his gaze. If she told him to leave, he would. She knew that, because the two of them had lived through a scene similar to this before, and when Cord had realized that she'd meant what she said, he'd turned around and walked out of her life.

But this time he had a child with him. And even though he couldn't have known that was the worst thing he could do to her, after that first quick glance she couldn't bring herself to look at the tiny figure in his arms.

"I know you never wanted to see me again. But what either of us wants doesn't matter a damn right now."

Against all her expectations, he shifted the child gently and used his free hand to open the screen door. He stepped inside, and those strong brown fingers that she remembered so well dropped briefly to the top of King's head. The dog grinned up at him, his tail wagging with pleasure.

"Whose—whose child is she?"

She forced the question out from between lips that felt as if they'd been frozen. Without waiting for his answer she reached under the sink for the small dustpan and whisk broom she kept there for emergencies, and avoiding his eyes, she started sweeping the shards of glass up. The whiskey was an amber pool that spread halfway across the kitchen floor, and the smell was so pungent that she felt as if she was going to throw up.

"Get her out of here, Cord. There's nothing I can do for her, so just turn around and take her away. You never should have brought her here."

Her head bent over her task, her words came out in a wrenching undertone and her vision blurred suddenly. The next moment she felt a slicing pain and through the sheen of tears she saw the blood already welling up from the ball of her thumb.

"I can't do that. She's mine."

Above her, his low voice delivered the information that she hadn't wanted to hear, had never wanted to know, and suddenly the pain in her hand was nothing. Julia felt as though the ground underneath her was slipping away, letting her slide back into the void that she'd so recently escaped, but this time she knew she'd never be able to climb out again.

It was true, then. He'd made a child with someone else, started a family that belonged to him and some unknown woman. She'd wanted him to do that. She'd wanted to be part of his past, to be left alone by him, but his confirmation of what she'd previously only guessed at was too much to bear.

Oblivious to the slow crimson drops that were falling from her hand and turning to bright umber as they hit the spilled liquor, she raised her head and looked at him.

"Where's her mother?"

One corner of Cord's mouth hitched up in that wry half smile that she had never quite forgotten, but the obsidian eyes held no hint of humor. "I said she was my child, Julia." He tightened his grasp on the silent little body. "I should have said she was ours."

Chapter 2

"**Y**ou're bleeding." His glance moved past her white, stricken face to the gash on her thumb, and his instant concern overrode whatever he'd been about to say. "Let me get her to a bed and I'll help you. Is Davey's—is the spare room made up?"

He took her silence for affirmation and strode down the hall, the child still motionless, her head tucked into the curve of his neck, a silky-fine swath of red hair mingling against the midnight-black of his. The heart-shaped little face was pale with what could have been exhaustion, but the blue eyes peering over Cord's shoulder were open wide and staring at nothing. It wasn't exhaustion, Julia thought suddenly. She'd seen that fixed, unfocused gaze often enough to recognize it, even after all this time. Something had happened to this child—something that had caused her to retreat temporarily to a secret place deep inside herself where no one could reach her.

She pushed the thought aside almost fearfully as she saw them disappear into Davey's bedroom. She was already letting herself get involved, and that could be disastrous. For the child's sake, she had to keep her distance.

Getting stiffly to her feet and moving to the sink, she heard him talking quietly in the bedroom, but if he was getting any answer from his small companion the child's voice was too soft to carry as far as the kitchen. King's ears pricked up with interest, and he trotted down the hall to the bedroom at the snicking sound that meant Cord had unlatched the window to get some air into the stuffy room. He knew this house as well as she did, she thought. He'd been in and out of here since they'd both been children themselves.

What the hell had he meant?

They'd never had children together—never would, now. She turned the cold tap on, holding her hand beneath the icy water and watching the crimson sluice away down the drain. When the bleeding slowed, she one-handedly reached for a clean dish towel and wrapped it around her thumb before bending again to pick up the dustpan.

"Let me finish that." He came into the kitchen, King at his heels. His movements were deft and economical, and within a minute all traces of the glass had been disposed of and the floor was almost dry. He stood at the sink, wringing out the rag he'd mopped the liquor up with, and Julia stood by silently, feeling the tension build inside her.

Whatever his reasons for coming here and whoever the little girl was, they couldn't stay. She had to make him see that. She had no idea why he'd said what he had about the child belonging to the two of them and she didn't even want to know. That part of her life was over.

Everything she'd once been had burned away in a single searing moment two years ago. Only through the grace of God had her self-destruction narrowly missed destroying an innocent victim.

She couldn't let him know that, but she wouldn't let them stay.

For a split second Julia saw again the heart-shaped little face with the blue, doll-like gaze. She thrust the image away from her.

"Whatever you want from me, the answer is no. I'm not responsible for that child, Cord, no matter what cryptic comments you choose to make. You'll have to go when she's had some rest.''

She felt the shaking start and she turned away from him, willing her body not to betray her. The muscles in her arms tensed as she hugged herself tightly, the dish towel still wrapped around her hand. Slowly the tremors subsided.

''But she is your responsibility. She's *our* responsibility.'' The husky voice behind her held a thread of incredulity. ''Dammit, Julia—don't you realize who she is?''

When she'd been a child she'd had a kaleidoscope. It had been the old-fashioned kind, with bits of colored glass that tumbled noisily every time she twisted the metal cylinder, and there had always been a slight delay between the sound of the glass rattling into place and the jewel-like pattern bursting into existence in the dark tube in front of her eyes.

It was as if she heard Cord's words clicking into place inside her brain, but for a moment she couldn't see what they meant. Then everything suddenly made a terrible kind of sense. Julia whirled around to face him, her unhurt hand flying to her mouth as if to hold back the words that spilled from her lips.

''Dear God—she's *Lizbet*, isn't she?'' She searched his expression apprehensively, and the pain she saw on his features sent a chill through her. ''Paul and Sheila—are they all right? What happened, Cord? Were they in an accident?''

Her voice had risen steadily on each unanswered question, and with two strides he was in front of her, pulling her to his chest and holding her tightly. He smelled of the whiskey she'd spilled, she thought incongruously. Her mind skittered away from the terror it already sensed was about to envelop it and frantically tried to busy itself with irrelevancies.

He was wearing a blue chambray shirt that she was almost sure she remembered from before. Blue had always looked good against the coppery tan of his skin and the blue-black sheen of his hair. His jeans still rode low on his lean hips, and her head still came to the exact place on his chest where she could hear his heart beating. She felt his hand on her hair.

''It's as bad as it can be, Julia. Get ready for it.'' His breath was warm against her temple, and his voice shook slightly. She felt the icy dread coalesce into a stomach-clenching certainty, and she cut him off before he could continue.

"I didn't recognize her at first. She's grown so fast, Cord! She must be four—no, five now. Remember when we went to her third birthday party, and the clown tried to give her a balloon and she started crying? And you'd just gotten King for me, and she gave him cake under the table and Sheila and I put a party hat on him and took pictures of him and Lizbet, both with their hats on and both of them with icing smeared all over their faces?"

She was babbling into his chest, her words tumbling over one another. Her throat felt as if it was constricting, and she raced on, refusing to meet his eyes.

"Remember when she was baptised and she wore the same antique lace gown that Sheila had worn, and her mother and grandmother before her? And you said that you wanted to be around when it was brought out for Lizbet's firstborn, and Paul said he wasn't planning on letting her start dating until she was thirty? And we all started laughing, and then when the priest called us forward to make our vows as her godparents I started—I started crying and I couldn't—I couldn't—"

Her throat had closed up completely, and the torrent of words came to an enforced stop. Inside her an intolerable pressure was building, desperately seeking release, but at the same time it felt as if her rib cage was being squeezed tighter and tighter by some cruel, gigantic hand.

She raised her head from his chest, unaware of the tears streaming down her face. Her eyes slowly met his. Her pupils were enormously wide, as if they were attempting to find and collect a glimmer of light where there was none.

"They're dead, aren't they?" With the harshness of ripping silk, her hoarse whisper sliced through the silence.

She'd never seen him cry before but now his skin was wet, and even as she watched, the shimmer at the outer corners of his eyes spilled over into slow silvery tracks that gleamed against his tan. He held her gaze and didn't attempt to hide his tears or brush them away.

"I like your version better," he said. "I like thinking about them the way they were when we were all together. But yes. They're dead." His voice cracked and his grasp on her tightened painfully. "They were killed, Julia. Somebody killed them."

"No!" The cry burst from her before he'd finished speaking.

"All the way up here I was trying to think of a way to break it gently. There isn't any." His eyes were shadowed and the faint lines around his mouth that hadn't been there two years ago deepened, but she was beyond noticing. She shook her head in refusal and tried to push herself away from him. He didn't release his hold on her.

"Cord, you—you're crazy! You show up here with some insane story about our best friends being killed and expect me to believe it? What the hell are you trying to do?"

In the corner by the door King looked up worriedly, aroused by her tone. "I won't accept it. It's all some crazy lie or you've got your information wrong or—or something! Paul and Sheila murdered? Things like that just don't happen!"

"Things like that do happen. Before you left the force you used to see it every working day of your life, Julia." His words were low and intense. "They're not supposed to but they do. I saw them myself, just minutes—" He stopped, and a muscle worked in his jaw. "Just minutes after," he continued bleakly. "I was just a few minutes too late."

She'd known from the first that it was true, but denying it was a way of keeping Paul and Sheila Durant alive for the space of another heartbeat or two. She hadn't seen them for years, Julia thought wrenchingly. She hadn't been able to see anyone. But in the back of her mind she'd always known that they were there—Sheila, with her glorious mass of red hair and her wicked sense of humor, and Paul, as far from the conventional conception of a cop as possible with his glasses continually slipping down his beaky nose, his gangling frame giving the impression of clumsiness and his wryly self-deprecating attitude never completely concealing the overwhelming pride he felt in his beautiful wife and the daughter he adored.

It had been enough to know that they were still a part of her universe, even if the probability of her picking up the thread of their old relationship was about as remote as the stars she stared at, sitting on the dock during those long nights when she was afraid to fall asleep.

And now they were gone—all Sheila's fire, all Paul's steady warmth, extinguished. Her world had suddenly become a colder, darker place.

This time when she drew away from his embrace Cord didn't attempt to stop her. She unwound the bulky dish towel from her hand and stared at the cut on her thumb as if she had nothing more important to occupy her mind and saw with dull surprise that it had stopped bleeding—which was strange, she thought hazily, since somewhere deep inside her she felt as if she was hemorrhaging.

As Cord walked over to the window and looked out into the night, his shoulders sagging with weariness and pain, she got a bandage out of the small first-aid kit she kept under the sink for emergencies and covered up the small wound. It was a clean cut. It would heal without a scar.

"Tell me what happened." She pressed the edges of the bandage down neatly, smoothing them carefully and methodically and keeping her attention focused on the trivial task. Her hand was trembling.

"The killer was after Lizbet, too." Fatigue made his voice grainy, but if he was surprised that her initial denial of what he'd told her had been replaced by an unwilling acceptance, he didn't show it. "Paul had been doing some renovating in the basement, and at the first shot from upstairs he put her in the crawl space behind the newly installed drywall and told her not to make a sound. Then he went upstairs and was killed himself. After that second shot Lizbet apparently heard the shooter going through the house room by room, calling her name, but she did what her father had told her and stayed silent. I'm not even sure if she knows exactly what happened to her parents, but she's one terrified little girl."

"Whoever did this *knew* them?"

She'd thought there was no new horror to come. It seemed she'd been wrong. Julia choked back the bile that rose in her

throat and as Cord turned from the window to face her she saw
that the same conclusion had already crossed his mind.

"Well enough to know they had a daughter and what her
name was." He met her stunned gaze. "Paul phoned me yesterday and told me that he'd had the feeling someone had been
following him the last few days. Added to that, Sheila had been
getting weird calls on her cell phone and one of the teachers at
the summer day camp Lizbet was going to in the mornings had
told them that all her artwork had been slashed—none of the
other kids' work was touched. He was worried enough to ask
me to fly out and stay with them for a while."

"But why not just alert the local authorities? For God's sake,
Cord, when a police officer's family is threatened that's priority
one with his co-workers! Why was his first impulse to call you
in all the way from California?"

His eyes darkened. They glittered like black diamonds in the
tan of his face, and all of a sudden she saw the hard-edged,
implacably committed detective he'd been when they'd both
worked together so long ago—the detective he still was.

"He knew he could trust me. He couldn't be sure about
anyone else, since whoever was phoning Sheila had to have
gotten her cell phone number from the precinct. You know why
she carried that damn phone. Only his work had the number,
and it was only ever to be used for one reason."

*"I pray it never rings, Julia. But if anything happened to
Paul and they couldn't get in touch with me I wouldn't be able
to forgive myself for not being with him. I carry it all the time—
just in case…"*

It had been the only time Sheila had confessed the fear that
lurked beneath her wholehearted support of her husband's career choice. She'd been haunted by the worst-case scenario that
every cop's spouse tried not to dwell on—that one day the man
she loved would go to work and never come home alive.

Instead, Paul had been killed in his own home. And Sheila
had been taken down first. The thought that one of his fellow
officers might have had something to do with it seemed the
most monstrous betrayal of all.

"I caught the first flight available." His words came out with an effort. "As soon as I got to their house I knew something was wrong—the front door was open wide. I ran in with my gun drawn and the first thing I saw was Sheila's body in the hall. She'd been killed instantly."

"Thank God she didn't suffer, at least," Julia whispered brokenly. She held back the tears that were threatening again and bit her lip to keep the sobs from rising to her throat.

"Paul had been shot at the top of the basement stairs. I found him half in and half out of the doorway, but he'd been rolled over onto his back." Cord's mouth tightened grimly. "He'd been stabbed in the chest, as well."

And the hits just keep on coming. Julia swayed and felt behind her for the familiar solidity of the countertop.

"I don't want to know any more." Her voice was barely audible. A sliver of panicky urgency ran through it. "They're dead—isn't that enough? I hope whoever did this to them is caught and brought to justice, but even justice won't bring Paul and Sheila back. There's nothing we can do to make it right again, Cord—absolutely *nothing*—so what's the use of going over every terrible detail?"

He looked at her as if she was speaking a foreign language. "Those details, as you call them, are clues. How the hell are we supposed to track down the killer if you refuse to examine the *details?*"

His voice had a raw edge to it, and with a quick glance at the hallway where the bedrooms were he went on more quietly. "I know you were planning on quitting when I left—when you told me to get out of your life. You wanted to come back to the kind of life and the kind of people you'd grown up with— people who knew a Monet from a Manet, whose carefully rustic summer properties cost more than the homes of the ordinary working stiffs that you'd been forced to rub shoulders with for too long, people who hired men like my father to work for them. I accepted that, finally."

"That's right," she said through stiff lips. "So now I leave the detective work to the professionals—like you, Cord. It's not what I do anymore."

"I'm beginning to realize that." His glance took in the

shabby robe she was wearing, the battered scuffs on her feet and the dark circles under her eyes. It rested finally on her bandaged hand. "But what I haven't figured out is what you have been doing for the past couple of years—aside from getting up in the middle of the night to reach for the bottle, that is."

"I haven't had a drink for nineteen months." Even as she snapped out the automatic reply she realized her mistake. Before she could gloss it over, he'd picked up on her slip. His eyes narrowed appraisingly on her.

"The only people who know exactly how long it's been since their last drink are the ones who found it damned hard to quit," he said slowly. "Just what in hell's been happening to you since you threw me out of your life? You're living here year-round, aren't you? You never returned to your old life at all—you just retreated from everything. For God's sake, Julia, have you been here by *yourself* for two whole years?"

For one dangerous moment she felt like pouring out everything. Then common sense reasserted itself. No matter how tempting it might be to reveal her demons to Cord, to respond to the note of wary compassion in his voice and finally tell him the truth that she'd successfully hidden from him so long, to do so would be fatal. He might tell himself that he understood her fears, Julia thought dully. He might even make an attempt to rebuild the relationship that had once existed between them— and at that thought, an irrational spark of hope flared within her. She quenched it immediately. In the end she'd have to send him away again, but this time it would be harder because he'd know why she was doing it. He'd insist on staying—out of pity, out of compassion, out of a sense of duty. But eventually the love would die.

He's the marrying kind. He wants a family of his own.

"My life isn't your concern anymore, Cord. Stop grilling me." She could feel her fragile self-control slipping away and she prayed she could hold onto it long enough to convince him. "Paul and Sheila were my best friends, too—but if you're determined to look into their deaths you're going to have to find someone else to work with. Investigation never was my field of expertise, anyway.''

"No. You were a Child Protection Specialist—one of the best." He ground the words out, stepping in front of her and blocking her path. His eyes were as cold and as threatening as black ice. "And now you're willing to put a little girl in jeopardy just because you don't want to get involved? What about that vow you took with me, promising to take the place of her parents if the day ever came that she needed us? Didn't that mean *anything* to you? For God's sake, she's so petrified that she hasn't said a word since she told me what happened—and you're the only person who has the faintest chance of getting through to her before she retreats into herself for good!"

"I'll get her *killed!*" The words spilled from her like acid, tinged with the corrosive terror of a hundred sleepless nights and the soul-destroying guilt of memory-laden days. Her face was colorless except for the pale fire behind her hazel eyes, a fire that seemed to be consuming her. "God help me, Cord— I'm no good at keeping them safe anymore! I'm a *liability!* She's in jeopardy just by being here in my home!"

She felt a pressure on her knee, and at her feet King whined loudly. He nudged her again with his muzzle, but she ignored him.

"You have to take her away." Her voice had sunk to a whisper, sibilant with fear. She clutched his arm. "I'll do something or say something that'll put her in more danger than she's in already, Cord. Get her out of here before another child pays for my mistakes!"

The remoteness had vanished from his features, to be replaced with baffled concern. Impatiently he shoved the whining dog away from them and searched her tortured expression. "What the hell are you talking about? You brought more children back than anyone else ever had. You were a damned legend! Lost children, children held hostage, abused children—you were the avenging angel that came in and scooped them up to safety! How many kids out there owe their lives to you, Julia? A liability? For more kids than I can remember, you were their last hope—and you came through for them!"

"You don't get it, do you?" Her arms were crossed tightly just below her breasts, her fists clenched, and her slim frame was hunched slightly forward at the waist, as if she was trying to protect herself from a blow. Her voice was despairingly ragged, and her eyes were blind with tears. "I'm not a damned *legend,* Cord—I'm a ghost story! The person you thought you knew is dead, and this is all that's left!"

She dragged in a shallow, shuddering breath, her lashes dipping briefly to her cheekbones. "I can't help you," she said dully. "I just can't help you."

He put a hand out to support her as she swayed. "What happened?" he asked harshly. His glance narrowed, searching her face intently. "What the hell happened during your last month at work? Sheila wrote and told me you'd resigned like you'd said you would, but she didn't go into any details. What in God's name went wrong, Julia?"

She'd never been able to tell him everything, not even when the bond between them had seemed unbreakable. She'd always held back, and now was no different.

"I don't want the responsibility anymore, that's all." It was almost too tempting to let herself lean against him, to let him take the full weight of her. She was so weary, Julia thought bleakly. She was so damned tired of being alone and fighting the demons single-handed. But it was her fight—hers and no one else's. She stood straighter, and his hand fell away.

"You should get some sleep yourself, Cord. You're going to need—"

Just then there was a sharp pain at her ankle, and she gave a startled little cry. Looking down in shock, she saw King, his tail tucked between his legs in abject apology but his stance defiant and stubborn. He barked once as he met her eyes, and then trotted a few steps in the direction of the hallway.

"He nipped me!" Everything else was temporarily forgotten in her shock at the shepherd's unprecedented behavior. "He's never done anything like that before!"

"Did he break the skin?" Cord bent down swiftly, and she felt his hand circle her ankle to inspect it. His touch should have felt impersonal, but instead it sent a shiver of sensation up her leg, as if instead of merely examining her ankle he'd taken it much farther…as if he'd stroked her calf, the back of her knee, her inner thigh, with those strong capable fingers that had once known every inch of her.

Hastily she put her foot down, her face faintly flushed. "He didn't hurt me. But that's not like him. He's usually the most gentle—"

King barked again, a sharp, urgent sound. Once again he trotted to the hallway and looked back at them, and suddenly Julia felt a terrible foreboding.

"Lizbet! My God—he's trying to tell us something's wrong with Lizbet!"

Her appalled gaze met Cord's, and the next moment she was running behind him down the hallway after King. The dog bounded ahead of them into the spare bedroom and then stood in the middle of the dark room, barking wildly. As they reached the doorway Cord felt for the light switch on the wall and snapped it on. Looking past him Julia realized that her worst nightmare had finally come true.

The bed was empty. The cushioned pad on the window seat that Davey had sat on for hours so long ago, enthralled with the collie stories of Albert Payson Terhune, had slipped onto the floor.

Lizbet was gone.

The corner of the screen at the low window had been pushed outward. It was small comfort, she thought numbly, but it was proof that the child hadn't been abducted by someone breaking into the room.

"She can't have gotten far. I'll check around the house and meet you down at the dock." His mouth was set in a grim line. "If she hasn't turned up by then we'll have to start searching the shoreline until sunrise, and then we'll take the boat out. While it's still dark we're going to have to try to locate her by sound, and I don't want a motor running until we can do a visual search."

"She heard me telling you she couldn't stay here." Julia's fist was knuckled against her mouth, her other hand splayed against the door frame behind her. "Why else would she have run away? I'm responsible for this, Cord.'' Her teeth started to chatter, and the shaking spread to the rest of her body as her unfocused stare darted wildly around the empty room. ''I told you I'd put her in danger, and I have. This is my fault. It's my fault!'' Her voice rose to a thin whimper that bordered on the edge of hysteria and then she felt strong hands on her shoulders, shaking her roughly.

''You're the one who's going to save her, dammit! You used to be able to get inside a child's head with some kind of sixth sense that no one else had, Julia! Whatever you say, you still have that ability—it's *part* of you. Use it, for God's sake! *Find* her.''

She tried to avert her gaze from his, but those black eyes seemed to draw her in until she felt as if everything nonessential was being stripped away and only her spirit remained—battered, bleeding and worn almost past endurance.

But not completely defeated.

The trembling stopped. Slowly but powerfully, like a current changing direction far beneath the surface of a river, an almost-forgotten strength began to surge through her limbs, and Julia felt a moment's fear as she let herself be swept into its flow. If she let it, it could take her over. There had always been that danger, and she was doubly vulnerable now. But she had no choice. Deliberately, she let the last instinctive shred of resistance fall from her, and almost immediately the night outside seemed to grow darker, the wind in the trees more threatening.

She pressed her lips together and nodded tightly, a restrained gesture totally at variance with the near hysteria she'd shown a few seconds ago.

''There's a flashlight in the cupboard above the stove. Take King with you—I can't let anything distract me right now.'' She saw the hesitation on his face. ''Go,'' she said hoarsely, her posture rigid and tense. ''You know how I work, Cord.''

He reached out and brushed his thumb lightly against the corner of her mouth. ''I know,'' he said. ''I just never thought I'd see the miracle again.'' He held her gaze for a single moment, and in that second their lives together raced through her mind as if she was drowning—a blur of frozen images, like a stack of photographs being shuffled swiftly before her eyes. Then he was gone, the dog a shadow behind him.

She was all alone. She was looking for a ghost to lead her to a child in danger.

Flicking the light switch off, Julia took a deep breath and closed her eyes, deliberately freeing her mind from everything around it and letting it reach out into the darkness.

The child—save the child...

Chapter 3

The lake had been bluer, the summers so much longer back then....

And Davey had been the center of her world—at nine years old, the big brother whose word was the final say on any question, the infinitely wiser and stronger being that a five-year-old little sister could only hero-worship and try to emulate.

Sometimes, if she was really lucky, she could tag along after him—like now.

Her job had been to sneak down to the boathouse after dinner the night before and hide the life jackets under the front seat of the little Sunfish so everything would be ready the next morning. She'd felt important that he'd trusted her with that. The life jackets were bright orange. Davey had told her that was so people could see you floating in the water if you had an accident and they were looking for you. He hadn't known why they smelled like wet dog, though, but they did, Julia had thought as she put them carefully in the little compartment under the boat seat.

They smelled the way King, Davey's old German shepherd

who'd died last winter, had smelled after he'd been playing in the lake with them, before his fur had dried off in the hot sun.

Now it was the next morning and she was in the Sunfish, and pieces of fog that looked like rags were blowing off the top of the water as Davey cast off and jumped from the dock to the boat. Watching him, Julia shivered, but she was careful not to let him see. What if one day he was too late, and he didn't make it back into the boat in time? What if he untied the ropes and pushed off and then stood there on the dock while she floated out into the lake alone? It was too scary to think about. Besides, Davey would find a way to get to her. He wouldn't ever leave her.

They really weren't supposed to be out here by themselves at all, but it wasn't the first time Davey had taken the boat out in the early morning. He was a born sailor, Dad had told the other fathers at the yacht club that day he'd taken them there. He'd ruffled Davey's hair proudly and bought him a white sailing cap with the club's crest on it, but there hadn't been any small enough to fit Julia. She hadn't minded. It had been enough just to be out with them, away from her mother's sad silences.

And right now it was enough to be here on the lake with Davey, even though he was kind of mad at her. She was wearing the fat orange life belt that jammed up under her chin so high when she was sitting down that she had to keep tugging on it to keep it from touching her mouth. It tasted like wet dog, too. But Davey wasn't wearing anything over his striped T-shirt, and that was her fault. Julia felt the heavy orange canvas creeping up her chin to her mouth again and pulled it down. She was sure she'd put both life jackets under the seat last night, she thought miserably. But when they'd gotten out onto the lake and Davey had told her to take them out, she'd only found one.

One of the very best things about having him for a big brother was that he didn't stay mad long, though. He was already smiling at her again, pointing at a blue heron flying low across the lake. His best friend Cord knew all about the birds and the animals that lived around the lake because his ancestors had always been here, not like their family, who only came here for the summers and then went back to their big house on Long Island for the rest of the year.

Cord was just as good a sailor as Davey was, but when Julia had asked him if his father belonged to the yacht club he'd scowled. Then one corner of his mouth had gone up in a funny kind of a smile and he'd pulled at her pigtails and told her that his dad didn't have time to belong to clubs. Afterward Davey had told her not to ask dumb questions, and if she had to, to ask him first. But she'd known that Cord hadn't really been angry with her, because he'd found a perfectly round stone later that day, and he'd given it to her for good luck.

They were changing direction. Davey had told her it was called tacking, and Julia had thought at first he'd said attacking, because when it happened the boom came across the boat and if you weren't careful it could hit you. She looked out across the water to where their house was, big and white, with the lawn that Cord's dad had mowed yesterday looking like green velvet.

Just then the heron circled back, maybe to have another look at them. Davey glanced up as the wide-winged shadow passed over him.

And the boom attacked him.

It was like watching one of the movies that Dad had taken the year Davey learned to dive off the high board. Dad had sat in the dark in their living room, running the movie over and over again, backward and forward and slowing it down so he could show Davey all the things he was doing wrong. After that, Davey had practiced and practiced until the instructor at the swim club had told him he wanted to put him on the diving team. But when his dive was finally perfect and he'd shown Dad, he'd never gone back to the pool again.

It looked just like the movie when Dad slowed it down, Julia thought, sitting scrunched up on the hard wooden seat and watching Davey with her eyes opened so wide they hurt. The boom swung over like it was going through molasses and then it hit Davey's head with a solid thunk just as he started to duck. Slowly she saw his neck snap sideways. Slowly the rope he'd been holding fell from his fingers, but it didn't hit the deck right away. It seemed to hang in the air at the level of his waist, and then it was down by his knees, and then it was tangled around his feet.

But Davey's feet were moving, too, rising up into the air with the same kind of slow motion that everything around her seemed to have, the toes of his shoes touching each other in a V shape as he started to fall over the side of the boat. He looked like a seesaw, Julia thought. His hip was on the edge of the boat and his feet were still sliding up through the thick air in that weird and frightening way but his head was already touching the water.

Any second now the seesaw would come up again. Any second now the movie would start running backward and Davey would slowly tip back into the boat and his feet would go down on the deck and his eyes would open and everything would be the way it was supposed to be and she would laugh and tell him how funny he'd looked and he'd start laughing, too, and then they'd go home together and maybe this afternoon Cord's mom might take them to town for ice creams. Any second now all that would happen.

Except all of a sudden the movie started running really, really fast.

She saw Davey's striped T-shirt sliding under the water and then his legs and his white sneakers, still tangled up in the rope, and the rope started snaking over the side of the boat until it reached the end and it stretched tight from the cleat it was tied to.

It felt like there was something big sitting on her chest, not letting her breathe. Holding onto the edge of the boat, Julia slid off the seat onto her knees. She was too afraid to stand up because the deck was moving up and down, and instead of going in a straight line the Sunfish felt like it was going to tip over onto its side. She bit her lip and scrambled over to where the rope was rubbing the white-painted wood and she tried to pull on it, but it stayed tight and the thing that was sitting on her chest seemed to be getting heavier and heavier and she couldn't get any air into her at all.

Then the wind shifted again and the little Sunfish picked up speed and the rope rolled over her fingers and she started screaming and screaming and far off by the shore she could see Cord Hunter, Davey's very best friend, jumping into his dad's old motorboat and heading out towards her....

Nothing had been the same after that. Julia stood in the dark bedroom and felt the predawn breeze coming through the pushed-out screen and went deeper into the past.

She was only five, and she was frightened. Her mother always had a glass in her hand and fell asleep downstairs with the television all fuzzy late at night, and when her father looked at her it seemed like he couldn't even see her. Sometimes she was scared that if she held out her own hand to look at it she'd be able to see right through it herself.

She needed somewhere dark and safe to hide—somewhere even if she *was* invisible, it wouldn't matter anyway. Somewhere so dark that everything was invisible and she could just wrap her arms around her legs and sit without making a sound and no one would be able to find her....

She moved like a sleepwalker out of the bedroom and down the hall to the side door that opened onto the garden where her mother had sat and pretended to read all those years ago, and as she passed by the broken redwood chaise that she'd never bothered to remove since she'd come back here to live she thought she smelled Shalimar, her mother's favorite perfume.

She shivered. She kept moving.

Somewhere dark, somewhere that was darker than the night and darker than the woods behind the house. Somewhere a little girl would be able to hide for as long as she wanted. Somewhere small and safe. Somewhere no one would look except another little girl who'd once gone looking for a safe hiding place.

Her feet, still clad in the backless slippers, moved through the wet grass as surely and steadily as if they were following a path they'd worn down themselves. Her eyes were closed, and her breathing was shallow.

Find the child. Save the child. *Be* the child....

She went deeper still, losing herself in the child she'd once been, and then even deeper, searching out the fear and pain of the tiny redhead who'd stared at her with the still blue gaze of a doll. In the silence of her mind she could hear a small, frightened whisper, almost inaudible.

Be the child. She concentrated, and the whisper became clearer....

The boathouse.

Julia stood like a statue on the wet lawn, her mind still operating on two levels and with both levels possessing the knowledge she needed. Only by letting herself become the child she'd once been had she been able to think like the little girl she was searching for, and she was certain now she knew where to find Lizbet. But Lizbet didn't need the help of another child—she needed the adult Julia to protect her. It was time to set aside the fearful little ghost who'd entered her for the last few minutes, time to struggle free from the faded memories that this recent reliving had brought to life once more.

It felt like she was tearing her soul in two.

The past was powerful, and its ghosts were the most powerful of all, despite their pain and vulnerability. The child she'd once been always came to her freighted with guilt and loneliness, but when it was time to abandon her again she clung to the adult Julia with a strength born of fear, terrified to be cast into the shadows and forgotten until the next time.

And even though Julia knew that the frightened little personality was no ghost at all, but merely a long-ago echo of her own self, she felt as if she was turning her back on a real child—a child who had haunted her all her life for some purpose that she'd never been able to understand.

A convulsion ran through her body, and she felt the desperate presence receding into the furthermost corner of her mind with all the other memories that she never allowed herself to examine. She felt as if she'd just run ten miles, and her limbs were shaking with exertion.

"She's nowhere around the house and I checked the woods as far back as the fence line." Cord melted out of the grayness, King—the present King, not the long-gone one from her childhood, Julia thought with a moment of shaky confusion—at his heels. There was just enough light now to make out the tortured expression on his features and the straight, grim line of his mouth, and she put her hand lightly on his arm. Her fingers were still trembling, and her voice was unsteady.

"She's in the old boathouse."

The hope that flared in his eyes was instantly tempered with apprehension, and she forestalled his reply. "I know. She couldn't have picked a more dangerous place—I've been meaning to have it pulled down since I came back here. You're going to have to let me go in alone, Cord. I'm lighter than you are and those rotten floorboards might take my weight long enough for me to get her out of there."

"No. I'll go." His tone brooked no argument, and her hand tightened on his arm.

"She was running from *me,* Cord! If you bring her back she'll only try again. Don't you see—she has to know that *I* came for her. She has to know that I want her enough so that I'll never stop looking for her until I find her, and that just won't happen if you deliver her to me like a package. She already trusts you—now I have to prove to her that she can trust me." She hesitated, and then added in an undertone, "Besides, I'm her guardian. She's my responsibility, too."

She was using his own words against him, but she felt no compunction. She couldn't wipe out the mistake that had ended her career—the mistake that no one knew about but herself and a dead man—but she could try to bridge the chasm she'd so unthinkingly created between herself and the child she'd vowed to protect.

She owed it to the best friends she'd ever had. Sheila and Paul had put their trust in her, and she'd let them down. She wanted the chance to make things right again, and her desperation must have shown in her eyes.

"I should know better than to try to talk you out of something you really want." Cord glanced at the dark shape of the old boathouse with resignation. "It didn't work when you were Lizbet's age, it didn't work when you were sixteen and wanted to ride my motorcycle, and it's not going to work now, is it? But be careful. I'll be standing right outside, so if you think the damned thing's going to go, call out to me."

He turned to the path that led to the boathouse and then paused. Swiftly he pulled her to him and kissed her hard on the mouth. Just as swiftly he released her, his expression unreadable. "Twenty-three months, four days and two hours," he said tersely. "You were my addiction."

He held her shocked gaze for the space of a heartbeat and then gave her an ironic half smile. "Walking out of your life was the one thing I never should have let you talk me into. I'm not going to let you do it a second time."

He lightly traced the corner of her mouth, still soft from his kiss. Then he turned and set off quickly down the path. After a startled moment she ran after him, her thoughts a chaotic whirl.

He hadn't changed at all, she thought in frustrated confusion as they hastened to the water's edge and the rickety building that ran alongside the dock. He'd always had more confidence in her than she'd had in herself, always seen her as strong and capable and supremely in control of any situation. Tonight had been the first time a crack had appeared in his golden-girl image of her, but already he seemed to have forgotten the messy vulnerability she'd displayed in front of him.

After she'd sent him away it had taken long enough for her to reach some kind of equilibrium in her emotional existence, as sterile and empty as that existence had been. How was she supposed to cope if he came back into her life again?

The door of the boathouse was slightly ajar, and Cord carefully pulled it open wide, wincing as it creaked on its rusted hinges. Shutting her mind to what had just happened between them with an effort, Julia narrowed her gaze and looked past him into the darkness, but it was almost impossible to see anything inside. She knew that the floor ran around the perimeter of the building and in the middle was the long-disused boat slip—in actual fact, a large square opening in the floor to the lake below. She could just make out the oily ripple of water where the floor abruptly ended, but there hadn't been boats kept there for years.

Lizbet was in there somewhere, behind the clutter of boxes and old tarpaulins and rusty motor parts. Despite any other doubts she might have, Julia knew she hadn't been wrong about that. The child was here and she was still in danger. As if to underline her apprehension, the wind from the lake outside freshened as it always did just before dawn, and the timbers creaked ominously. The structure was in worse repair than she'd realized, she thought in alarm.

As Cord held the whining King back and followed her with a worried gaze, Julia stepped nervously into the darkness and started edging her way toward the back of the boathouse.

With her first step she felt the sponginess of rot underfoot, the unexpected give where there should have been solidity. Through the flimsy soles of her scuffs she felt the pebble-like pressure of a nailhead that had risen higher than the floorboard it originally had been meant to secure. She gingerly put her full weight onto her leg and held her breath. The floor sagged, but didn't break.

There was a rustling sound by the far wall, on the other side of the dully gleaming rectangle in the middle of the boathouse, and then a muffled splash as something slipped into the water. Julia tried to control her shudder, but she couldn't prevent the unpleasant prickling sensation that lifted the skin at the back of her neck. Water rats. It was bad enough knowing that they were scurrying around her in the dark, but feeling something bump against her underwater would send her right over the edge of panic. She only hoped that Lizbet didn't know what those scuffling noises meant.

She was halfway to the pile of boxes now, and she paused. Keeping her voice low, she spoke into the darkness, praying that her presence wouldn't frighten the little girl into any sudden movement.

"It's me, Lizbet—your Aunt Julia. Uncle Cord's waiting outside for us."

She slid her foot carefully a few inches forward and felt the sickening emptiness of a missing section of floor. Sweat beaded like ice water on her forehead as she realized that Lizbet must have come this way herself only a short time before. That the child had made it safely to her dangerous refuge had been nothing short of a miracle, Julia thought shakily. She felt for a more secure footing and edged closer.

"I don't blame you for running away, and no one's going to make you come back if you're not ready to. But I've got something important to tell you. I want you to know I'm really, really sorry for making you feel sad back at the house."

She'd reached the pile of crates. Listening intently, she thought she could hear the soft sound of an indrawn breath behind one of them. The floor where she was standing felt more solid than the surrounding area, and she cautiously lowered herself to her knees. It was frightening enough here in the unfamiliar dark. The child whose trust she was trying to win didn't need a disembodied voice floating down at her from on high.

"Do you know what a good luck charm is, Lizbet? It's like a rabbit's foot or maybe a shiny penny that you keep in your pocket for luck." She saw a gleam of white sneaker edging from behind the crate, but she went on with careful casualness. "But there are bad luck charms, too—and that's what I thought I was for you. I thought if you stayed with me I would bring you bad luck, Lizbet. Thinking that that made me so afraid that I thought you'd be safer somewhere else."

Slowly a tiny, heart-shaped face peered out from the pile of boxes. In the gloom, Lizbet's eyes were wide and solemn. She looked ready to dart back into her makeshift sanctuary at any sudden movement.

"Except then I remembered something that I had when I was your age—a good luck charm so strong that I figure it can cancel out any bad luck that I might bring."

Slowly she reached into the pocket of the chenille robe and felt the smooth, perfect roundness of the stone that Cord had given her so long ago. Once it had been a talisman for a scared, confused little girl. It was time its protective magic was put back to use. Julia drew the stone out of her pocket and held it in her open palm.

"Take it. It's yours now."

A small hand reached out toward hers and touched the cool stone with minute fingertips. The next moment Lizbet's fingers closed around the rock and whisked it to the safety of her own

jeans' pocket. Julia let out the breath she hadn't realized she'd
been holding.

"I'm kind of hungry—how about you? If you want, we can
go up to the house and I bet I can get Uncle Cord to make us
both some of his famous buttermilk pancakes. He's a way better
cook than I am."

It was going to be a long time before she'd be able to coax
a giggle out of that serious little mouth, Julia told herself. Right
now it was enough to see the pinched, white look replaced for
a split second by the tentative flicker of a smile. She held out
her hand, feeling somehow as if she was facing the biggest and
most important test of her whole life.

"It's pretty dark in here. I'm going to need you to hold on
tight to keep me from falling into the lake."

Through the cracks in the boathouse walls came a thin shaft
of dawn light, enough so that she could see the heart-shaped
face looking at her doubtfully. Then the two silky wings of red
hair swung forward as Lizbet nodded silently. The little hand
was cold as it slipped into hers and gripped tightly.

"Your mom was my best friend, honey."

Julia's whisper was uneven. Somewhere deep inside her she
felt a painfully sweet sensation, as if a patch of ground that had
been parched for too long had suddenly been split by the slender
green shoot of a seedling. Despite the tears that prickled behind
her lashes, she kept her eyes on Lizbet's hesitant blue gaze, but
when she spoke again her words were so soft she almost could
have been talking to herself.

"I think she'd like it that we're finally getting to know each
other."

Chapter 4

He'd gotten about as much sleep as she had, Julia thought distractedly the next morning—a couple of hours, maybe less— but at least she'd done her tossing and turning in her own bed. The obviously weary man in front of her had wrapped himself up in an old quilt, pulled one of the ancient overstuffed armchairs from the living room into the hall and had catnapped outside of Davey's room.

Despite the sun it was early in the season, and although by mid-June the earth itself would have absorbed enough warmth to dispel the last cold dampness of spring, right now the breeze blowing off the lake still held more than a hint of its northern origins, and the distinct green scent of the nearby pines sharpened the atmosphere like tiny slivers of ice. The trees on the property—the hickories, maples and the massive old oak that shaded the house in the summer—had leafed out, but their foliage hadn't thickened to the dense canopy that it would create in a few more weeks. Through the tangle of branches above, the sky looked like well-bleached denim. Julia stopped by a grove of tamaracks that had once provided an almost Oriental background to a long-vanished rock garden.

"What are we going to do about Lizbet?"

She flicked a quick glance over her shoulder at the house. The child was still sleeping, and King had been left on guard in her room in case she awoke. Earlier Cord had told her that he'd informed Sheila's mother last night that he had her granddaughter, and Betty Wilson, devastated by the news she'd just received, had been all too grateful that the child was with them. Betty had been battling cancer, Julia knew, and even if she hadn't been stricken with grief she was no longer able to care for her beloved Lizbet.

"I've thought about that. Since Dad moved some friends of mine have been living in our old place down the road. Dad said the place held too many memories of Mom for him to want to sell it." Cord's voice held affection. "Anyway, Mary and Frank Whitefield will take Lizbet in for as long as we need to keep her out of sight. I don't want her around while we're trying to track down her parents' killer."

He bent down and pulled a tuft of dried choke grass out of the garden, revealing a pale green spear pushing stubbornly through the dead weeds. "My father planted these for your mother one year," he said softly, clearing the earth around the shoot.

With a gentle thumb he touched the young plant, and then he straightened up and sighed, still not looking at her directly. "I didn't like it out in California. It wasn't home."

Julia knew what he meant without him spelling it out. He hadn't just grown up in New York state, he had his roots here, and they went back a lot farther than the *Mayflower*. Part of him had always seemed inexorably bound to a more elemental way of life, and in the past, coming back to this place where his family had lived for generations had seemed to be a necessary ritual of renewal for him. He would blend in anywhere, she thought, and if he had to he would find a way to survive in a desert. But his soul would always thirst for a sunrise over a still lake, the dark red blur of cardinals against a snowy bough in the dusk, the crumbly feel of lichen on granite underfoot.

"La-La Land too rich for your blood?" she asked negligently, not wanting him to know how closely attuned she still was to his thoughts. "All those California babes—didn't you have even the slightest urge to kick loose a little and enjoy yourself?"

As soon as the words left her lips she wished she could take them back. Indulging her almost desperate need to know what had happened to him over the last two years—whether he'd met anyone, if he'd fallen in love—was an area that had to be out of bounds if she had any hope of hanging onto her self-control while he was around. She couldn't let things get personal between them. She was no good at personal anymore.

"It's none of my business anyway," she added swiftly, but she was too late. Cord rubbed the dirt from his hand carelessly against the seam of his jeans.

"You've got to be crazy," he said. His tone was conversational and uninflected. "I only ever loved one woman, and that was you. Did you think that would change just because there was a continent between us? Did you really think I wouldn't be hearing your voice, seeing your face—for God's sake— smelling the scent of your *skin* every waking hour that I was away from you?"

He spoke as quietly as he always did and he made no move to touch her. He stood there, solid and big and about as flighty as the damned oak tree arching protectively over the house behind him, and she stared at him, unable to think of a single thing to say in reply.

"I met a man one night in a bar." His low voice overrode her thoughts. "He said his people could shape shift and that he himself had flown like an eagle across mountain peaks. He'd had too much to drink, and maybe I had, too. But while he was talking I believed him, and all I could think was that I wanted to shape shift, too, to take on the wings of some bird strong enough to fly day and night until I was back with you again. I thought I would land on your window ledge and look into your room and make sure you were sleeping and safe, and then I would rise into the moonlight again and fly away before you awoke."

One corner of his mouth lifted unexpectedly in a smile. Reaching out, he tucked a stray strand of hair behind her ear and then let his palm linger gently on the shape of her skull. "Like I said, I was a little drunk. I remember waking up stiff and cold on a hill hours later and feeling sure that I really had become that eagle and had seen you, but I never could make it happen again. So I dreamed about you instead. I had you in my arms every night."

She didn't want to hear any more. "I don't believe in magic, Cord. And if you held anyone in your arms at night, she was a fantasy woman." Her eyes met his steadily. "Whatever there once was between us is over. I tried to tell you that two years ago. If you won't accept it I don't see how we can work together on finding out who killed Paul and Sheila."

"I could accept it if it was the truth. But you're lying to me. I still can't look at you without needing you so bad I'd crawl over ten miles of rough road on my hands and knees to get to you, and whether you admit it or not, you want me, too, Julia." His fingers slid under her hair to the nape of her neck. "But go ahead and prove me wrong if you think you can. Kiss me."

Her breath caught in her throat with a noise that sounded more like a startled gasp than the laugh she'd attempted. "Kiss you? What's that supposed to—"

"Kiss me like it means nothing." He drew her slightly closer to him, his fingertips warm against the fine bones at the back of her neck.

With heightened awareness, she could feel the coarser texture of the last few grains of soil still remaining on his hand. He was leaving his *fingerprints* on her, she thought foolishly, and as soon as the ridiculous notion entered her mind it was followed by a rush of desire so raw and unexpected that it felt as if the air around her had turned to warm water, immediately drenching the cotton sweater and the jeans she was wearing and soaking through to her skin. Cord's mouth was only inches from hers.

"All we've got is history, Cord," she said tightly. "Let's leave it at that." Her body was tense against his touch.

He exhaled softly, still holding her gaze. Shifting position slightly so that he was blocking the sun from her eyes, he shook his head and let the ghost of a smile cross his defeated features.

"My God, you're one mule-headed woman. Why couldn't you have held on to what we had just as stubbornly?"

He let his hand slide from the back of her neck and shrugged, that ironic smile still lifting one corner of his mouth. A crazy mixture of relief and disappointment swept through her, but she forced herself to concentrate on the former instead of the latter. He started to turn away, and suddenly her limbs felt like lead.

Then he stopped and turned back to face her. His eyes were unreadable.

"Hell, no. Not this time." With one fluid movement, he bridged the space between them, pulling her to him so swiftly that she had no chance to react. "Good God, I just have to have this," he muttered, his mouth coming down on hers.

She could taste salt on his top lip and the same sweat slicked her exposed skin where the vee neckline of her sweater dipped as he gathered her to his chest, his arm tightening around her. With his other hand he pushed her hair from her temple, his opened fingers sliding through it until they reached the back of her head, and then spreading wider. Individual sensations fell away, overwhelmed by the shock of sudden mindless need that tore through her.

She'd first kissed him when she'd been seventeen and he'd been twenty-two. Now it was ten years later, and if she'd had to guess a few seconds ago, she would have said that after all the years of intimacy between them there was nothing about Cord Hunter that was unfamiliar to her. She couldn't have been more *wrong,* Julia thought incoherently.

Never, not even in the last few months of their relationship when everything had been falling apart, had he ever seemed to forget the physical disparity between them, and his size and strength had always been downplayed when he'd been with her. But this kiss was different from anything she'd experienced with him in the past—harder and hotter, his mouth open against hers with an almost adolescent lack of finesse. Once he'd been able to maintain some semblance of control even at the height of their lovemaking. Now not only had he lost that control, but he seemed to have forgotten any subtlety he'd ever possessed. All that was left was urgency.

He wanted her. He wanted her now, and badly enough that he hadn't been able to ease into the moment or prolong the waiting. Despite the warning bells that were shrilling frantically in that part of her brain that was still functioning, there was no real choice left to her.

She kissed him back, opening herself fully to him, and he immediately took advantage of her lack of resistance and moved in even closer, his biceps tensing against her breasts. Liquid fire flashed through her. She could *taste* him, Julia thought disjointedly, and even that was different from the way she remembered it—he tasted ripe and dark, like cherries flamed in brandy, burning their way down her throat and exploding sweetly as they reached the pit of her stomach. Hardly knowing what she was doing, she felt her fingers fumbling at the buttons of his shirt, impatiently opening them. Her hands slid possessively against his skin, and she felt the faint ridge of scar tissue that followed the line of a bottom rib.

Another woman would have to ask him how he'd gotten that, Julia thought fiercely. Another woman could question him for years and still never know Cord the way she did. Once she'd lain in bed beside him, touching every mark on his body with gentle fingers and recalling the circumstances of each while he'd watched her, a faint smile playing on his lips as she went through the litany—falling from the oak tree when he was nine; getting a fishhook in his shoulder when he was teaching a tourist how to cast; being hit by a piece of flying debris when, as a member of the community's volunteer fire department, he'd arrived at the blaze that had leveled the old box factory in town just as an ancient propane tank had exploded.

She knew him—every *inch* of him, Julia thought. He was hers and no one else's, and not having him had been like existing in hell for two years. She arched her body to his and his grip around her tightened convulsively. His mouth moved to the corner of her lips, and she could feel his lashes flicking against the line of her cheekbone.

"Right about now I usually wake up," he whispered hoarsely, his breath warm on her upper lip. His words were muffled against her skin. "Every time I do it's like dying. Tell me it was the same for you."

The scar on his ribs was from a stray round he'd caught the year before they'd separated. He'd been instrumental in tracking down the Donner "family," a chillingly twisted group of serial killers who in the end had chosen to die in a violent confrontation with the authorities rather than surrender. Her fingertips passed over it gently, like a blind woman touching her own features in a reaffirmation of something she'd always known.

"It was the same for—"

The words died in her throat. Past the scar on his ribs her searching fingers had found another—a raised weal that snaked down from the side of his torso to the top of his hip. It felt ugly. It felt unfamiliar. She had no idea how he'd gotten it or when it had happened. All she knew was that it had to be less than two years old.

It had to be less than two years old, because two years ago their life together had come to an abrupt end. Two years ago she'd sent him away, knowing that it was the last acceptable option she had.

He still loved her. He still wanted her. But he'd made some kind of a life for himself that didn't include her—the proof was right here, under her fingertips.

She still loved him. She would never love anyone the way she loved him. And the only thing of value she had left to give him—the last token of love she could place before him—was his freedom.

"I felt the same way, Cord." She drew slightly away from him, bringing her hand up to his mouth and tracing the line of his bottom lip. His gaze darkened with desire. "We were fabulous in bed together and you were right—there's no way I could kiss you without feeling *anything*. But..."

She hesitated, avoiding his eyes and imprinting every minuscule detail of his mouth on her memory. "I guess what I'm trying to tell you is that it wouldn't be fair for me to let you believe we could rebuild a relationship, based only on a childhood hero worship that I outgrew long ago and the fact that we both like fu—"

"Don't." Cord's hands fell from her to his sides. He took a step back, his eyes narrowed to black slits. "That was never what we did in bed together. We made love."

He rubbed the side of his jaw wearily, still watching her intently. "Honey, I was the boy from the wrong side of the tracks who taught you how to lie, remember? You got good at it, but not that good. It doesn't take a detective's badge to see that your life's fallen apart just as badly as mine has, and for the same reason. We belong together. And this time I'm not leaving until I find out why that terrifies you so much."

She only had to hold herself together for another minute or two, Julia told herself shakily. She met his gaze with her own, the sunlight turning the hazel in her eyes to a clear bronze, the rich chestnut glints in her hair contrasting with the lack of color in her face. "I'm not the stubborn one, Cord—*you* are. I'll work with you on this case, but that's all. We're temporary partners, and nothing more."

High in the sky above them a windblown cloud passed over the sun, and its shadow raced across the tops of the pines, the porch of the house, Cord's features. Something flickered behind his eyes for the briefest of instants.

"Sometimes you almost convince me," he said softly. "Maybe I'm not as stubborn as you think."

Then he turned, striding along the overgrown path toward the house. Julia deliberately didn't watch him go, but instead turned her face to the lake. She hugged her arms across her body, her hands so tightly clenched that her nails, short and blunt, pressed into her palms. The light cotton sweater was no protection against the breeze that came in off the lake, but the freshness soothed the hot, burning sensation behind her eyes.

She'd been wrong to feel even the slightest antagonism toward the woman she'd fantasized about over the last two years—that blue-eyed, blond, tennis-playing Californian that she'd feared would take her place in Cord's heart. Whoever he eventually made a life with, and whatever she looked like, Julia thought painfully, the woman who would one day make Cord forget he wasn't her enemy.

"I'll never know you, but one day you'll learn about me."

Tears blurring her vision, she forced the nearly inaudible words past numb lips, her gaze fixed on the whitecaps near the middle of the lake where the water was choppier. "You'll wonder what kind of a woman could let him go. You'll think I couldn't have loved him—but you'll be wrong. You'll be so *wrong*...."

She'd missed her period, and she hadn't been able to tell him. She'd told herself it was because she wanted to be sure before giving him the news, but when the home pregnancy test showed positive she'd been glad that she'd waited until he was out of the apartment before taking it. Hunched over like an old woman, she'd sat down on the edge of the bathtub and started to shake.

It was what they wanted, she'd told herself, staring at the pink-tinted stick in front of her as if it was a snake about to strike. Wasn't it what they'd wanted—a family of their own someday? Two boys, two girls, and Cord had always joked that he'd teach the boys how to be as good a cook as their father if she'd show the girls how she caught five lake trout to everyone else's one.

He would be the perfect father-to-be, worrying about her health, indulging her quirks and cravings, attending Lamaze classes with her. Finally the day would arrive when he bundled her into the car, drove like crazy to the hospital, and she gave birth to their baby—a tiny, perfect, *fragile* human being that they would be responsible for.

And she wouldn't be up to the task, she'd thought with cold certainty. Of all people, she knew how swiftly tragedy could strike, how no amount of precaution could totally insure a child's safety. The world was a dangerous place, and more often than not its victims were the innocent, the defenseless—

The children that she hadn't been able to save.

She'd taken each failure personally—the instances of abuse that she had been informed of too late, the Have You Seen This Child? photos that eventually faded and curled on bulletin boards and telephone poles around the city, the confused bereavement of parents who berated themselves and each other with a barrage of if onlys—if only I hadn't let go of her hand, if only we hadn't let him sit in the front seat, if only we'd taken her with us, if only we'd kept him at home...*if only we could have kept our child safe.*

What it all came down to was if only they'd known, they would have done things differently, Julia had thought. But she *did* know. And, having that knowledge, what had she been thinking of by making a child with Cord—a child that would be born into such a capriciously violent world?

When she'd eventually learned that her pregnancy result had been an error, she'd felt as if she'd been given a second chance to avert a tragedy, and more than ever she'd been glad she hadn't told Cord anything yet. She'd left the doctor's office and had sat in a nearby park until afternoon grayed into dusk. When she'd finally risen from the park bench, her limbs stiff from the hours of frozen immobility, she'd known what she had to do. Her job was to save the children she could, and even at that there were dozens who slipped through the cracks. But she could ensure that no child of hers and Cord's would ever be lost through her inadequacy.

She would send him away. She would tell him any lie it took to make him leave her, but the one thing she would never tell him was the truth. If he ever knew her fear he would try to make things right for her, and because losing him would break her heart Julia was afraid she might weaken enough to listen to the lies she knew *he* would tell *her.* He would tell her that a life without children wouldn't devastate him, he would tell her that he wouldn't ache for the feel of a baby's fist holding his, he would tell her that he wouldn't envy the friends of his who were fathers themselves.

And he might even believe it himself for a while. But as the years passed the sense of loss would grow in him, because more than any man she knew, Cord wanted children of his own. And no matter how much he loved her, he would always know that but for her he could have had them....

"You'll never know me," Julia whispered. Back at the house King barked playfully on the porch, and a flock of mourning doves flew fussily into the trees. "But one day you might learn that there was a woman before you in his life. Don't let that worry you."

Their children would look like Cord. They would grow up beside the Pacific. They would be tennis players like their mother.

"I let him go because I love him so. I always have." Blinking the tears from her eyes, she started up the path toward the house. Then she turned and looked one last time at the blue lake, the far shore, the distant horizon. "I always will," she whispered to herself.

Chapter 5

"*Ashes to ashes, dust to dust...*"

Her spine ramrod-straight, Julia stood beside Cord's immobile bulk and stared unseeingly ahead. The job of a police officer was no picnic. The hours were grueling, the respect often nonexistent and the danger ever-present, but when an officer was killed there was always a good turnout at the funeral. It was one of the few benefits of being a cop, she thought, her black-gloved fist clenched tightly around the shoulder strap of her purse. She'd known how Paul and Sheila had scraped along on his salary when he'd been a rookie, how for years they'd celebrated Christmas the day after or the day before because Paul had always been working on December the twenty-fifth, and how Sheila had lain awake nights when Paul had been working a case, wondering if this would be the night when her cell phone rang.

But now that he was dead and especially since the job had claimed Sheila, as well, his fellow officers, many of them in dress uniform, had gathered to show the world that however scant the material rewards of their career were, the profession and those who chose it were worthy of the highest honor. It was all about solidarity, Julia told herself tightly. The grim-faced men and women around her were there to bid farewell to one of their own, knowing full well that the next funeral could be theirs.

It had been a touchingly beautiful service. But here at the graveside under a cloudlessly perfect blue sky nothing could blunt the terribly symbolic sight of the token shovelful of earth falling onto the two polished mahogany coffins that were even now being lowered into the ground. Sheila's mother, Betty Wilson, was sobbing quietly a few feet away, her frail figure flanked by friends and relatives, and most of the other mourners' faces were distorted by grief.

Who in this crowd had betrayed them? Which grieving face hid a lying heart?

"How are you holding up?" As people began to move away from the graveside, Cord took her arm and met her watery gaze. "If you think you can manage it, I'd like to stick around for a while and talk to a few people. But if you'd like to leave—"

"Someone here isn't who they seem, Cord. Someone here was no friend to Paul or Sheila," Julia cut in flatly. "I know that as well as you do, and of course we'll stay and find out what we can. Stop treating me like I'm a basket case."

"You remind me of a sweet little girl I once knew who told me she could recognize poison ivy without my help," Cord said dryly. "Oh, yeah—that *was* you. Still as prickly as ever, aren't you? I only thought you might feel out of place here now that you aren't on the force anymore."

"Oh." Julia was nonplussed. "I thought you were worried that I might…" Her words trailed off, and a faint color mounted her too-pale cheeks.

"Worried you might what?"

She shrugged. "I don't know. I guess I thought you might wonder if I could handle an emotional situation like this without a—a crutch." She looked at her hands, unconsciously twisting the strap of her purse. "Without needing a drink," she said quietly.

"Do you?" His question held no condemnation. When she didn't answer his hand gently cupped her chin and tipped her face back so that their eyes met. "*Do* you need a drink to face something like this?"

"Once, I would have," she said simply, looking into his gravely sympathetic face. "And for the rest of my life I'll be aware that it's a trap I could fall into again if I let myself."

In the strong sunlight, dappled by the overarching elm boughs, his eyes darkened, the thick lashes throwing sharp shadows onto his high cheekbones. "Were you going through this when we were together?"

The conversation, personal as it had been from the start, was straying into forbidden territory as far as she was concerned, Julia thought. She withdrew from his grasp and shook her head. "No. There was an incident at work that..."

She closed her eyes as the familiar images flashed through her mind like a home movie from hell—the narrow ledge of the office building, the stalled traffic far below, the hopeless and hate-filled expression of the man holding the child—

She drew a deep breath and forced her eyes open. The day was still perfect, the peaceful park-like setting around her a watercolor-like blur of soft greens and the gray of weathered stone as her vision wavered and cleared. "I was stressed out and I chose the wrong way to handle it. It had nothing to do with us."

Her tone was deliberately final in an effort to shore up the barrier between them—a barrier that had somehow dangerously weakened in the last few minutes. He'd always been able to slip under her defenses, Julia thought nervously. It was one of the reasons she'd been relieved yesterday when he'd decided to make his base of operations a motel room in town rather than the lake house with her. He'd said it was more convenient that way, but they'd both known that living under the same roof, however temporarily, would be too emotionally distracting at a time when they needed to focus on working smoothly together.

She looked past him to a nearby group of mourners—fellow officers of Paul, she realized, recognizing one or two—and then her own edginess vanished as she took in the uncomfortable expressions on the group of faces and saw the reason for them.

"Good Lord, isn't that—" she began, but Cord, following her glance, finished her thought.

"Dean Tascoe, damn him. And it looks like he's spoiling for a fight." His lips thinned and he scanned the area swiftly. "Betty must have left already, thank God, but even so, I'm not about to stand by and let Paul and Sheila's funeral be turned into a free-for-all by that bastard. Emotions are running high enough as it is."

Turning on his heel and striding purposefully across the lawn, he was already several yards away from her before Julia gathered her wits together and hurried after him. Ahead of her, Cord's back was rigid with anger, the broad shoulders set stiffly under the somber and well-cut suit jacket. His hair, as glossy as a raven's wing, gleamed with blue-black highlights under the buttery afternoon sunlight.

Tascoe had chosen the wrong place to air any grievances he might feel he had, she thought apprehensively. Cord had dealt with the man in the past and had made no secret of the fact that he considered him a disgrace to the uniform he'd once worn. To have him attempting to sully this solemn occasion was intolerable.

"Hey, Chief—long time no see." Breaking off from the heated discussion he'd been having with an attractive but angry-looking woman—Paul's partner, Cindy Lopez, Julia realized with belated recognition—the stocky ex-cop fixed a grave expression on his heavy features. "Hell of a note, isn't it? The thin blue line just got a little thinner, but we all know that comes with the territory. To take out Durant's lady too, though…"

He shrugged meaty shoulders. "Well, I guess we're agreed that when this scumbag gets caught, the odds are pretty damn good he's going to suffer a fatal accident long before he gets the chance to go before some bleeding-heart jury and tell them how misunderstood he is, right, folks? We know how to handle cop killers—all of us except for Chatchie here." He shot a disgusted look at Lopez, and her lips tightened.

"Tascoe, I just lost the best partner anyone could have, so don't tell me I wouldn't know what to do if I found his killer," she said, her dark brown eyes hard with contempt. "I'd read the bastard his rights, cuff him and expect justice to take its course—because that's the way Paul would have handled it. I swore to uphold the law, not take it into my own hands.''

"You sound pretty cool for someone whose partner just got whacked, *chiquita*. I thought you people were supposed to be hot-blooded,'' Tascoe drawled insinuatingly. "Or do you just reserve all that passion for your girlfriend? Now, that's one *hell* of a waste.''

"Your kind of policework got you kicked off the force, Tascoe.'' Stepping in front of the other man, Cord gave him a tight smile, his eyes glittering like chips of black ice. "Too bad you still haven't figured out we're supposed to be the good guys. If you came here to pay your respects to a decent cop and his wife, you're going the wrong way about it.''

"He's right, Dean. Don't start anything.''

For the first time Julia noticed the thin, middle-aged blonde standing beside the burly ex-cop. Her face, like the faces of many there, bore traces of tears but Julia had the distinct impression that in her case grief was a constant companion rather than a reaction to today's funeral. She tugged again at Tascoe's arm.

"Please, Dean. Let's go home.''

To Julia's surprise, instead of shaking her off impatiently, Tascoe looked down at the woman with uncharacteristic gentleness. He patted her hand awkwardly.

"Don't worry, Jackie. I know you've got to work with these people, and I've said what I came to say, anyway.'' He raised his gaze to Cord, still standing in front of him. "I've got to admit, Chief, when I learned it was you who blew the whistle on me I was hoping for a long time that I'd run into you in a dark alley some night. But that's all water under the bridge as far as I'm concerned—you did what you thought you had to do, and I'm on easy street these days. I've got my own investigation agency now. If you're ever looking to change jobs, give me a call.''

He fished a dog-eared business card out of the breast pocket of his blue suit and handed it to a silent Cord, but as he did, his glance fell on Julia, and the slightly bloodshot eyes widened in recognition. Then, curiously, his glance slid uncomfortably away from her and back to Cord again. He addressed him with insincere enthusiasm.

"Hey, you two lovebirds made up! I'll tell you, Chief—this little girl just fell completely apart when you dumped—"

"Not one more word, Tascoe."

Cord's voice barely carried, but its very lack of emphasis was a threat in itself. If he was forced to take on Dean Tascoe he wouldn't even break a sweat, Julia thought with a flicker of gratification that she instantly suppressed. Although clearly the other man had once been formidably muscled, much of his bulk had turned to fat, and despite his bullying manner it was obvious that he knew he'd pushed Cord to a dangerous limit. He gave an unconvincing shrug.

"No offense, Chief. I just thought—"

"Calling me Chief is offensive, Tascoe." Cord sounded suddenly weary. "But today all I want is to say goodbye to my two best friends in peace. Just go."

"We're going." The blond woman Tascoe looked pasty and ill, and her voice was thready. "I—I'm sorry about your friends. What happened to them was—was terrible. *Terrible.* Especially since there was a—a child involved." The thin hand on Tascoe's sleeve trembled visibly.

Tascoe bent his balding head once more to his companion, and again Julia was struck by the complete change in his personality as he did so. His arm around her, he nodded to Cord, ignoring Cindy Lopez and the others, and led the distraught Jackie away.

"I can't believe he used to be a cop." Darting a disgusted look at his retreating figure, Cindy raked strong fingers through a swath of shining hair and then patted her pockets. "I don't want anyone ragging on me for this," she said belligerently, pulling out a pack of cigarettes and scowling. She lit one with a quick nervous gesture and took a deep drag. "I'm trying to quit, but having to deal with that yahoo right after a funeral is too much."

"Jerks like that aren't worth it, Cin." A slender, almost fragile-seeming woman in the group spoke up, her voice attractively husky. Chestnut hair curved in elegant feathers around the delicate bones of her face and her arched brows knitted together as the other woman drew agitatedly on the cigarette. "Why don't we go home and I'll brew up some maté? We can have it out on the balcony."

Her clear green gaze rested on Cindy with a mixture of love and concern that seemed oddly familiar to Julia. With dawning comprehension, she realized that it was the same look that she'd seen in Sheila's eyes when the stress of the job had gotten to Paul. The knowledge took her aback, but only for a moment. Although she hadn't guessed at Cindy's lifestyle when she'd met her after Cord had transferred out two years ago, Paul certainly would have known shortly after being partnered with her. He'd counted her among his friends, and that was good enough for Julia. Lopez sighed.

"I know, Erica." She frowned and looked at Cord. "Dammit, he was grilling me for details like some stringer for the *National Enquirer*—asking me whether Paul was shot and then stabbed, or stabbed and then shot, wanting to know exactly where Sheila's body had been found, what she'd been wearing..." Her voice shook. "Hell, after everything I've seen at work you'd think I'd be handling this better."

"He used to be my partner. I'm not handling it too well, either," Cord said bleakly. "Being a cop doesn't mean you stop feeling—unless you want to end up like Dean Tascoe."

He squinted through the elm branches at the cloudless sky, his hands shoved negligently in the pockets of his trousers, his jacket open. Against the crisp white of his shirt Julia glimpsed the worn brown leather of his shoulder holster, and at the sight a small jolt of fear ran through her. He'd come armed. What was he expecting to happen *here,* of all places?

"It seems all wrong, somehow, doesn't it?" Cindy's friend Erica looked at the perfect sky as Cord had and sketched a small, graceful gesture that encompassed the beautifully landscaped grounds, the freshly leafed trees, the golden sunlight bathing the scene. "If this was an opera the heavens would be splitting open with thunder and lightning, the sky would be dark, and we'd be rending our clothes and cursing the gods."

"This is my only decent pantsuit," Lopez said with a lop-sided smile. "But that cursing the gods thing sounds good to me. Erica designs stage costumes," she added to Julia with a note of pride in her voice. "She gets a little Wagnerian once in a while, but this time she's right. I'd feel better if I could just be *doing* something."

As they'd been speaking, the crowd around them had gradually thinned. Lopez's frustrated comment brought forth a ragged and dispirited chorus of agreement from the few remaining officers clustered nearby, and one by one, men and women in uniform shook hands or clasped each other in brief, wordless hugs before heading toward the high and ornate iron gates enclosing the area. Beyond the gates, parked cars lined both sides of the winding, graveled drive that entered the cemetery.

"I guess we should be heading out, too, Cord," Lopez said heavily. "Although tonight I don't think a nice hot cup of maté's going to cut it." She shot a defiantly guilty look at Erica that under different circumstances might have brought a smile to Julia's lips. "I've got a date with an almost full bottle of Scotch that I've been saving for a rainy day. Right now I feel like Noah."

There was a heartbeat of silence after her words, and then her appalled gaze found and held Julia's. Her color rose under the smooth tan of her cheeks.

"God—sorry, Julia. I didn't intend to—I mean, I know it's probably something you'd rather..." She raked her hair back, her expression contrite and her words trailing away. "Me and my big mouth," she mumbled.

Great, Julia thought dully. Her only consolation these last two years had been that at least the people she'd once worked with had no idea of how completely her life had disintegrated. Now it seemed that her personal problems and weaknesses had been common knowledge right from the start. It was humiliating, and shameful, and...

...and strangely *liberating,* she thought with a slight sense of shock. She wouldn't have to watch what she said or concoct any elaborate excuses—make that lies, she told herself—in the event that she found herself in a social situation. It felt as if a weighty load had been lifted from her shoulders—a weight that she never would have had the nerve to shrug off without Cindy's faux pas.

Although she *had* been able to tell Cord, she realized, surprised.

"Please don't think that Paul violated any confidences—" Cindy stammered, but Julia cut across her apologies.

"I know he didn't. I thought it was such a terrible secret that I didn't tell anyone about it."

Seeing the stricken look in the expressive brown eyes watching her, she laid her hand tentatively on Lopez's arm. The disconcerting thought came to her that it had been a long time since she'd reached out to comfort another person.

"Cindy—it's okay. I'm not upset." She attempted a grin. "I'm certainly not about to run off to the nearest bar and knock back a dozen tequila shooters because of this."

It was time to change the topic, she thought, wishing all of a sudden that she was back at the lake, alone in the big house with no one but King to intrude upon her solitude. But the German shepherd was with Lizbet at Mary Whitefield's house, where he would stay until all danger to the child had passed.

"You must have your own theory as to who targeted Paul and Sheila." She directed her comment to Lopez, but she was conscious of Cord beside her. "I know neither of us has any official standing in this matter, but maybe the very fact that we aren't as close to the investigation as you are might help us see a pattern here."

"I think I see the pattern," Lopez began, but then she broke off, darting a quick glance over her shoulder at a cluster of overall-clad workers standing by the discreet, foot-high chain that surrounded the rectangles of fresh earth a few dozen yards away. Julia followed her glance. Just beyond the two new graves the rolling landscape took a slight rise, and from somewhere out of sight she could hear the rumbling noise of a piece of machinery idling. It sounded like construction equipment, more suited to the side of a highway than to this pastoral setting.

Cord had heard it, too. Julia saw the pain that flashed across his features without understanding the reason for it. A second later she understood.

"I think we're holding up their work." His hand moved as if to touch her, but then he checked himself. "Let's go," he said quietly. "They want to fill in the graves."

"Oh."

The startled exclamation that escaped Cindy's lips made her suddenly sound much more vulnerable than her tough exterior suggested. Erica, taking in the situation at a glance, laid a hand on her back, shepherding her gently toward the gates that led out of the cemetery.

"You said you thought you saw a pattern?" Cord's question was a timely diversion. Erica shot him a grateful look. Julia heard Cindy take in a deep, shuddering breath and saw her square her shoulders.

"Yeah. And I think we were *supposed* to see it." She frowned at the velvety turf underfoot, and Julia realized that the dark-haired woman beside her was back in the unassumingly comfortable suburban house that she'd visited so often before as a guest, but that now had turned nightmarishly into a crime scene, with her partner and his wife as the victims.

"It was the way Paul was killed, of course," Lopez said haltingly.

Julia knew she was reliving the moment when, after getting the call at home and racing to the scene, she must have run up the pebbled walkway to Paul's house, her badge held wordlessly out to the phalanx of uniformed officers. She would have had to put away all personal feelings at the time, Julia thought with aching compassion, and it couldn't be done. She knew that from her own experience. But Lopez, with her cigarettes, her nervous mannerisms and her obvious stress, was tearing herself apart trying. Julia only hoped that Erica would be there for her when the inevitable emotional crash came.

"The shot to the head killed him, and the killer would have known that. Anyone would have known that, just—" her throat worked convulsively "—just by looking at him. It was bad. Real bad."

Her eyes were luminous with sadness. As they passed

through the iron gates and headed toward the private road, now almost empty of cars, she continued with an obvious effort. "So the stabbing had to be some kind of sign. Its only purpose was symbolic, and once we accepted that, it was obvious what it was meant to symbolize."

"You and Paul had been trying to destroy the heart of the DiMarco organization." Cord's statement was matter-of-fact. "The authorities were being warned off the mob investigation, and killing Paul that way was a brutal example of the retaliation in store if the case continued."

"Yeah. You're good, Detective Hunter." Lopez shot him a twisted smile. "That's the way I read it, too. We'd targeted Vince DiMarco's chain of Laundromats because we knew there was more getting washed in them than just clothes." She gave a short laugh. "Now that heroin's trendy again, thanks to a couple of irresponsible movies that impressed the hell out of a whole new generation of kids, DiMarco—ever the savvy businessman—has gotten into it in a big way. Which means big money. Big *dirty* money that he's passing through his legit operations, including the Laundromats, so it loses that unpleasant smell of dead junkies and ruined lives."

This time Erica's comforting touch couldn't stop the shaking. Her hair falling like dark brown silk around her face, Lopez stood stock-still at the edge of the drive, fists clenched at her sides, her head bowed. Julia looked up at Cord helplessly. He met her stricken gaze and this time she welcomed the brief moment of closeness. Then he stepped away, facing Lopez and gripping her shoulders.

"You had a cousin. She died of an overdose, didn't she?" His words were gentle and barely audible, but at them Lopez's tearstained face jerked up.

"How did you know that? *Nobody* knows that!"

"Before I left for California I needed to be sure that whoever was replacing me as Paul's partner was someone I could trust. I won't apologize for investigating you, Lopez. If you'd been in my position you'd have done the same. We both cared too much for Paul to leave anything to chance where his partner was concerned."

The woman in front of him nodded slowly. Julia felt some of the tension of the moment ease, and beside her Erica let out a pent-up breath.

"Tina and I were as close as sisters. She was a few years younger than me, but the difference in our ages didn't seem to matter. We did everything together. But at the time I decided to become a cop she was dating this guy that no one in the family liked, especially me. I knew he was bad news and I couldn't see what she saw in him." She shrugged, her eyes clouded with memory. "Well, you two know how consumed your life becomes when you're in training. Then, after I found out I'd made the cut and took my first rookie position, I seemed to have even less of a personal life. I was working crazy shifts, pulling doubles a lot of the time, taking more training…" Her voice broke. "I should have *made* time for her. The day I made my first arrest I came home to tell my family. My mother was just hanging up the phone when I walked into the house. She told me Tina was dead. She was only seventeen, and when I saw her body at the funeral home I thought I was looking at an old lady."

"So right from the start investigating DiMarco was personal," Julia said. "Now it's even more so. Have you thought about asking for another assignment?"

Lopez looked at her as if she'd suddenly started talking Urdu. "Another assignment? I'm like you—I'll go down in flames one of these days. But until then I'll give the job everything I've got, whatever the consequences."

Julia didn't dare look at Cord. "I didn't go down in flames," she said shortly. "I made the decision to leave because I wanted to do more with my life."

"That's not what I heard. I heard—"

"You heard wrong." Julia's tone was a clear signal that the topic was closed, and Lopez stared at her, obviously taken aback. Then she flicked a glance at Cord's impassive face, and her dark eyes widened.

"Sure," she agreed smoothly, her features a bland mask. "There's a lot of scuttlebutt when someone leaves. I should have known better than to listen to rumors."

"Where are you parked?" Cord's question was directed at Lopez and Erica. He didn't look at Julia.

"Around that curve," Erica said. "When we arrived there was a line of cars almost all the way up to the main road. We couldn't get any closer."

"Would I be pulling a Dean Tascoe if I offered to hike up there and get my vehicle first? It's a little closer, and then I could drive you back to yours." His grin, although it didn't reach his eyes, brought forth an answering smile from Erica.

"I think I'd even put up with Tascoe's chauvinism if it would save me another walk in these heels." Although her companion was wearing a creamy silk blouse and a charcoal pantsuit, she'd opted for a tailored skirt and jacket. Her shoes, elegantly narrow, didn't look like they'd stand up to the graveled road for long.

"I'll go with you, Cord." Lopez raked her hair back with one hand. Julia saw her reach toward the pocket that held her cigarettes with the other, and then stop. "Don't worry, I won't sneak one when I'm out of sight," she told a watching Erica with a guilty smile. "I just need to get Cord's advice on a couple of details that bothered me about the crime scene."

"Julia?" Cord gave her a politely inquiring glance. The current that had flowed between them when he'd met her gaze earlier might never have existed. "Do you want to wait here or walk up with us?"

He was distancing himself from her. She knew he was, because she'd used the same techniques herself—the impersonal courtesy, the meticulous consideration for her convenience, the painstaking inclusion of her in an activity. Those had been her tactics in the weeks leading up to that final discussion when she'd told him that she didn't want the future they'd planned together.

The last thing she'd ever wanted to do was to hurt him. Now she realized just how wounding her inexplicable coolness must have been.

"I'll stay with Erica. My heels aren't as high as hers, but since I practically live in Weejuns, my feet aren't too happy with me, either," she replied, hoping she sounded convincing.

Apparently she did. In a few minutes Cord and Lopez were out of sight around the bend in the road, despite the fact that he had to be shortening his stride to match hers.

"Cindy put her foot in it again, didn't she?" Slipping her shoes off, Erica sat down on a small ornamental bench just outside the iron gates. Julia remained standing, but she was careful to keep her gaze averted from the grounds themselves. She could hear the same rumble of machinery that she'd heard before, but now the varying timbre of the engine signified that it was in use.

"You're a nice woman, and Lopez is lucky to have you for a friend," she answered stiffly. "But touchy-feely isn't my style, Erica. I don't feel comfortable discussing my personal life at the best of times."

Her words were just short of rudeness but Erica wasn't put off. "I knew someone like you once," she mused. She looked at her dark blue linen skirt and flicked a nonexistent speck of lint from it. "She was wound as tightly as a top, but everyone saw her as a competent, unflappable success. She never let anyone get close enough to her to realize that she was screaming inside. She was me, of course," she added quietly.

"You?" Julia stared unbelievingly at the other woman. "But you seem so—so *centered*," she protested.

"And you seem so detached." Erica met her gaze. "But you're not, are you? You didn't stop being a cop because of a cool and rational career decision—you left because you were hemorrhaging to death, and you didn't know any other way to stop the bleeding."

Those clear blue eyes saw too much—*way* too much, Julia thought. With relief she heard the crunching of tires on gravel and turned, surprised but grateful that Cord and Lopez had returned in time to terminate this excruciating tête-à-tête.

But the vehicle slowing to a stop in front of them wasn't the sports utility that Cord had rented yesterday. As the gleaming black limousine idled a few feet away, she realized that it had to belong to the funeral home that had taken care of the arrangements today.

"They'll be bringing more flowers. The church was full of them," Erica said in a low tone, but Julia wasn't listening.

Her intuition, after two years of disuse, was rusty. But once upon a time she'd relied on it, not only for her own safety, but for the very survival of the children she'd been assigned to protect. She'd been trained to see below the surface—to notice the incongruity of a little boy who wore long sleeves on a hot summer day to hide bruises, the terrible secret that a little girl might signal by mutilating a favorite doll, the puppy chew toy in a household where there was now no pet—a possible sign of a murderous violence that was just one step away from claiming a tiny, human victim.

And now that intuition was telling her that a limousine with windows tinted so darkly that its occupants were invisible was not the vehicle that would be used to transport floral tributes. "Erica, get up and run back inside the gates," she commanded in a terse voice, her lips barely moving as the door to the limousine unlatched with an audible and solid-sounding thunk. "Make your way back to those workmen as fast as you can."

"What's the matter?" Alerted by her tone, Erica had risen. Her shoes lay on their sides on the grass where she'd kicked them off.

"Now!" Julia snapped. "It's you they want—you're supposed to be an object lesson, just like Sheila was. *Run,* Erica!"

The car door was opening even as she spoke, but the slender, elegant blonde was already moving through the gates and over the manicured lawns, her escape witnessed by the two burly men hastily exiting the rear doors of the limousine. As they approached, Julia saw the telltale bulges in their jackets. Her leg muscles tightened unconsciously as if to ready herself for instant flight, but logic told her that DiMarco's men weren't interested in her. To kill indiscriminately would nullify the message they wanted to send—that they were targeting specific individuals who were somehow linked to the investigation of their boss.

"I know you're not here to pay your respects to the dead," she said flatly. "What do you want?"

"You Julia Stewart?" The man who spoke had a curiously

light voice, as if something had damaged his larynx. She was surprised into a slight nod. At it, he smiled, reaching into his jacket.

"You're making a mistake." She'd left it too late to run, Julia thought. The best she could do was stall for a few precious seconds and hope that Cord and Lopez would arrive in time. The burly man's hand withdrew from his jacket as the frantic hope raced through her mind, but instead of a gun he was holding what looked like a short leather stick. It was a blackjack, she thought, confused.

"No mistake, Miss Stewart. You're the one we want," he said in that oddly delicate voice. Before she could react he stepped nimbly behind her and brought the weapon down on the base of her skull.

Chapter 6

They were out in the Sunfish and the boom had swung around, but it was different this time—this time the boom had attacked her, not Davey. She'd started to fall overboard, but he'd jumped up and saved her. This was the way it was *supposed* to have happened, Julia thought happily. She was crying, but not because her head hurt so much. Davey had never died. Dad wouldn't make her invisible anymore and Mom wouldn't be sick so much and she wouldn't know, always and for the rest of her life, that she was responsible for the terrible thing that had torn her family apart....

"This is the way it was *supposed* to have happened," she insisted groggily, struggling to hold onto the dream as futilely as she so often struggled to escape the nightmares. She could hear muffled music and then a voice that stirred a faint chord in her memory, although she couldn't immediately place it. It was an older man's voice, very slightly accented and tight with anger.

"I told you not to lay a *hand* on her—what didn't you understand about that, you fools? This was *not* the way it was supposed to be!" The words alone held no threat, but the thread of icy fury that ran through them was clear. She knew who he was now, and felt dazedly thankful that his anger wasn't directed at her.

Vittorio Falcone's displeasure, though less easily roused than it once had been, was still something to be avoided at all costs. His enemies had a way of vanishing.

There was the sound of a door being opened, and as it did the music got briefly louder. Then it closed and the room fell quiet. Julia opened her eyes and met the knowing gaze of the man watching her.

"Hi, Vittorio," she said in a voice that sounded nothing like her own. "I take it I'm at the strip club?"

"Yeah. I heard you were out of a job."

The thin lips stretched into a smile as he sat down behind a battered metal desk overflowing with papers and cash register receipts.

"But the customers aren't paying to see ribs, *cara.* You'll have to put some meat on that scrawny frame before you can work here at the Bootie Palace."

His hands looked a little more arthritic than she remembered, but Don Vittorio's hooded dark eyes still reminded her of the bird of prey that was his namesake, and the aura of ruthless power that hung around him as palpably as a cloak had never depended merely on physical strength. Despite the fact that he based his operations out of this shabbily utilitarian office and made a point of knowing everything that went on in the club, he could never have been mistaken for an elderly small-time businessman. There was something about him that commanded respect.

He still had a full head of thick, steel-gray hair, and he still dressed the way he had when she'd first met him—a soft white shirt, its sleeves rolled halfway up forearms that had once been more muscular than they were now, gray flannel pants and always a vest. He kept his shirt buttoned up to the collar, but once she'd seen the small gold medallion that he wore around his neck. St. Jude, he'd told her with an oddly rueful smile— because he himself was probably a lost cause.

It had been a telling remark, and when he'd made it Julia

had known without asking that any favors Vittorio Falcone
might request of St. Jude would be for his grandson, not himself.

He had lost his wife years ago, and his only son had been
killed during a brief but bloody power struggle between rival
mob families. Falcone had paid a high price for his power and
wealth. He was determined that his beloved grandson's life
would follow a different path.

"I have to make a phone call, Vittorio," she said firmly.
"The people I was with when I left so abruptly for this meeting
will be worried."

Cord wouldn't just be worried, she thought apprehensively—
he'd be going crazy blaming himself for having gotten her into
this.

"They know where you are by now. I sent one of my men
with a message as soon as those fools told me how they'd
handled things," Vittorio said with a grimace. "Again, my
apologies, my friend."

She sat up cautiously, her immediate worries subsiding, but
still determined to contact Cord herself as soon as Vittorio Falcone had told her what he'd brought her here to say.

Friend. Vittorio Falcone didn't use the word lightly, she
knew. He had acquaintances, associates and underlings by the
score, but he could count the number of people he called friends
on the fingers of one hand. She was one of those few.

"How is Anthony these days, Don Falcone?" She seldom
used his title, but the old man had just honored her, and she
wanted him to know she was aware of that.

"He's been accepted at Harvard Medical—can you believe
it? A Falcone at *Harvard.*"

"He'll make you proud of him. One day you'll have to call
him *Dottore*," Julia said huskily. The old man gave an unsteady
little laugh, his eyes suspiciously bright.

"He still asks about you, you know," he said gruffly. "He
knows how much he owes you. I do too, *cara.*"

Anthony Falcone had been a vulnerable teenager on the road
to self-destruction when Julia had first come in contact with
him years ago. He'd been one of her earliest cases, and at first

no one had realized that the rebellious young runaway recovering in the emergency ward from a near-fatal sample of angel dust laced with strychnine was the grandson of Vittorio Falcone. Anthony had refused to identify himself to Julia when she'd questioned him in the hospital, and the next day when she'd shown up again she'd been told that he'd gone.

With a workload that she could hardly keep up with, it would have been easy for her to simply chalk him up as one more runaway who didn't want to come home and go on to her next case. But in her brief interview with the underage teen, Julia had sensed the terrible emotional turmoil that he'd been going through, and for the next two weeks she'd spent every off-duty hour scouring the city for him. By then the papers were full of the news that Don Vittorio's grandson was missing and believed kidnapped, but no one linked that information with the young boy who'd walked out of the hospital.

She'd found him, finally, and not a moment too soon, unconscious in a cardboard box in a garbage-strewn alleyway. This time when he'd been rushed to the hospital someone had recognized him, and Vittorio Falcone had been notified.

He'd sat by his grandson's bed for three days and three nights, never leaving his side, until the boy was out of danger and on the mend. Then he'd paid a visit to Julia. She could name her price, he'd told her harshly. Whatever he had was hers, in return for saving his Anthony's life.

She'd turned down his money incredulously. If he really wanted to repay her, she'd told the mob boss, he could get his grandson into counseling to ensure that whatever problem he'd been trying to run away from was resolved. Vittorio himself was probably partially to blame for the situation, she'd gone on heatedly. Armed and stone-faced minions had stood stolidly by, sure that the slender young woman angrily chewing out their impassively silent boss was signing her own death warrant.

Instead, Don Vittorio had kissed her hand as he'd left with his phalanx of bodyguards. He'd followed her advice and repaired his relationship with his grandson, and over the following years he had kept her apprised of Anthony's achievements.

And he had added her to the very short list of people he considered friends.

"You should be proud, Vittorio. You brought up a fine young man," Julia said with affection.

"He would have been dead if it hadn't been for you." Under shaggy gray brows, the hawk-like eyes bored into hers as he delivered the blunt statement. "How many others like him have there been?"

Disconcerted, she looked away. "It was my job. There were too many I lost."

"And now you have another one to protect, eh?"

Shocked, her eyes flew to his. "Don Vittorio—how did you know that?"

He calmed her agitation with an upraised hand. "Don't worry, it's not common knowledge. But me, here—I'm like a spider sitting in the middle of a web. Anything happens at the edges of my web, I hear about it. I put all those pieces of information together and do some thinking and I come up with answers." He frowned. "Then I tell myself, Vittorio—maybe your friend Julia, who two years ago walked away from everything she cared about and who told you she didn't need your help when you offered it—maybe she just might need your help now. They think the killings of the detective and his wife were ordered by Vince DiMarco, don't they?"

Julia hesitated. "It's the only possibility they've come up with so far," she admitted slowly. "And his death seemed designed to—to send a message."

It was still unbearably hard to talk about. If Vittorio Falcone had been involved, even peripherally, in arranging Paul's gruesome murder and Sheila's senseless execution, Julia thought suddenly, her friendship with him would disappear as if it had never been. She would destroy the old man herself if she had to, but he would pay for his crime.

"Don't look at me like that, *cara*." He sounded testy. "I wasn't part of—"

With a violent crash, the door to his office flew open. From the club beyond, the sound of high-pitched screams and angry shouts drowned out the music, but all Julia's attention was focused on the two men entering Don Vittorio's inner sanctum.

One of them was Cord. The other was a stranger, but whoever he was, he was holding his right arm close to his chest and his face was drained of all color. He stumbled ahead of Cord into the room, and only then did she see that he was being propelled forward by the barrel of the automatic Cord was pressing into his spine.

"Are you all right, Julia?" Cord's question was tersely urgent.

Vittorio held up his hands in a placating gesture. "She's fine, my hotheaded young friend. I brought her here to give her some information, that's all." He rose and walked to the door calmly, flashing a disgusted look at his disarmed minion. "Come. We must talk, Julia—but I advise that your impetuous Detective Hunter conceal his weapon before the rest of my men see it."

He pushed open the door to the public area of the club, leaving them no choice but to follow him. Julia darted an incredulous look at Cord.

"You were aware that I knew Falcone. What the *hell* were you thinking of?" She kept her voice low, but it throbbed with anger.

"Some thug collars me in the precinct parking lot where I was just about to start setting up a search for you and tells me not to worry, you're with your old pal the crime boss," he whispered back at her. "That was supposed to *reassure* me? You don't know me at all, do you?"

His face was inches from hers and his voice was a furious whisper. Her lips parted in shock. "I'm the man who's loved you since the day you stopped wearing pigtails. Didn't it occur to you that I wouldn't believe you were safe until I heard it from *you?* You've got my damn cell number—was it too much to expect that you'd phone me yourself? I thought you'd been *killed,* dammit!"

She'd known he could get angry. She hadn't realized he was capable of directing that anger at her, no matter what the provocation. Cord had always had boundless patience and infinite forbearance where she was concerned.

"You're right, I should have—" she began.

"Shove it, Julia," he snapped tiredly. "It either comes from the heart or it doesn't. I don't need the Emily Post version."

He strode ahead of her. Even the back of his head looked rigid with anger, she thought, dismayed and oddly disconcerted by his curt dismissal.

As she sat at the secluded corner table the old man had selected, Vittorio sighed.

"I have a grandson. He will never conduct his business in such a place as this." He inclined his head toward the large stage in the middle of the room, where a woman with impossibly platinum hair and even more impossible breasts was going through her routine.

"You despise me because of who I am and what I do. Fair enough. We are enemies, in a way." Vittorio turned to Cord, who was watching him with narrowed eyes. "But no one will ever despise my grandson. As he grows into manhood he will be honored and respected, and one day the name of Falcone will come to stand for something very different than it does now. This I owe to my friend here." He nodded at Julia, his expression softening as he did so. "But she has never let me repay her, and Vittorio Falcone, as you may know, does not like unpaid debts. So when I hear what has happened to her friends, and I learn who is thought to be responsible, I know that this is my chance to pay back some small portion of what I owe. The whole debt, of course, can never be paid in full," he said softly, the fierce brown eyes brilliant with emotion.

"Short of having Vincent DiMarco gift-wrapped and delivered to us for questioning, I don't see how you can help us," Cord said dismissively. "And that's not about to happen. Even the police haven't been able to locate him—the man's gone underground."

"Ahh…" Vittorio spread his callused workingman's palms out in an expansive gesture that took in the darkened club, the garishly lit stage, the afternoon drinkers. "But this *is* the underground—and I rule it."

As soon as the words left his lips, she heard the sudden sound of a commotion coming from the main entrance of the club. A group of businessmen who had been enjoying the show from a nearby table turned their heads to look, their slightly befuddled expressions turning to sharp alarm. Hastily grabbing the suit jackets they had shed and tossing bills down beside their latest round of drinks, they exited hurriedly. Other patrons were exhibiting similar signs of nervousness—either leaving as quickly as the table of businessmen had or turning to stare straight ahead at the stage, their faces carefully blank.

"Not gift-wrapped," Vittorio said, his lips thinning in distaste. "But yours to question."

The reason for his distaste was as apparent as the reason for the sudden consternation that had swept the club. Weaving their way through tables that emptied as if by magic before them came four of Vittorio's men, all of them solidly built and grim-faced. The man they were frog-marching toward the corner table looked to be in his thirties, with fleshy good looks that were right now distorted by rage and humiliation.

He had to be Vincent DiMarco.

All he was wearing was a silk dressing robe that stopped well short of his bony knees and was dangerously close to slipping completely open in front. Even as the thought went through her mind, the opulent fringed tie belt came undone. He was also wearing a pair of chartreuse silk boxers, she saw in relief.

"How the hell—" Cord was staring at Vittorio, who returned his look blandly. "The department's been looking for him for *days!*" he exploded.

"Obviously not in the right place," Vittorio said. "There are two highly accomplished Swedish girls he's been seeing lately…twins. You think we interrupted his language lesson?"

"Let me go, damn you!"

His robe flapping ridiculously open, revealing a chest that looked like a bear rug and a number of glinting gold chains, Vincent DiMarco shouted into the impassive faces of the men propelling him forward.

"This is a *betrayal,* Vittorio!" As Falcone's men shoved him roughly toward their table, his arms still firmly pinioned to his sides, the man's attitude was blusteringly outraged but his Adam's apple bobbed as he spoke, betraying his fear.

"A betrayal of what?" Falcone's voice was icy and Julia knew she was seeing a side of him that she had deliberately closed her eyes to before. "You've been dealing in *eroina,* no? Heroin?" DiMarco opened his mouth but before he could speak the old man waved a contemptuous hand. "No lies, remember? You have been watched for some time now, Vincenzo, and I know almost all of it already. This interview would have come soon enough, but this way I can do a favor for a friend. You thought to expand your turf, and you decided that maybe the old falcon was too blind and too weary to know what was happening in his territory. That was a mistake, but not your first one…and not your biggest one."

He frowned. "However, for now we want to know what your involvement was in the deaths of the police detective and his wife. Again—lying is not in your best interests, Vincenzo."

There was steel in the old man's voice, but something else too, Julia thought. The hairs at the back of her neck prickled apprehensively. It came to her that for the first time in her life she was hearing what pure, unadulterated hatred sounded like— not anger, not fury, but a hate so dark and so deep that it seemed like no human emotion at all.

The flip side of hatred was love. Suddenly she knew why Vittorio Falcone, Anthony's grandfather, hated Vincent DiMarco so thoroughly and so well. She was looking at a dead man, she thought. Her stomach lurched.

The next moment Cord's hand had reached for hers under the table. His attention was still fixed on DiMarco, awaiting his answer, but his strong fingers wrapped around hers firmly, as if he knew how much of an ordeal this was for her.

She'd told herself she couldn't start depending on his strength again, that it wasn't fair. *To hell with fair,* Julia thought, gripping Cord's hand as tightly as she could and wishing she never had to let go. Tomorrow she could start being fair and sensible and detached again. Right now she needed him, and the touch of his hand on hers made her feel like she'd come home after being lost for a long, long time.

"*No,* Don Falcone! That was nothing to do with me—I swear it!" DiMarco's complexion was ashy. He had been trying ineffectually to pull the edges of his robe together, but now he abandoned the attempt. "I may have been considering how best to deal with the problem—yes, I confess, I had set up a small sideline that I had not yet informed you about, but—"

"You're lying again. I have no time for this." Falcone made a small motion of dismissal and turned to Cord. "I will call you in a few hours. We will have the truth for you then."

"I can *prove* it, Don Falcone!" The half-clad man looked as though he was about to faint. He swayed in his chair, and his hand clutched at Falcone's arm desperately.

"*Never touch me.*" Vittorio repressed a shudder and Julia knew that her suspicions had been correct. "An alibi is worthless. You paid someone to do the deed for you, Vincenzo."

"*Yes*—I did." Sweat glistened on the pallid face. "I paid someone to attach a device to his *car,* Don Falcone! If Durant had lived until the next morning, when he started his car it would have exploded. *That's* what I had planned."

"He's telling the truth," Cord said flatly. He turned to Julia. "Lopez told me this afternoon that they'd seen signs that Paul's vehicle had been tampered with. Luckily somebody used their head and called in the bomb squad before another cop got killed. And that information hasn't been released to the media, Falcone," he added to Vittorio. "Even you weren't aware of that detail, am I right?"

The old man shook his head. "I have my sources, but there wasn't even a whisper."

"You're lucky, DiMarco." Cord stood up. Even beside Falcone's men he gave a formidable impression of sheer physical strength and dangerous power, but unlike them he had a quality of restraint holding that strength in check.

"This was not what you had hoped for. I'm sorry," Vittorio started to get to his feet.

"I can give you a *name,* Don Falcone!" DiMarco had been dabbing at his forehead with a paper serviette, but now he leaned forward eagerly.

"We should leave," Cord said in an undertone. "If he starts

spilling information about mob business I'll have to pass it on, and that could implicate Vittorio. Come on.'' He started to turn away.

''No—wait!'' This time DiMarco's clutching fingers fastened on to the edge of Cord's sleeve. He half rose from his seat, but sank back when one of Falcone's men took a step forward. ''This is to do with the killings! It's not *me* you should be talking to—you should be looking in your own back yard!''

''*What are you talking about?*''

Cord turned to the man. Bending over and bracing himself on the tabletop, his palms flat on its surface, he brought his face to within inches of DiMarco's.

''What do you mean, in my own back yard? Was it another *officer* who did this?'' With a sudden, violent movement he straightened, grabbing the gaudy lapels of the silk gown and pulling DiMarco from his seat. ''*Tell* me!''

''I don't *know!*'' He struggled ineffectually in Cord's grip, his breath coming in harsh, labored gasps. ''But a man came to us weeks ago—said he was willing to sell us inside information about the investigation that your friend was conducting. He said that whatever we wanted to know about Durant, he could find it out for us.''

''His *name,* dammit!'' Cord's face was so close to DiMarco's that they were almost touching. The seam of one of the silk lapels ripped.

''He *said* he was a cop—but when I looked into it I found out he'd been fired a few years ago.'' With a mighty effort DiMarco wrenched out of Cord's grasp, his chest heaving. ''His name was Tascoe—Dean Tascoe.''

Chapter 7

"I don't want you going back to the house tonight. We'll phone Mary and Frank and tell them we won't be coming by to see Lizbet for a day or so." Cord tapped the brakes of the rented Bronco as a driver in front of him made an illegal lane change. His fingers tightened on the steering wheel. "Tascoe could be following us right now, and I'm not about to lead him to the child."

"We don't know that DiMarco was telling the truth. You saw the man, Cord—he would have said *anything*." Julia swallowed. "Do you—do you think the police will get to the club in time?"

As soon as they'd left Vittorio she'd insisted that they phone Lopez and tip her off to DiMarco's whereabouts. Cord had seen her distress and had complied, but now he glanced quickly at her.

"They would have been there within minutes of our leaving, believe me—it'll take a lot to convince them that he's not their number one suspect in the murders." They were driving into the setting sun, and he flipped the visor down. From the breast pocket of his jacket he pulled out a pair of Ray-Bans and put them on.

With his eyes concealed by the dark lenses he looked like a stranger, and Julia found herself studying his face as if he was someone she'd never met, as if he wasn't Cordell Hunter, the boy next door who'd loved her all his life, the familiar best friend of her big brother who'd substituted for Davey after he'd died and until she'd grown up enough to see him in a more adult role.

If she was just meeting him for the first time now, she thought, she would never guess at the tenderness he was capable of. If all she had of him was a passing glance on the street or a few moments of sharing an elevator in silence, she would see the firm mouth, the high, hard cheekbones with the tiny but obvious scar, the thick, midnight-black hair that he raked out of his eyes in an impatient, unconscious gesture now and then. He would seem dangerous and tough and forbidding.

And for a split second, passing by him on that street or brushing his sleeve as she exited that elevator, she wouldn't be able to repress a sudden weakness, a momentary breathlessness, as she wondered what he would be like in a more intimate setting.

He exuded total *maleness,* she thought. And it was foolish pretending that she would only be susceptible to that overwhelming physical aura if she met him as a stranger. He geared the Bronco down and the impenetrably dark lenses were turned her way.

"Why are you so worried about him, anyway? Falcone's one of the few who draws the line at hard narcotics, I know, but he's not going to have one of his top men whacked for it."

"DiMarco supplied Falcone's teenage grandson with angel dust six years ago," Julia said flatly. "He had to be trying to get to Vittorio through his family, or maybe he wanted to eliminate the next generation of power so that he could take over when the old man stepped down. I don't have to be a palm reader to know that his lifeline just got abruptly shortened, now that Falcone's guessed it was him who tried to eliminate Anthony."

"I knew I was missing something during that meeting," Cord said slowly. "You're sure about this?"

"I saw the hate in Vittorio's eyes." Her own were bleak as she looked at him. "You're right. He wouldn't let a business problem bother him. What he felt toward DiMarco was very, very personal…and maybe I don't blame him for what he wants to do to the man."

She felt guilty even for admitting it, but along with the guilt was a flicker of defiance. Vittorio Falcone's code was simple, and if someone broke it his retribution was brutal, but there was one part of it that she couldn't argue with. Children were to be protected. No matter what internecine war was raging around them in his world, they were to be kept out of it. DiMarco had violated that code.

"It's easy to let the boundaries blur when you're dealing with scum like DiMarco." There was a warning note in Cord's voice. "Look at Dean Tascoe—he used to be a pretty decent cop before he decided he could mete out his own brand of justice. Now there's a good chance he's a murderer."

"How do you figure that? Even if DiMarco was telling the truth, all we know is that Tascoe was willing to sell information," she argued. "He's bitter and he blames everyone except himself for losing his badge, but why would he target Paul specifically—even to the point of killing Sheila and wanting to hurt a little girl?"

"Paul backed me up on that report I made on Tascoe," Cord said shortly. "Without his corroboration it would have been my word against a detective who'd been on the force for almost twenty years. Tascoe had major clout, and there I was trying to get him ousted because Paul and I had walked in on him and a buddy pistol-whipping a sadistic little pimp that everyone thought deserved it anyway." He hesitated, and Julia saw his mouth tighten. "Hell, even *I* wouldn't have shed any tears if I'd been told that Billy Wolfe's body had been found in an alley somewhere."

"So why *did* you report Tascoe, if you felt like that?"

"Because sometimes it doesn't matter what you want or what you need or what you feel—you just have to take a stand and do the right thing," he said softly. They had come to an intersection and he had stopped for the red light, but he kept his gaze fixed straight ahead. When he spoke it seemed as if he was telling her something that he'd told himself many times before. "Maybe making that decision tears you apart. Maybe years later you still sit up nights wondering how your life would have turned out if you'd acted differently. But I have to look at myself in the mirror every day, Julia. I didn't want to be ashamed of the man I saw looking back at me. I couldn't stay quiet about what I saw Tascoe doing to Wolfe, and neither could Paul."

The light changed. Accelerating through the intersection smoothly, he went on, his voice hardening. "Anyway, Tascoe might see the loss of his career as motive enough for murder."

He signaled and slowed the Bronco, turning into the parking lot of the motel that he'd checked into two days previously. Her car was parked outside Cord's unit around the back where she'd left it after driving in to meet him before the funeral— had that only been a few hours ago? It felt like days, at least, she thought. There was a No Vacancy sign in the window of the office, so she wasn't going to find a room there, Julia thought wearily, noticing for the first time the grass stain on the front of her blouse—from where she'd fallen after Falcone's eager muscle man had coshed her, she surmised. She didn't even have a change of clothes with her.

"Maybe you should get out of town for a while." Pulling up beside her car, Cord turned off the ignition. He made no move to get out. She stared at him, her weariness suddenly forgotten.

"Why?" Her voice rose in astonishment.

"Because Tascoe saw you with me today and he knows that you're important to me. If he killed Sheila, what's to stop him from coming after you?" He reached up and took off his sunglasses, tiredly pinching the bridge of his nose with his thumb and forefinger. "If Tascoe's our man, then I'm the second half of his revenge equation. He knew he wouldn't have to come hunting for me in California, that I'd be back to attend Paul's funeral."

"You're forgetting something. *You* came to *me,* Cord."

Her angry retort was loud enough so that an older couple exiting the motel looked apprehensively toward them.

"Let's discuss this inside. Among other things, it's probably not good police procedure to shout out our theories to all and sundry," Cord said shortly.

Slamming the Bronco's door behind her with more force than she needed, Julia waited while he locked the vehicle and then stiffly followed him to the door of the unit. As soon as they stepped inside she whirled around to face him.

"You came to *me*—because we're *both* responsible for what happens to Lizbet! It wasn't just you standing alone at that baptismal font five years ago promising to take care of her if the day ever came that Paul and Sheila couldn't. I was there, *too!* I made the same vow! And now you expect me to simply walk *out* on her when her life's in danger?" She had never been so angry with him. But then, he had never misjudged her so completely.

"I came to you because I hoped she'd be able to tell you what she saw, give you some clue as to what the killer looked like or what he sounded like—*something.*" Cord shucked off his suit jacket and threw it on the bed. He loosened his tie with a jerk. "But dammit, she hasn't said one word since I got her out of her house. Mary told me that she won't even talk to the other kids when they're playing."

"She's responding to me better than before," Julia protested quickly. "She lets me hold her now, and yesterday when King chased a squirrel she actually laughed a little." She paused and then went on reluctantly. "But no, I don't think she can help us much with what she saw that night. Not in the near future, anyway."

"And now you won't even be able to visit her." Cord looked at her with a frown. "When I showed up on your doorstep the other night you made it crystal clear that you didn't want to become involved. I don't understand why we're even arguing about this."

"Because I *did* get involved, dammit!" She faced him, hazel eyes blazing. "You pulled me back in and now you want to push me back out again. *I've* got to look in the mirror every day too, Cord—and for the last two years I haven't felt that proud of the person I see staring back at me."

She stopped. She'd said too much, she thought.

"Lopez said you'd gone down in flames. Exactly what the hell happened in those last few weeks after I left, Julia?" She was standing close enough to the bed so that he could reach out and touch her, and he did, his hand grasping her wrist lightly. "You told me you were planning to give the job up, but it wasn't as simple as that, was it?"

"I screwed up. In that job screwing up can cost a child's life, so I handed in my badge a little sooner than I'd planned. That's all you need to know, Cord—that and the fact that I'm staying on this case."

Pulling her wrist away, she turned and walked into the bathroom, leaving the door slightly ajar. She stripped off her jacket and draped it over the shower rod, then unbuttoned her blouse and shrugged out of it, her back to him.

"When I was on the force I worked with people who were under stress, people who were lying or who had something to hide. I learned to read them pretty well. Tascoe might have been a dirty cop, but I just don't see him gunning down a woman in cold blood. It doesn't fit with his profile."

"He profiles as violent and ruthless. What doesn't fit?" From the room behind her Cord's voice took on an edge. "And by the way, it would be a whole lot easier on me if you'd keep your clothes on while we're discussing this."

"You've seen me with less on hundreds of times." Bending over the sink, Julia filled it with cold water and threw the blouse in to soak. "And I'm not Bootie Palace material. You should be able to keep yourself under control for a minute or two. Can I borrow one of your shirts?"

She was wearing a plain white cotton sports bra—no more revealing than a bathing suit top, she thought, and sensible rather than sensuous. Bras and panties were about the only clothing purchases she made these days, and the most erotic undergarment she owned were the panties she had on under her skirt. They were pale blue with a pattern of dancing carrots on them, for some Freudian reason.

"Take your pick." Without getting off the bed he gestured expansively at the small wardrobe beside the bolted-down television. "Nothing I own will fit you, anyway. And in case you're interested, I still think you're the most beautiful woman I've ever seen, bony elbows and all. I used to love the way your breasts would fit exactly in my hands—no more, no less."

Julia had crossed to the wardrobe, and now she was glad she had her back to him. Making a pretence of flipping through his selection of shirts—white, white and white with a faint off-white stripe—she felt a ridiculous prickle of tears behind her eyelids even as her mouth curved into a shaky smile.

Damn Cord Hunter anyway, she thought, pulling the racy off-white striped number from its hanger and struggling into it awkwardly. He'd never been one for flowery speeches, but he'd always had a habit of coming at her out of left field with some devastatingly heart-melting observation like the one he'd just made. He would drop it into the conversation casually, as if he was just stating a simple fact that he figured she already knew, and every single time he did it she felt like her heart took a little skip in her chest, as if it thought it could fly.

Stupid heart, she thought, blinking away the incipient tears. And stupid her, for letting her guard down, even for a minute.

"Tascoe might profile as violent, but he treated that woman he was with as if she was fine china," she said, cinching the tails of Cord's shirt around her waist in a knot and rolling back the sleeves. It still billowed extravagantly around her. "As misguided and twisted as the man is, he sees women as something to protect, not to harm. He takes it way too far, but doesn't it prove that it's unlikely he would kill Sheila and then hunt through the house for Lizbet?"

"It's a theory, Julia. It's not proof. And we can't overlook Paul's conviction that whoever was watching his family had ties to the police department." Cord stood up. "Dean Tascoe might have been booted off the force, but a lot of the hardliners in the department think he got shafted. He's still got contacts. Hell, Jackie's the chief's personal secretary."

"Jackie? The woman he was with?"

In the process of taking off his tie he paused, alerted by something in her tone. "Yeah. Jackie Redmond. Nice enough woman, and her life hasn't been easy. Why?"

Facing the dresser mirror, he slowly unbuttoned his cuffs, but his attention was focused on her reflection in the mirror. She shook her head as if to clear it, her expression troubled.

"Didn't you find her reaction at the funeral a little over the top? I mean—" she struggled to pinpoint her impressions "—she appeared so *shaken*."

"Everybody there was shaken by what happened to Sheila and Paul, even if they didn't know them personally," he said with a touch of confusion. "What's your point?"

"But her hands were actually *trembling*, Cord. And when she mentioned Lizbet, she seemed almost desperate."

"Like I said, her life hasn't been easy." He glanced over his shoulder at her, one eyebrow raised. "You haven't lost your touch, Julia. I was so busy concentrating on Tascoe that her reactions went right by me. I heard her daughter left home a couple of years back—just took off without a word and vanished. That would explain a lot of what you saw."

"She lost a child?" Julia remembered the haunted expression of the woman with Dean Tascoe, the impression she'd given of being so tightly wound she was about to snap. She felt a rush of compassion for Jackie Redmond. "Oh, Cord—the poor woman!"

"Her daughter wasn't a child when she left. She was about nineteen or twenty," he informed her. Bending his head, he turned his attention to unfastening his cuffs. "Still, that's got to be rough. The woman's a widow and her daughter was everything to her. I guess no matter how old your kids get, some part of you still thinks of them as the children they once were."

"Maybe." Julia sat on the edge of the bed, suddenly bone tired and uncomfortably aware that his words, as nonjudgmental as they'd been, could just as well be referring to her relationship with her father.

Except Willard Stewart hadn't fallen apart over the fact that he barely ever saw his daughter anymore. As far as her father was concerned, he'd only ever lost one child, and the child he still grieved over had never been her, Julia knew, although in the past Cord had disagreed with her on this point. His theory was that father and daughter were too much alike for the relationship between them to ever have been an easy one—but that Willard Stewart, despite his reticence on the subject, loved her more than he'd ever been able to express.

Beneath that rock-hard exterior beat the heart of a marshmallow, Julia thought wryly. Cord Hunter believed in happy endings. She was a little more pragmatic than that.

"Maybe we should stick to topics we can agree on," she said without rancor. "Like the fact that I intend to see this investigation through with you." She lay back against the headboard of the bed and pursed her lips thoughtfully. "Oh, right—I don't *need* your agreement on that."

"No, I guess you don't." He slanted a sardonic glance at her in the mirror and resumed unbuttoning his shirt. "It's not like the time Davey and I went rock climbing at Maiden's Leap and made you stay at home, is it?"

"I followed you until I couldn't see you anymore." She smiled reminiscently. "Since you were on your bicycles and I was a pudgy little five-year-old, I lost sight of you pretty fast."

"If I tried that today I suppose you'd just get your own bicycle." A corner of his mouth quirked up as she nodded, but his eyes were serious. "Okay. We work together—but I want you staying here with me. We should get you something to wear before the stores close, and then if you're lucky I'll buy you dinner."

Removing his shirt as he spoke, he brought his face closer to the dresser mirror and rubbed his jawline appraisingly. He opened a drawer, pulled out a pair of jeans and a dark blue T-shirt and tossed them on the bed beside her.

"Stay here with—" Julia broke off in the middle of her sentence, her eyes widening. "What the *hell* do you think you're doing?"

"You've seen me with less on hundreds of times—a lot less, as I recall." He gave her a blandly innocent look, the dark lashes dipping down briefly to touch his cheekbones as he un-

buckled his belt and unzipped his trousers. "It isn't an option,
Julia—while we're on this investigation we're joined at the hip.
We eat together, interview suspects together and sleep together.
You can have the left side of the bed," he added generously,
stepping out of his pants. "I was here first and I like the side
nearest the door."

Now he was the one standing close enough to the bed for
her to reach out and touch him, but she kept her hands rigidly
at her sides.

He was wearing white boxer shorts, of course. She'd bought
him a pair of red bikini briefs one Christmas, more to see the
look on his face when he unwrapped them than in any real
conviction that she could effect a change in his hopelessly conservative sense of style. It had been the year King was still
teething. A day later they'd found the bikinis shredded into
festive ribbons between the puppy's paws, though Cord had
sworn up and down that he had put them away out of the dog's
reach.

And the only reason she was dwelling on *that* long-ago memory, Julia told herself in frustration, was to keep her mind occupied with something other than the sight of those perfectly
muscled long legs, that hard, flat stomach and that broadly massive chest. Against the tan of his skin the boxers looked as crisp
and white as a flag of surrender.

But if anyone was surrendering here, it wasn't going to be
her, she thought.

"I can't stay with you, Cord." She forced her gaze away
from him with what she hoped looked like casual disinterest,
praying that the faint heat she could feel in her face wasn't
visible. "It just wouldn't work."

"You're blushing." He studied her, his brows raised in mild
surprise. He bent toward her, and her eyes flew to his face
nervously. Slowly he picked his jeans up off the bed and gave
a sigh of sharp exasperation.

"For crying out loud, let's just get this over with. Having
you jump out of your skin every time I so much as brush against
you is making *me* nervous. Is this what we're supposed to be
so afraid of?"

Tossing his jeans aside, he bent over her again, this time so swiftly that she didn't have time to react. One knee was suddenly warm and tense beside her thigh and one arm braced on the bed behind her, and his mouth was on hers even as her lips parted in surprise. His other arm was around her, cradling her securely as she sunk backward onto the bed, and then a white heat tore through her as the borrowed shirt she was wearing fell slightly open and she felt the intimate touch of his chest as he kept on going, lowering himself lightly against her.

When he'd kissed her two days ago at the lake there had been an edge of desperation in their embrace. Now the overwhelming impression was one of frustration, of impulses kept too long in check that couldn't be held back any longer.

Except she wasn't just getting that impression from the signals *he* was sending out, Julia thought breathlessly, feeling his tongue searching her mouth, and meeting it with her own. It was all too evident from the way her nails pressed into the tough, tanned hide of his shoulders, the way she was arching her neck as if to present the vulnerable line of her throat to him, and the way every nerve ending in her body felt like it was sizzling—*all* too evident that the suddenly unleashed frustration she was sensing came just as much from her as from him.

If this was a crime scene, she thought dazedly, both of them would be cuffed and charged. Hardly knowing what she was doing, she found herself fumbling awkwardly at the buttons on the shirt she was wearing. She couldn't stand having *anything* between them, she thought—she needed him against the skin of her stomach, the curve of her breasts.

"It's my shirt. I get to rip it," Cord said huskily, lifting his mouth from hers the barest fraction of an inch. His breath was warm on the corners of her lips, like an echo of his kiss. With one effortless movement, he grasped the edges of the shirt and tore it open. Like tiny flat pearls flying through the air, buttons scattered, falling to the floor beside them.

"It's my bra. I get to remove it," Julia managed to say. Was that really her voice? she wondered light-headedly. It had sounded more like a *purr*.

"Too late, honey. I was always better at undressing you than you were yourself."

Through thick lashes his eyes glinted like chips of onyx as his hand reached around to her back, unclasping the garment and slipping it from her arms. His voice had the same velvet quality as hers, deepened and hoarsened into a growl, but as he looked down at her the growl caught in his throat.

"Sometimes I used to tell myself that I was remembering everything all wrong, that no one woman could have been so flawless, so completely desirable. But it wasn't a fantasy." He bent his head to her. "You're real. *This* is real."

It *was* reality. It felt like a dream, an erotic dream that she could move through languidly, receiving the touch of his sure, hard hands on every inch of her body, finding with her own hands the places that she knew could drive him over the edge and taking no responsibility for anything that might happen because it was a dream, and dreams had a life of their own.

But it wasn't a dream. It was real—and reality had consequences like pain and regret.

"I can't do this, Cord." She forced the words out past lips that felt like they had been turned to ice and felt him tense immediately. "It's—it's *wrong*."

He raised his head, his eyes on hers. "It's not wrong, Julia— how could it be? I'm not some stranger you met on the street that you're passing an hour or two with, for God's sake. This is the way it's *supposed* to be between us. The last two years were wrong—we're just making it right again."

"There's no future for us."

She delivered the pronouncement flatly, meeting his gaze directly so that he would see the certainty in hers. She needed to convince him, she thought desperately, and she needed to convince him *now*. Every minute she spent with him she could feel herself weakening, and if she let this go on any longer, sooner or later she would give in.

And you'd be giving in to yourself, not to him. You'd like to tell yourself that the two of you could work everything out, even get married like you once planned to, wouldn't you? You'd have what you always wanted—him. But he'd have to put the rest of his hopes and dreams away forever.

That stern little voice inside her head was her conscience, she thought drearily. As hateful as it could seem, it was right, and she knew it.

"Why don't we have a future? What's stopping us?" His face was a mask, his eyes unreadable. "Or is it just that you don't want it?"

"I don't want a future with you." She sat up abruptly. "Is that what you need to hear?" Her voice rose and she pulled the torn edges of her shirt together defensively. "I don't *have* to explain myself to you—we went through this two years ago, settled everything, and the situation we're in today has nothing to do with what went before."

She pushed her hair from her face. "I've got to go—I have to find a place to stay tonight. I'll meet you back here early tomorrow morning and we can decide where we're going to go on this investigation."

"No." He stood, his posture rigid and his mouth a grim line. "I crossed the line. It won't happen again."

He turned his back to her and stepped into his jeans. Turning to face her again, he stood there, his hands on his hips. "Look—this wasn't some devious ploy of mine to lure you back into my life. I've been up-front with you, Julia. I never stopped wanting you, I never stopped loving you and, yeah— I'll admit it—I never stopped hoping that one day I'd get a second chance at making this work. Some adolescent part of me might have had the crazy notion that as soon as I saw you again, a miracle would happen and you'd run into my arms. That first night at the lake house I realized that miracles weren't in the cards. You looked at me like I was the last person in the world you wanted to see."

There was a thread of pain in his voice that she couldn't bear to hear.

"You startled me, Cord. For a minute I—I thought you were a ghost."

She attempted a smile but she knew it wasn't reaching her eyes. He looked at her, and suddenly she saw the changes the last two years had wrought in him—the sharper line of his jaw, the slight deepening of the lines bracketing his mouth, the tenseness in his posture. He hesitated a moment, and then sat down on the bed beside her.

"I never played games with you, honey. I wouldn't know how," he said softly. "I want you with me because every second you're out of my sight I'll be imagining that you're in danger. I respect what you say about Tascoe, but we can't know for sure that he'd balk at hurting a woman. And if I'm wrong and he didn't kill Paul and Sheila at all, then we have no idea who the real murderer is or what his agenda might be. I need to know you're safe."

He was such a *good* man, Julia thought, meeting his gaze. He was good and honorable and loving, and she had never wanted to hurt him. All she'd ever wanted for Cord Hunter was the whole world—happiness, love, the children that he longed for. But the only thing he was asking of her now was peace of mind.

She could give him that, at least.

"I'll stay here with you." She saw the relief in his eyes and felt ridiculously like crying. "I—I'll even let you have the left side of the bed," she added with feigned reluctance. One corner of his mouth rose in as failed an attempt at a smile as hers had been. His hand reached out and, so lightly that she might have thought she was imagining it, he stroked her hair from her face.

"We were something, once, weren't we?" That soft, husky voice that she'd heard all her life—had heard in her dreams even when he'd been three thousand miles away—was barely above a murmur. "I know that time's behind us, but weren't we something great together, you and me?"

The tears that had been threatening for the last few minutes spilled slowly over as she rested her cheek against his palm and felt his other arm slip around her shoulders, snugging her closely against him. She could feel his heartbeat, Julia thought, looking at him, her vision glazed and shimmering.

"That time's gone, Cord," she whispered painfully.

''But...you're right. We really were something. Once upon a time—'' Her voice broke, and it felt like her own heart was cracking in two. ''Once upon a time we had it all,'' she said softly.

Chapter 8

"Tascoe's disappeared." Cord rejoined Julia at the table and then fell frustratedly silent as their waitress approached.

The small Vietnamese eatery was a far cry from the prohibitively expensive French restaurants that her father favored, Julia thought as the petite and dark-haired woman poured a steaming stream of delicately tinted green tea into first her cup and then Cord's. Then again, it had been ages since she had done more than grab a burger and bolt it down during her visits to town to pick up supplies. The leisurely and surprisingly pleasant meal they'd just shared had been a welcome plateau in the events of the day—and judging from Cord's interrupted announcement just now, that day was far from over.

At the mall she'd made her necessary purchases as swiftly as possible—a couple of T-shirts, some jeans and the pair of khaki pants she was wearing right now, among other things—and then had tried to beg off when he'd looked at her wan face and drooping shoulders and had insisted that she needed to eat something. Now she was glad he'd overridden her halfhearted protests.

He was one of those rarest of men—a true protector, she thought wistfully. The few times she'd seen him with Lizbet and the Whitefield twins he'd been in his element. The day they'd brought the silent child to Mary and Frank Whitefield she'd watched him pushing each child in turn on the back yard swing. Terry and Tessa, the twins, had shrieked with excitement and urged him to push them as high as they could go. But when Lizbet's turn came Cord had stood in front of her, letting the swing, with her in it clutching the ropes, arc slowly away from him. Every time it came back, he held it still for a moment, as if to emphasize to the little girl that she was never completely on her own, and that he would always be there, watching her and waiting for her.

He was a born father, Julia thought. He needed children of his own. However hard it became over the next few days to remember that, she couldn't allow herself to forget it.

"Tascoe's disappeared." Repeating his earlier pronouncement as their waitress walked away, Cord kept his voice low, but he couldn't hide the edge of anger in his tone. "DiMarco apparently couldn't stop talking when they hauled him down to the station—waived the phone call to his lawyer, asked for a pair of pants and spilled the beans about everything he could think of. Lopez said she wouldn't have been surprised if he'd come up with the identity of the man on the grassy knoll in Dallas back in sixty-three." His mouth tightened. "He gave them the same story he gave us about Tascoe, and although I got the impression Lopez still prefers DiMarco himself as a suspect, she sent a car out to pick Tascoe up for questioning. They can't find him."

"Maybe one of those old cronies you said he still has tipped him off that the police wanted to talk to him," Julia said dubiously. "But I don't know, Cord—Tascoe didn't seem like the type to run at the first hint of trouble. He probably thinks he can outbluff and outmaneuver someone like Lopez. Doesn't it seem more likely that he'd welcome the chance to cross swords with her just to prove what a mistake the department made when they let him go?"

"I don't know." He took an absent sip of his tea and fell

silent. Then she saw his eyes narrow thoughtfully. "How beat are you?" he asked her abruptly.

Julia blinked. "Beat? As in tired?" If he'd asked that question an hour ago she would have said she was exhausted. But the light meal and the hot tea had energized her, she realized in surprise. "We're going to pay a visit to Jackie Redmond, aren't we?" she said with sudden certainty. "I'm game, Cord. If Tascoe really is on the run, he's already got a head start—there's no sense in giving him more of an edge over us than he has."

"That's the way I see it."

He flashed a briefly impersonal grin at her, and she felt an inane little feather of happiness uncurl somewhere in the vicinity of her stomach. As he paid their bill and left a tip for the waitress, she tried to get herself under control, but it was no use.

Just being with him, even under these grim circumstances, was more than she'd ever expected to have again. Over the last two years she'd never forgotten the long, sweet nights tangled up in each other's arms, the look in his eyes when he told her he loved her or the feel of his mouth on hers.

But she'd somehow forgotten just how good it felt to simply *be* with him.

Jackie Redmond's apartment was on the other side of town. As they drove there, a light misty rain began to fall, and when Cord switched on the windshield wipers, the rhythmic swishing noise they made was almost mesmerically calming.

She needed calming, Julia admitted. Before they'd left the motel she'd seen Cord arm himself, and he'd looked momentarily taken aback when she'd told him she wasn't carrying a gun.

"You're still licensed to carry one, aren't you?" he'd asked, frowning, and when she'd told him that she was he'd nodded. "We'll have to get you one tomorrow. When you were on the force you didn't go out on a case unarmed."

Cord was right—she had to start thinking like a cop again. The brief sense of calm the last hour had brought had already dissipated, and she clasped her hands tightly in her lap. She had

to start acknowledging that violence could be just beyond a
doorway, that danger was all around her, because once again it
was her job to take care of that danger before it could reach
out and harm a child—harm *Lizbet*. She'd failed once. What
made her think she wouldn't fail again?

"Vittorio's grandson—what's his name again?" Cord's
voice held careless curiosity.

"Anthony."

The streets were a rainwashed blur of lights and reflections
from passing cars. She *couldn't* fail this time, Julia told herself
tightly, squeezing her eyes shut. She saw again Lizbet's doll-
like face and silky red hair, so like her mother's, and bit down
on her lower lip. What if they didn't find Paul and Sheila's
killer in time? What if even now the child was in danger? No
matter what anyone else said, she just couldn't bring herself to
believe that Dean Tascoe had been responsible for killing
Sheila—Paul, maybe, but never a woman. And even Tascoe
would have no reason to inflict that final, unnecessary wound
on Paul's already dead body. Cord had theorized that the man
had been trying to throw suspicion on the mob by doing so,
but she wasn't satisfied with that explanation.

Shot, then stabbed. In heaven's name, *why?* Sheila's murder,
as terrible as it was, had been a clean kill. Why hadn't Paul's?

*Sheila was shot because she was supposed to be shot. Paul
was shot because he came up those basement stairs faster than
the killer expected.* The thought came into her mind with the
force of certainty, and she turned swiftly to Cord.

Then she stopped herself. A paralyzing fear gripped her.
What if she was wrong? She'd been wrong that last time—and
that time, too, she'd been so certain she had the situation under
control. That time, too, a child's life had hung in the balance.
She couldn't *trust* herself. She couldn't trust her reactions, her
perceptions, her instincts—

"Falcone said Anthony was going to medical school?"
Again the quiet voice broke into her thoughts.

"Harvard, Vittorio said." Her reply was terse. Cord had
given her an excuse tonight, she thought frantically. He'd

wanted her out of this investigation. She could tell him she'd thought it over, changed her mind—

"One of the first you saved. Whatever he does in the future, you'll know you had a part in it."

"What?" Distracted, she looked at him. In the darkened interior of the vehicle she could only make out the strong lines of his profile.

"He wouldn't even exist now, but for you. You gave him the gift of life." He shrugged, his attention on the rain-slick road. "But I guess that's a feeling you got used to, right?"

"No." She shook her head in the dark. "No, I never even thought of it that way. There were always others. There were always so many others."

"You never sat back sometimes and took stock of the ones you rescued?" There was a note of incredulity in his voice. "I'll bet every single one of those children remembers you."

"But, Cord—"

"Anthony Falcone will have children of his own someday. They'll become adults and raise a new generation. Maybe they'll never know it, but they'll owe their very existence to the woman who didn't give up when everyone else did—the woman who searched for a young boy in danger until she found him and brought him home." His hands tightened on the steering wheel. "You made a *difference,* Julia. Never forget that."

For the rest of the drive he was silent, and she was too absorbed in the image he'd planted in her mind to break into his silence. Anthony Falcone's children—and their children, and the ones after them, stretching into some future so dim and faraway that her path and theirs would never cross. Long after she was gone, was it possible that some part of who she'd been would live on in children's laughter, a newborn's cry?

It was a shattering concept, and one she couldn't take in all at once.

"We're here. It's really coming down now—we're going to have to make a run for it."

She blinked and looked up. The man she'd spent the evening with, the man who'd held her in his arms earlier, was suddenly gone. In his place was a watchful, cautious professional. The situation they were about to walk into was probably innocuous, Julia thought, feeling her adrenaline start to flow. But they couldn't assume that. She looked down and saw that her hand had unconsciously gone to her hip, as if to check for the holstered gun that wasn't there.

It seemed some old habits died hard. She was glad of that. Clearing her mind of everything extraneous, she nodded curtly at him.

"Let's go."

The rain that had only minutes ago been a light mist had turned into a solid curtain of water as they dashed across the street and ducked under the inadequate protection of the building's awning. There were two bulbous globe lamps flanking each side of the old, glass-paned door, and in the hazy, rain-shimmered light they cast, Julia saw drops of water sparkling like diamonds against the blackness of Cord's hair.

"We might as well have taken our time," he said wryly. "Honey, you look like a drowned rat."

"You look a little damp yourself." Without meaning to, she raised her palm and slicked some of the water from his face, and before she could withdraw it he'd caught her hand in one of his.

"I'm not expecting any trouble—but that's just when it comes from out of left field. Worst-case scenario is that Tascoe's hiding out here, so don't leave my side and don't take any chances." He was holding her hand close enough to his mouth so that she could feel the faint exhalation of breath he gave. "I'd feel better if you weren't unarmed," he admitted.

"I trust my partner to watch my back," Julia said softly. "You be careful, too, Cord."

He held her gaze and then gave her hand a quick, hard squeeze. "Right. Let's hope we're worrying over nothing."

The security of the building was nonexistent. Cord simply opened the green-painted main door, and they walked in. The cramped lobby they entered was little more than an area where tenants could pause to peer at the brass-plated mail slots set into the wall, and straight ahead was a short flight of shallow wooden stairs protected by a vinyl runner from any dirt an inconsiderate occupant might track in.

"No one's been up here since the rain started," Cord said, glancing at the slightly damp tracks he was leaving. "Which means exactly zero," he added with a shrug. "Tascoe, if he's here, could have come at any time."

They mounted the stairs to the third-floor landing, and ahead of her he paused. The apartment in front of them was labeled 3B. It boasted an ornate pewter knocker in the shape of a braying donkey, and outside on a rubber mat was a pair of shoes that looked like their owner had to be at least sixty and female.

"Trusting souls. A lot of these places have had the same tenants for years," Cord murmured. "They think a peephole and a five-and-dime chain lock on the inside are the cutting edge of home security. Jackie's apartment must be at the end of the hall."

The woman they'd seen at the funeral with Dean Tascoe might not have been from the same generation as some of her fellow tenants, but it seemed she was just as trusting. Even as they were still halfway down the hall, the door to her apartment opened and she peered out at them as they approached.

"Mrs. Redmond? Jackie?" The woman's lack of precaution had taken him by surprise, Julia realized. "It's Cordell Hunter and Julia Stewart—we talked with you at the funeral today. Can we come in and ask you a few questions?"

"What about?"

The trust that had led Jackie Redmond to open her door so naively was rapidly evaporating. She'd been expecting someone else, Julia thought.

"Please, Mrs. Redmond." Cord looked over his shoulder at the apartment they'd passed. "It really would be better if we talked inside."

"I was just going to bed," the woman said reluctantly, but she stepped back and allowed them to enter. Cord went first, his wariness apparent.

The Redmond apartment was spacious enough—certainly more spacious than anything being built these days, Julia thought—but instead of the feeling of airiness that it should have given, the overall impression was almost claustrophobic. There were photos and ornaments on every surface in the living room, and the decor was a stuffy mix of colors and heavy textures.

Her attention was drawn to a picture of the Last Supper on the wall. The frame glowed with a dim light, and Julia realized that it was not only electrified, but that there was something odd about the picture itself. She looked again as Jackie gestured for her and Cord to sit and saw that it had been created to give a three-dimensional effect. One of the disciples seemed to be following her with his eyes, and with an unpleasant start she realized that he must be Judas.

"I don't understand why you want to talk to me."

Jackie drifted to a nearby table, distractedly rearranging the placement of a gilt-framed picture, and suddenly Julia saw that all the photos in the room were of the same girl, from childhood to young womanhood. The daughter she'd lost, she thought with a pang of compassion. The woman had surrounded herself with images of the child who was no longer with her.

"Is this—is this about the murders? I hardly knew Detective Durant and his wife."

She hovered uncertainly by the sofa where Julia was sitting. The satin quilted dressing gown she wore gave her almost painfully thin figure some much-needed bulk, but her hands, nervously fluttering around patting pillows and touching objects, were so bony they looked as though they could snap.

"It's about the murders, yes." Cord's voice was even softer than it usually was, Julia noted. She took her cue from him and smiled reassuringly at Jackie.

"We're hoping you can tell us where to find Mr. Tascoe," she began. "He's not at his house, and—"

"Captain Tascoe isn't here," Jackie cut in quickly.

Cord leaned forward, resting his forearms on his knees. "I'm not here in any official capacity, as you know, Mrs. Redmond, but—"

Again the woman spoke before he could finish. "Oh, I know that, Detective Hunter. Don't forget, I'm the chief's personal secretary." She perched on the arm of a chair and smoothed the lace edges of her cuffs. "You were very close to Detective Durant, weren't you?" Her edginess had returned, and she flicked a speck of dust from the shade of the small, fussy lamp beside her. "Captain Tascoe told me after we spoke today that you were his daughter's godparents."

For the second time today Jackie Redmond had maneuvered the conversation around to Lizbet, Julia thought slowly. Fluttery and strained as she might seem, she couldn't be a fool. Beneath that faded, little-girl helplessness was a woman who'd had the determination to make a life for herself after her husband had died, who'd brought up a child alone and who'd ended up in the plum position at her place of work. She even had Dean Tascoe wrapped around her little finger. Maybe they'd been handling her *too* gently.

"I'm Lizbet's godmother and Cord's her godfather." Julia nodded. "What happened to that little girl was something that *no* child should ever have to experience." She heard the hard edge in her voice and made no attempt to soften it. "You're a mother yourself, Mrs. Redmond. I'm sure I don't have to explain to you."

"Was she—was she *there* at the time? Was she *hurt?*" She had Jackie Redmond's attention now, Julia noted as the woman's hand flew to her throat. Her blue eyes were wide, and what little color there had been in her lips had drained away. "There was *nothing* about the child in the news reports! I assumed she'd been out of the house at the—at the—"

"At the time her parents were murdered?" Julia saw Cord's quick glance. "No. Lizbet was there, too. The deaths of Paul and Sheila were terrible enough, but..."

She let her voice trail off.

"Oh, dear *God!*"

There was the sound of something shattering, and Julia's head jerked up. On the cluttered table beside the woman across from her were the broken shards of a china basket of flowers, but Jackie didn't seem to realize what she'd done. Her face was so white that for a moment it seemed she was about to faint, and Cord must have had the same fear, too, because he leaped from his chair and caught the thin, pink-quilted arm. She shook him off, swaying.

"The child was killed *too?* No—he *promised* that nothing would—"

"What the hell are you doing here?"

The angry voice of Dean Tascoe ripped across Jackie's horrified whisper. Standing at the threshold, his keys still in his hand, he took in the scene with a thunderous expression on his face and then strode swiftly across the room to her.

"Why didn't you *tell* me?" As Tascoe reached for her, Jackie drew away from him, her arms wrapped tightly around her thin body. "You said that the child was *safe,* Dean. *Why didn't you tell me?*"

"The child *is* safe—for now, Mrs. Redmond. I didn't tell you she'd been killed," Julia said coldly. "But you're hiding something, aren't you? Who are you protecting—him?" She flicked a glance at Tascoe, his arms around Jackie's shaking shoulders.

"I—no, I—"

"Don't say anything, Jackie. Let me handle this." The beefy ex-cop's face was dangerously red, but his hand on the blond woman's hair was gentle. He nestled her head into the crook of his shoulder as if he was shielding her with his body. "I told you I'd take care of this for you, didn't I?"

"Lopez is looking for you, Tascoe." Cord's voice was flat. "DiMarco's in custody, and he's talking like crazy, trying to cut a deal. He mentioned your name."

"In connection with what?" The red face flushed even deeper. "I told you I run my own investigation agency now, Chief. So I slip Vince DiMarco my card—what harm is there in that? The man has plenty of legit operations, and every businessman can use a little outside help once in a while."

"That'll probably fly." Cord's gaze hardened. "For a while, at least. But Lopez, no matter what you think of her, is a good cop. She'll dig into that story, so if I were you I'd pray it holds up. Talking about outside help, maybe you should phone a lawyer before you say anything more. I wouldn't want to taint the court case against you by not informing you of your rights."

"You don't have the jurisdiction to arrest me, Hunter."

It was the first time he'd used Cord's name. There was a touch of fear in the man's angry eyes, Julia noted, although not once had he turned his gaze directly to her. She remembered his odd attitude toward her at the cemetery and wondered what it was about her that made it impossible for him to meet her eyes.

"I don't, but then I'm not going to. I'm phoning Lopez right now to tell her to come and pick you up." Keeping a wary gaze on Tascoe, Cord reached toward the pastel-pink telephone sitting in a nest-like frill of lace on the table beside the sofa. "And don't even try to run, Tascoe. Paul and Sheila were my best friends. Just looking at you makes my trigger finger itch."

"*That's* what this is all about? You think *I* killed them?"

If the man was acting, he'd missed his calling, Julia thought. The bloodshot blue eyes stared at Cord in shock. The meaty hands gripping Jackie's thin shoulders tightened, and almost absently he put the woman from him. She sank onto the sofa, both hands to her mouth.

He turned to Cord, his fists balled at his sides, but his attack came in the form of words.

"I gave you people twenty years of my life. I worked my goddamned *tail* off building cases against scumbags who made more money in a month than I did in a year, knowing that it was useless—that they'd just hire some high-priced mouthpiece who would have them back on the street before I'd finished the paperwork. Yeah—I cut some corners in the end. Why not? I didn't see the other side respecting any freakin' Geneva Convention, Chief! But to suspect me of being a *cop killer!*"

The last word came out in a roar of rage, and he lunged for the man in front of him, but even as he leaped for Cord's throat, those huge hands outstretched, Cord pivoted and smashed the side of his shoulder into the burly ex-cop like a battering ram, both of them crashing into the small telephone table. Tascoe fell heavily to the floor, but Cord retained his balance and stood over him, his gun suddenly in his hand.

It had all taken only a second. Julia let out a shaky breath, feeling like she'd been holding it for hours.

"Dean! Are you all right? You're bleeding!"

Her pink quilted gown crumpling stiffly around her, Jackie sank to the floor beside a dazed Tascoe. She was right—along the side of his face was a long cut. Blood had trickled into his eye, and with the back of his hand he wiped it away.

All the fight had gone out of him. Rising painfully to his feet with the thin blond woman nervously fussing over him, he seemed somehow defeated. As he stood he looked at Julia for the first time.

"I used to hear about you. They called you the Guardian Angel, did you know that?"

"I've been called a lot of things," she replied, disconcerted by his question. "But I'm not on the force anymore."

"Because of Christie Hall."

Tascoe wasn't asking a question, he was stating a fact. She stared at him in shock. Not only were her personal problems common knowledge, she thought with sudden anger, but the events leading up to them seemed to be known by everyone—even Dean Tascoe, who had already left the department at the time of the incident. It wasn't something that would be in her file, because she'd never divulged to a single soul what had prompted her abrupt departure from her job.

"How do you know about—about Christie?"

Instead of answering her, Tascoe turned to Cord. "I'm not a cop killer. I know why you think I might have wanted to see Durant dead—because you and he got me fired. And like I told you today, there was a time when I wanted revenge on you two so bad I could taste it. But not now. Not for a long time."

"What changed?" Cord's voice was skeptical, his eyes watchful. He was still holding the gun on Tascoe.

"I got it," the ex-cop said simply. "I got my revenge. I haven't been able to live with myself since." He passed a big hand over his eyes, but this time he wasn't wiping away blood. "Harry Hall was one of my informants," he said to a frozen Julia. "I know why he jumped with his daughter. And you weren't responsible—*I* was."

Chapter 9

"So I guess we're back at square one."

Julia wearily tossed her shopping bags onto the motel bed as Cord laid his keys and his gun on the nightstand and shrugged out of his jacket.

"Looks like," he replied, his back to her. "But Tascoe's not out of the woods yet. Lopez is going to keep him for questioning a few hours, at least."

After his shattering revelation, the ex-cop had allowed them to notify the authorities of his whereabouts and had voluntarily agreed to meet with Cindy Lopez. Whether or not he'd really had a choice was a dubious point, Julia thought, but telling himself he was cooperating with the people he used to work with was obviously more palatable to his pride.

She didn't want to think about Tascoe. The man had ripped her life apart, had accelerated her descent into two years of hell. But tonight he had tried to make amends, and unwillingly she found herself replaying the scene in her mind...

"Harry was one of my informants before they took my badge away." As he'd stood there facing her, Julia had had the feeling that Dean Tascoe was barely aware that there was anyone else in the room. His words had been directed solely at her, and in his eyes she could read self-condemnation. His mouth had worked soundlessly before he'd been able to go on.

"He was small-time all the way—a petty thief, sometimes tried the odd con job. But he'd have made more money flipping burgers. Harry wasn't very successful at what he did, and I guess that was part of his trouble."

He'd sighed. Jackie had been watching him with wide, frightened eyes, and Cord had still been holding his gun, but Tascoe might have been in a confessional, with no one to hear him except the one who could forgive him.

"Anyway, when he heard what had happened to me I guess he felt like we were supposed to be buddies or something. Once in a while he'd meet me in a bar and buy me a beer, just to have the chance to talk. He'd been going through a rougher patch than usual, and he was worried about his little girl."

"Christie," Julia had said woodenly. "Her name was Christie."

"Yeah, Christie. She was the only person that sorry son of a bitch ever cared for in his life, and when he found out he had cancer he was crazy with worry, wondering what would happen to her. He'd heard about you, and he asked me if I thought you could help him find a family to adopt her before he died."

"Why me? Why not contact Family Services? That would have been the normal course to follow." She'd felt as if her knees were about to buckle, and beside her Cord put a supportive arm around her shoulders.

"I told you—he'd heard about the Guardian Angel, the woman who went to the wall for kids that no one else gave a damn for, the cop who seemed to be able to get inside their heads and know exactly how to help them." He'd shrugged wearily. "It had taken a few months for it to sink in that I was really through with the force, that no one was about to stick their neck out for me and get me reinstated, and that night I thought I saw the perfect way to get back at the bastard who'd wrecked my life."

"Me." Cord's voice had been a knife slash. "I was the one

you wanted, so why didn't you take me on directly? Why the *hell* did you involve Julia?''

''Because I knew hurting her was the worst thing I could do to you. That was just before you left for the coast, and I didn't know that you two were about to break up.'' Tascoe's grimace had been full of self-loathing. ''All I could think of was how much I hated you for the way my life had gone. I figured you'd broken the code—betrayed a fellow officer—and so I decided to do the same to your lady here. I told Harry to stay away from her, that if she ever got Christie away from him she'd have the girl into foster care so quick he'd never know what had happened to her. I told him that it was all a sham, good publicity for the department, that this Guardian Angel stuff was crap.''

''You made him afraid of me?'' Julia had felt the color drain from her cheeks. ''You made him *afraid* of me?''

Wrenching out of Cord's grasp, she'd grabbed Tascoe by his jacket. *''Do you know what you did?''*

Cord had moved forward and then stopped.

''God help me, of course I know.'' Tascoe had stood there unflinchingly, making no attempt to defend himself. His face had been a mask of grief. ''I knew as soon as I heard what had happened that what I'd told him about you a few weeks earlier had turned him against you. I—I wanted to tell you. I knew you would take it personally, think that something you'd said or done had caused him to jump with Christie—''

''I left that same day. I never went back. For two years I've seen that child's face in my nightmares, Tascoe—seen her falling away just as her fingertips touched mine, heard her screaming in terror because her father had decided to take his seven-year-old child with him on a suicide leap.''

Slowly Julia had released her hold on him, but her eyes had never left his. ''You almost caused her *death!* Thank God for the miracle and the SWAT member who saved her—because if Christie Hall had been killed I swear I—''

She hadn't been able to look at him any longer. Shaking with reaction, she'd turned on her heel and walked to the door of the apartment, waiting there silently while Cord had made the call to Lopez and Dean Tascoe had sat, his head bowed and his shoulders slumped, on the sofa. Jackie Redmond had approached her once.

"He's made some terrible mistakes, Miss Stewart. But we *all* have—every one of us." Her hands had been trembling but she'd gone on, with more force than Julia had thought she was capable of. "Are you so blameless that you can afford to judge him? Can't you even *try* to understand that sometimes people make the wrong choices—or that sometimes it seems like they don't have any choice at *all?*"

But Julia hadn't been able to answer her. She'd simply stared at the woman, until finally Jackie Redmond had turned and walked back to Tascoe....

"I asked the front desk for an early wake-up call." Cord's offhand statement broke into her thoughts, bringing her back to the present, and she looked up. He was standing beside the dresser, his arms folded. "I thought we'd try to get some more information on the DiMarco-Tascoe connection tomorrow."

"You don't think Tascoe was responsible for the killings, either, do you?" She frowned, her temples throbbing. "What really bothered me was the way Jackie reacted when she thought Lizbet had been killed along with Paul and Sheila. She's hiding something, and Tascoe's part of it."

"But you just said you didn't think he was responsible for the killings." He shook his head. "No—after tonight I can't see it. All we ever had against him was the word of a mobster who would have said anything we wanted to hear and a possible motive for revenge that had its roots in an incident that took place years ago."

Shot, then stabbed...because he came up those basement stairs faster than the killer expected. Paul wasn't supposed to have been shot at all—the killer wanted him to die in a particular way. The pattern...the pattern got messed up....

"What is it?" He was beside her, his hands on her shoulders, and she realized that she was shaking.

"Nothing. I just keep having these flashes, but then they disappear again." Julia put her hand to her forehead.

"Is it like the feelings you used to get when you were trying to connect with a child?'' Cord drew in a tense breath. "You're not trying to get inside the head of the *killer,* are you?''

"No.'' She shuddered.

"Is it possible that you've unconsciously picked up some clue, some faint impression from Lizbet? I know she hasn't talked to you, but I've seen you with her. Your eyes are always on her. You note her every reaction.''

I watch her because I'm afraid for her. I watch her because I'm terrified something's going to happen to her, and I won't be able to prevent it.

Julia kept her expression calm. "I'm not picking up anything from Lizbet. I doubt that anyone could right now—that little girl's completely closed off whatever she saw that night, and that worries me. If we don't find the killer in the next few days, Cord, we're going to have to get her into some kind of treatment.''

"I know.'' A shadow crossed his strong features. "We're running out of time. I don't want her out of hiding just yet, but I agree—if we haven't caught whoever did this within a couple of days she's going to have to see a professional.'' His eyes darkened. "I saw Paul's body, Julia. Someone out there is filled with rage, and I don't want him catching even a scent of Lizbet's presence.''

"I still think Tascoe knows something that he's not telling us.'' Her brows drew together. "He's a vigilante type—even when he was on the force he took matters into his own hands. Do you think it's possible that he might have been investigating this on his own and stumbled across some information that he's keeping for himself?''

"Thinking that if he solves the murders of a detective and his wife in a blaze of glory he'll be offered his old job back?'' Cord raked his hand through his hair, his eyes narrowed. "That fits his style. Even before the Billy Wolfe incident Tascoe was always skirting the edge. He was assigned to the Donner case before Paul and I took over, you know.''

"No, I didn't know.'' Julia looked up, repressing the shudder that always ran through her at the memory of the Gary Donner killings. "What happened? Why was he taken off the investigation?"

"He was doing his usual cowboy thing—conducting searches without a warrant, grilling suspects on his own, withholding information from the rest of the investigative team. He was a damn good detective, but he was a loose cannon, and that case was just too high profile. The department couldn't afford to have him on it, so he was quietly moved to another assignment, and Paul and I took over."

"At which point the two of you borrowed a leaf from Tascoe's book and acted like cowboys yourselves," Julia said sharply.

"Me, a cowboy? Now, that's a low blow." His teeth flashed briefly white against his skin. "My folks were always on the other side, remember?"

"You know what I mean." She looked at him, not amused. "You almost got *killed* on that job, Cord. You became obsessed with tracking down the Donner family, and I had to stand by and watch you turn into someone I didn't know. You were going through hell and you wouldn't let me help you. I couldn't even get *close* to you during that time."

It still hurt. But she'd made a mistake in revealing herself to him, she realized belatedly. He smiled at her again, this time with no humor at all in those dark eyes.

"Now you're the one who's crossed the line."

Walking over to the window, he stood to one side of the slatted metal blinds, bending them open slightly and looking out into the darkness for a minute. His back was to her, and she could see the slight bunching of muscle in his shoulders under the T-shirt. He spoke without turning around.

"But since you've made this conversation personal let's keep it that way." He let the blinds snap shut and turned to face her. "Why the *hell* didn't you tell me that your whole life was falling apart? Why did I have to find out about tonight—and from Dean Tascoe, for God's sake?"

"You weren't even around when it happened, Cord. You'd *left* by then," she started defensively.

"I'd been gone a couple of weeks, dammit—and because

you *wanted* me gone! But before that we'd been *everything* to each other. You knew all you had to do was pick up the phone and I'd be there for you.''

Slow comprehension spread across his features. ''It started way before the Christie Hall incident, didn't it? All the time we were together for those last few months you were just barely holding on, and you didn't think that was something I should know. You let me believe everything was just fine—you made *sure* I believed that. I was out of your life long before you told me it was over, wasn't I, Julia? I was just too damn stupid to figure it out.''

''It wasn't *like* that!'' Taken off guard, she tried to deflect his accusation with one of her own. ''Yes, I was stressed—it came with the territory. We *both* were, sometimes. Like I said— when you were working the Donner case I felt like I didn't *know* you anymore!''

In the silence that followed her outburst she could hear the steady whine of nighttime traffic speeding by on the road beside the motel. Cord, standing by the window a few feet away, was just outside the pools of light cast by the twin table lamps that flanked the bed. Looking at him in his dark T-shirt and jeans, Julia suddenly had the unsettling impression that he was merely a deeper shadow in the shadowy room—a shadow that would at any moment melt back into the darkness. He lifted his head and met her eyes.

''I felt like I didn't know myself for a while. I felt like I didn't *want* to know what I was turning into during that investigation, Julia—and when it was over I vowed I would never let a case get to me like that again.''

She stared at him in appalled compassion, but before she could speak he went on. ''Maybe I should have talked to you about the things we uncovered during that investigation, the unspeakable horrors we witnessed. Maybe I should have shared the nightmare—but I just couldn't *do* that to you. What we found in that farmhouse...''

He passed a hand across his eyes, and she saw him swallow heavily. ''God help me, I needed to keep that out of our life. I needed to be able to come home and have you in my arms at night and know that there was one part of my world—the most important part—that Gary Donner and his evil hadn't tainted.''

The rawness in his voice was a revelation. She hadn't realized that the man who'd headed the Donner investigation—the man who'd been photographed striding grim-faced and uncommunicative from crime scenes that had seemed chillingly mundane, like the Bradley farmhouse, the man who in the end had put his life on the line to bring about the end of Gary Donner's psychopathic "family"—had taken strength from her. She hadn't *known*, Julia thought. She hadn't known. She'd never even thought it possible.

"I'm glad," she said in a low tone. Lifting her head, she met his bleak gaze. "I'm glad I could help you through that. I'm glad I was your—your refuge."

"Yeah." His voice was toneless. He'd been standing with his back against the wall, but he straightened and let out a deep breath. "I wish I could have been yours. But that wasn't the way you wanted it. I never really knew you at all, did I?"

"How can you say that? How can you even *think* that? Of course you knew me—you knew me better than anyone, Cord!" He had it all *wrong*, she thought swiftly. Whatever she'd done, she done it because she *had* loved him.

"Oh, I thought I did. But I only saw what you wanted me to see, and you obviously kept the real Julia Stewart out of sight." He searched her face with sudden intensity. "Why? What were you so afraid of?"

"I wasn't *hiding* myself from you." She averted her eyes from his piercing gaze. "All my life I'd run to you with my little problems, told you all my secrets. Maybe I'd just realized it was time to stand on my own feet and try to handle things by myself—"

"We're not talking about the time you broke the boathouse window with a softball, dammit!" With an impatient stride he moved toward the bed and looked down at her in sudden anger. "We're talking about two people who were planning to get married—and you couldn't even trust me enough to tell me that you were on the verge of a nervous *breakdown!* Did you think I'd walk away from you if I found out? Is that why you sent me away first—because you didn't think my love was strong enough to see us through?''

His voice had a hoarse, incredulous rasp. From the unit next door she could hear the canned laughter of a television sitcom, and with stiff edginess she got to her feet and crossed to the dresser, needing to put some space between them. The room was so damned *small,* she thought with a flicker of resentment, hugging her arms around her body. And why did it suddenly seem so cold?

"I gave you my reasons two years ago. Why can't you accept that people change...that *I'd* changed? It's simple enough, Cord—I wanted a different life than the one we had all mapped out for us. I was tired of beating my head against the wall in a heartbreaking job, and what happened with Harry and Christie—"

"I don't even know what happened that day. You still haven't told me."

She tensed, waiting for the tremors to overtake her, but to her surprise they didn't come. Tascoe's confession had released her, she thought shakily. For the first time since those terrible and tragic hours on the ledge she was capable of relating the events of that day with some semblance of self-control.

"Hall had botched a bank holdup. From what Tascoe said tonight I guess it was a last-ditch attempt to strike it rich so he could provide for Christie when he was gone. Anyway, he managed to make his way back to the apartment of the woman who was baby-sitting Christie for him that day, and then within minutes the police arrived to arrest him. He panicked and ended up on a ledge just past the apartment's balcony—with Christie."

"And once they knew a child's life hung in the balance, you were called in." Cord nodded. "Go on."

She'd relived the scene so many times in her dreams, she thought sadly. It never could have had a completely happy ending, she knew that now.

"I was called in," she agreed. "I had a harness attached to me, and I stood on the outer edge of the balcony, getting as close as I dared to Harry and Christie. I couldn't look down."

She shuddered. "I was there for two and a half hours, talking to Harry, telling him he didn't want to do it, telling him that however bad things seemed we could help him. I promised that *I* would help him, that I'd make sure Christie was taken care of."

"After the way Tascoe had poisoned his mind against you, he would have read that as a threat." Cord's eyes were dark with remembered anger. "You never had a chance to talk him down."

"I never had a chance," she echoed softly, seeing for the last time the desperate expression on the man's face, the terrified child in his arms. "I didn't know that then. Finally he started to edge toward me, and I thought I'd somehow gotten through to him, that he was coming in. I told him to hand Christie to me. He looked at me—we were only about five feet apart by then. I saw his eyes, Cord, and right then and there I knew that somehow I'd miscalculated terribly. He—he *jumped*. We were on the tenth floor."

"But Christie was saved?" Even though he'd heard what she'd told Tascoe earlier, the corners of his mouth were white with tension.

"A SWAT team had been put into place during the situation. I don't think Hall even realized what was going on, but a team member had rappelled down from the roof to within a couple of feet of where we were." The tremors had come back, Julia realized. But this time she was able to overcome them. "He was the real hero that day—when Harry jumped, the SWAT member jumped, too, and managed to grab Christie out of her father's arms before Harry plunged to his death."

"Dear God." He was obviously visualizing the scene she'd so tersely described. "There must have been a moment when you thought—"

"A moment?" She gave a brittle laugh. "Not a moment, Cord. *Years*. Every night for the last two years I've dreamed about that split second—Harry stepping off that ledge, Christie's eyes, my hand reaching out and missing her. Except in my dreams I watch her fall all the way to the street below. In my dreams I was always responsible for her death."

"But it didn't play out that way. Even if it had, and even if Hall's decision to jump hadn't been influenced by Tascoe, there was no way you should have held yourself responsible for a tragedy that was unavoidable." His expression was once again guarded, his tone reserved. "If you hadn't shut me out of your life months before, I would have been there for you. We could have faced this together."

She'd started this day by attending the funeral of her two closest friends, Julia thought, her temples pounding, and then she'd gone through the emotional turmoil of Tascoe's shattering revelation. Now the man she'd loved all her life was coming too close to finding out the one thing she'd never wanted him to know.

Something inside her snapped.

"But you thought I was *perfect,* Cord!" The words rushed from her like an accusation. "You thought the woman you loved was *perfect! That's* why you loved me—that's why you haven't been able to forget me these last two years. How was I supposed to come to you and destroy that flawless image— reveal just how damn far from the truth it really was? How *could* I have?"

"That's right—that would have been a mistake. I'd have stopped loving you right there and then, Julia." His tanned face had paled with anger. "I'd have been out of there so goddamn fast you wouldn't have known what had happened. Good thing you ordered me the hell out before I could let you down."

"That's not what I'm saying." Her eyes blazed. "But you—"

"That's *exactly* what you're saying. You should have come right out and said that two years ago, so that I could have gotten on with my life." With a swift stride he was before her, his hands on her arms, his face in hers. "Yeah, you're right—I thought you were perfect. I saw the flaws, I saw the stubbornness, I even saw the fear sometimes when you forgot to hide it, and you *still* were perfect in my eyes. You were everything I'd ever wanted in a woman, Julia. You had me—*all* of me— and you thought it was all a lie."

"Let me go, Cord." She had to tip her head back to meet his furious gaze. "Let me go or I'll—"

"You'll what, Julia?" He was so close to her that she could see the single fleck of green in his right eye that she'd teased him about in the past under vastly different circumstances. "Anything you could do to me, you've already done. There's nothing left to take away." His hands dropped to his sides, and he shrugged. One corner of his mouth lifted slightly. "I'll let you go. You've been telling me to for long enough, haven't you?"

He turned away from her. Walking to the dresser, he emptied the pockets of his jeans, tossing a handful of change into the glass ashtray that sat there. He met her eyes in the mirror.

"Do you want the shower first?"

There was nothing at all in his voice but casual courtesy. Julia shook her head, and even that small movement was an effort. "No. No, go ahead and use it. I'll—I'll have mine later."

"I'll leave you a dry towel, then." Cord gave her an impersonal smile and stepped into the bathroom, closing the door behind him.

I'll let you go. You've been telling me to for long enough....

When he'd left the first time some part of her had known, even if she couldn't acknowledge it, that the tie that bound them together hadn't been severed completely. It had stretched like an invisible cord across a whole continent—she'd known in her heart that distance and time meant nothing, that it was capable of bridging *worlds,* if necessary, and that it would endure beyond death.

On one particularly bad night at the lake house she'd been lying in bed, King twitching fitfully in deep sleep on the floor beside her. Her eyes had been wide open in the dark, and outside the bare branches of the trees had been turned to silver foil by the full moon. It had only been weeks since her hard-won battle against the destructive crutch she had come to rely on, and she'd wondered if she had the strength to keep up the fight—wondered if she even cared enough to keep fighting.

She'd heard the rush of great wings from just beyond the window and had thought at first that an owl had pursued some terrified prey right up to the porch. A huge silhouette had momentarily darkened the moon, the silken rush of wings had come closer, and then she'd seen the bird alighting, noiseless and massive, on the low, wide sill of her bedroom window.

It had been like no owl she'd ever seen. Even in the moonlight she could tell it was some kind of eagle. Its beak curved dangerously down and its eyes seemed almost luminescently golden, and her first reaction had been fear. King had lifted his head, aroused by her indrawn breath, and she'd expected him to lunge at the silent shape only feet away.

Instead, his tail had thumped once, solidly, against the floorboards, and he'd given a curious puppy-like little whine—the same whine he gave when he saw her coming down the stone-pebbled path after being away for the day.

Unmoving, her gaze fixed on the apparition, she'd felt the fear slowly dissipate. A deep calm had overtaken her, and when she'd finally fallen asleep, the bird still standing guard at her window, the nightmares for once had remained at bay that night.

Cord's mother had told her that the Senecas' name for themselves was the *Nundawaono*—the People of the Great Hill. They were rich in legends and stories of otherworldly encounters. Cord had grown up with that heritage.

A few days ago she'd told him she didn't believe in magic. She'd lied. Where Cord was concerned, she'd always believed—from the day he'd given her the perfectly round, perfectly smooth lake stone for luck, right up until a few minutes ago when suddenly all the magic had gone out of her world.

The dull drumming roar of the shower had been providing a subconscious background to her thoughts, but now she heard it being cut off. There was a clanking metal sound as the outdated shower mechanism abruptly switched the running water to the taps of the bath, and then the slight squeal of the taps being turned off.

Cord didn't like getting caught in cold water. He'd always ended his showers that way, and at one time it had been something she'd teased him about—that she suspected his aversion to cold showers could be part of the reason he so often came back to bed with her in the mornings, his skin still damp and warm, his desire for her urgent and heated. They'd made each other late for work more times than she could count, Julia remembered.

In a few moments he would step into the room, and instead of hours of sweet, langorous lovemaking, there would be a few stiff, awkward exchanges between them. She would have her shower, and when she came back he would probably pretend to be asleep. She would slip into the bed, taking care to keep from accidentally touching him. His breath would be too even, her limbs would be kept rigidly still.

She wasn't going to be able to do this, Julia thought hopelessly.

But this time she had no badge to turn in, no gun to hand over, and the option of turning her back on this case and walking away simply didn't exist. She'd made a vow—a vow that still held, even though Sheila and Paul were gone. If she believed in anything, she had to believe in the sanctity of the promise she'd made five years ago, standing beside Cord in a small, unpretentious church, with a tiny, red-haired baby squalling lustily at a baptismal font.

They were still bound together, she thought—but by an old obligation that neither of them could ignore. Until they tracked down Paul and Sheila's killer, Lizbet could still be in danger, could still be snatched away, never to be heard from again, just as Jackie Redmond's daughter—

That was the key.

Julia froze. The *daughter* was the key—the key to the fear in Jackie Redmond's voice, the guilt in her eyes when she'd asked about Lizbet. She'd been the traitor—who better to hand over information about the department than the woman across whose desk every vital document, every confidential piece of information passed before being given to her boss? Paul had been right, except that the person betraying him hadn't been a fellow officer, she'd been the chief of police's personal secretary.

And like the most famous betrayer of all, she'd been stricken with guilt when she'd realized the enormity of what she'd done.

Redmond would have been vetted thoroughly before being

given such a sensitive position, Julia thought, her mind racing. She would have been assessed as completely trustworthy. For her to act so out of character could only mean that whoever was manipulating her had discovered the one threat—or promise—that she couldn't withstand.

They had her daughter. She had dozens of photographs of the girl—photographs that she hadn't been able to take her fearfilled eyes from this evening—but whoever was threatening her had the girl herself. And from Tascoe's protective attitude, he was well aware of the situation.

Except now the situation had changed. Tascoe was in custody, Jackie Redmond was all alone, and the killer she'd unwillingly aided would be wondering if her usefulness to him had come to an end. Julia heard Cord moving around in the bathroom beyond, and all of a sudden she made up her mind.

Grabbing a sweater and snatching her keys from the dresser, she slipped outside into the night.

Chapter 10

Twice on the drive to Jackie Redmond's apartment Julia almost turned around and headed back to the motel and Cord. He'd be furious when he found she'd gone, she knew—furious and alarmed. No matter what had passed between them tonight, he still thought of her as his partner on this case. He was her backup. She was his. He wouldn't understand why she'd ignored that basic rule.

She was finding her reaction hard to understand herself. All she knew was that Cord's remoteness was unendurable, but that made no sense at all. If anything, eliminating the last remnants of any kind of personal relationship between them would make it easier for her to concentrate on the task in front of her—finding and catching a killer before he could strike again. But as she parked in front of the apartment they'd left only an hour or so earlier, she found that she had to force herself to get out of the car.

What she really wanted to do was to fold her arms over the steering wheel, put her head down and cry, she thought with a flash of impatient honesty. Only the knowledge that Lizbet's safety was at stake kept her going.

The front door was still unlocked. It was a wonder that Tascoe hadn't taken steps to beef up the security himself, since Jackie's well-being was obviously all-important to him, but the man was an enigma in more ways than one. Running lightly up the first flight of stairs and rounding the landing to the second floor, she frowned.

How much *did* the ex-cop know about Paul and Sheila's death? What was his agenda? She'd based her belief in his innocence on a conviction that he was incapable of harming a woman or a child, but his confession tonight had proven her wrong. He'd nearly caused the death of Christie Hall two years ago, and by doing so his actions had almost destroyed Julia's life. She was suddenly glad that the likelihood of him returning while she was interviewing Jackie Redmond was almost nil.

Reaching the next landing, she halted abruptly, momentarily disconcerted. Above her, the third floor hallway was in darkness.

It was an old building. If there was a superintendent on the premises, which was a dubious possibility in the first place, it was now well after midnight and not even the most dedicated handyman would be replacing light bulbs at this time of night. Giving herself a mental shake, she forced her suddenly leaden feet up a few more stairs. She was here now, and Tascoe was otherwise occupied—if the woman was ever going to talk, this was probably the best time to catch her off guard. Scuttling away because of one burned-out light was just plain stupid.

As she reached the third floor, her nervousness eased. There in front of her was the braying pewter burro door knocker, easily visible in the illumination coming up from the second floor. The same pair of old-lady shoes she and Cord had noticed before still stood side by side on the rubber mat, and the very homeliness of these details was somehow reassuring. Nothing sinister had happened here. Nothing was *going* to happen.

Something crunched underfoot.

Without even having to think about it she knew exactly what it was, and with that knowledge the fear came flooding back in full force. She'd thought there was nothing about the job she'd forgotten, but this was one aspect she'd pushed to the back of her mind—the way that fear became a physical entity. It swept over her like a wave, cold and wet.

She'd stepped on broken glass. The bulb hadn't burned out. It had been deliberately taken out and smashed by someone who preferred the darkness to the light.

Sheila was shot. Paul was stabbed—pierced through the chest. Two down, two to go, and then the child, alone and unprotected...

Her mind was trying to operate on two levels, and although she knew that the theory it was desperately scrambling to put together was nearly complete, she shut it out with almost brutal force in order to focus all her attention on what her senses were telling her.

When you're a rabbit, think like the rabbit. Don't think like the fox, because the fox will always be able to do that better than you.

With crystal clarity the memory came into her mind—Cord's father, Davey and Cord walking beside him in the woods, herself perched high on his shoulders as he pointed out the twin tracks of a desperate flight for life and a pursuit of prey in fresh-fallen snow. He'd shown them the spot where the fox must have sat waiting in ambush, and the deep, twisting claw marks in the earth where, a split second before he could have known for sure he was in danger, the rabbit had reacted instantaneously to nebulous alarm and had escaped.

She was the rabbit here, and already her pupils had opened as widely as possible, taking in light she hadn't even known was there and catching the dim gleam of the brass knocker on Jackie Redmond's door. The angle was wrong, Julia instinctively realized. Without analysing it she knew that she was seeing the knocker as it would appear if the door wasn't completely closed, and immediately she froze, her back against the wall and her lips slightly parted to minimize the sound of her breathing.

She was the rabbit, and danger was near. She should run—her thigh muscles were already tensed, waiting for the command, and her heart was working overtime in her chest, pumping the oxygen-laden blood that it knew she would need to her limbs.

But she was also the fox. She hadn't expected to find her quarry tonight—the best she'd hoped for was to catch a glimpse of his tracks through Jackie's eyes—but if he was here she had no right to put her personal safety first. She was the fox, and she was protecting her own.

She inched cautiously along the wall, her palms flat against it. No doubt she was leaving her own tracks, Julia thought, trying to judge just how far away she was from the slightly open door. Tomorrow there would be smeared handmarks on the smooth painted plaster.

And then her sixth and last sense belatedly kicked in.

She was being watched. *He was right here with her in the dark and he was watching her.*

Everything happened at once. She felt rather than heard the presence behind her and she spun instantly, but at the same moment an arm snaked around her chest and a hand clamped over her mouth so hard that her neck jerked backward. Reacting without thought, her arms pinned uselessly at her sides, she stamped down with all the force she could muster on her attacker's instep.

His hand tightened on her mouth. She bit it and tasted the salty tang of blood and heard the almost inaudible whisper right in her ear all at the same time.

"Dammit, Julia, it's me!"

She twisted her head around as far as she could, her eyes wide with shock. They met Cord's, and even in the near-total darkness she could see the fury he was holding back. Slowly his hand moved from her mouth, but as she took a breath to speak he silenced her once more. He bent to her ear again. Even at that, she had to strain to hear him.

"I'm going in. You stay out here and wait for me." Before he'd finished she was shaking her head angrily, and his arm around her chest tightened. "Don't goddamn *argue* with me. I'm the one with the gun—and if I have to shoot you in the foot to get you to stay here don't be too sure I won't." He released her so abruptly that only the wall behind her kept her upright, and then he moved noiselessly toward the door.

As soon as he pushed it farther open a dim glow limned the edge of the door. It seemed almost ghostly, and she remembered the eerie picture on the living-room wall with its electrified frame. She controlled the shudder that threatened and found herself holding her breath as Cord swung the door open wide.

He paused, and she knew he was doing the same thing that she was—recalling the layout of the apartment and remembering the position of the two other rooms that led off the short entrance hall before it opened into the living room. There'd been an open walk-through to the Hollywood-style kitchen on the left, and almost opposite it had been a closed door that had presumably been the bathroom. Her nerves, already vibrating, tightened almost painfully as Cord slipped inside and disappeared into the shadows.

She stood there in the dark, hugging herself in an agony of apprehension and straining her ears to catch any slight sound from the apartment, but there was nothing. Her wishful theory about Jackie waiting for Tascoe to return obviously had been blown out of the water, she thought edgily.

But where would she be at this time of night? If she'd wanted to wait for Tascoe at the station she would have left at the same time the cruiser had arrived to collect him. Would she have gone to a friend's? Did she *have* any, besides Tascoe?

She'd been upset and alone. It was just conceivable that she'd sought out the company of the nearest acquaintance at hand— her neighbor.

Julia hesitated. There was still no sound coming from the apartment, and more from the need to be doing something— *anything*—to relieve the unendurable tension of waiting for Cord to give the all clear, she edged quietly down the hall until she could see the burro lady's door.

It was completely dark. If the woman had been entertaining a distraught Jackie Redmond, there would have been a chink of light coming from under the door, at least.

About to turn and head toward Jackie's apartment again, she suddenly felt the tiny hairs on the nape of her neck rise atavistically, but this time as she whirled around she realized almost at once that her concern was groundless. She bumped against the solidity of Cord, and he grasped her arms just above the elbows, steadying her in the total blackness.

"Redmond's been hurt," he hissed into her ear before she could say anything. "She's in there unconscious—I'm going outside to use the car phone to call the police and an ambulance. Stay with her until I get back."

There was a curiously flat tone to his whisper, as if he was reining in a terrible anger that he knew he couldn't afford to release. Her lips parted in shocked dismay.

"Dear God—she's been *attacked?* How—"

But even as the hushed questions poured from her he was gone. He had to have the vision of a cat, Julia thought uneasily, stumbling to the apartment he'd just left and feeling her way along the wall. Of course, part of her shakiness was due to the realization that her earlier forebodings had been proven right— Jackie *had* been in danger all along. She *had* been a threat to someone, and that someone had taken the first opportunity to silence her.

She should have listened to her intuition, she thought. She'd known there was something badly wrong here as soon as she'd realized that the hall light had been broken. Even before that her senses had been on full alert, so why had she grasped so eagerly—almost desperately—at any other explanation for her unease?

You didn't trust yourself to read the situation, she told herself sharply. *You've spent the last two years convinced that your gut feelings couldn't be relied on, because of the way you thought you'd mishandled Hall on that ledge—but you were wrong. Tascoe was responsible for the man's reaction, not you.*

It was true, she thought slowly. She'd *forced* herself to ignore the alarm bells going off in her mind. She would have to relearn what had once been second nature to her—to listen to them unquestioningly and react accordingly.

And they were still going off.

She didn't even think. The danger was behind her—it was *behind her!*—and she spun around in the dark to meet it, knowing that he was there, but even as she turned her foot came down on something and she felt herself overbalancing. And then she was falling, unable to save herself, unable to defend herself against the danger she was facing, the threat that was coming from the hallway—

The *empty* hallway? Even as the realization flashed through her mind Julia fell heavily onto the object that she'd stumbled over. Her hands flew out to break her fall, and her fingers came in contact with something that felt like fabric—soft, thick fabric, she thought in confusion. Soft, thick, *quilted* fabric.

She heard a low moan and realized it was coming from her own throat. For a moment her limbs refused to work, and then she was frantically scrambling to her knees. She put her weight down on something and immediately moved, her stomach doing a slow roll as she fought down a sudden nausea.

It was Jackie. She'd fallen over the woman's body in the dark—why hadn't Cord *warned* her—

Her head jerked up a split second before the man came out of the apartment, his huge silhouette blotting out the faint glow rimming the doorway, and even as she rose to her feet and went for him she saw his hand move upward and she knew that the next thing she would feel would be the bullet tearing through her, the same way one had torn through Sheila. Cord's face flashed into her mind's eye—not the way she'd seen it an hour ago, but the way she wanted to remember him, the way she would remember him in these last few seconds of life and beyond.

The apartment light snapped on, and for one moment she thought her need and love for him had conjured his image in front of her. She closed her eyes against the sudden brightness.

"What the *hell*—"

Her eyes flew open. The last of the blood drained from her face. It *was* Cord—but that was *crazy.*

"My God—did he hurt you? Are you all right?" He was grasping her shoulders, gently drawing her away from Jackie's still body. His glance flicked comprehensively over her frozen features, and she managed a nod.

"I—I'm okay, Cord. But Jackie—Jackie's..."

The woman's face was mercifully turned away from them, but above the lace-trimmed collar of the quilted robe her neck was canted at an unnatural angle. Cord bent swiftly to the body, and Julia looked away.

"She's dead. Her neck's been broken." He straightened. "I should have kept you with me, dammit. It could have been *you* lying there right now."

His voice was uneven, and as if he couldn't help himself he reached out for her, pulling her close. Julia didn't resist, but her body was rigid against his.

"You don't *have* a car phone in the Bronco, do you?" Her query came out on a high-pitched and wavery note, and Cord frowned in confusion.

"We can use the phone in the living room. I left my cell phone back at the motel."

"But there *isn't* one in the Bronco, is there?"

His arms around her, she stared over his shoulder down the shadowy hall. It felt like a thin skin of ice had formed around her, she thought hazily. But any minute now this blessed detachment would shatter and she would have to face the nightmarish truth.

"No, but that doesn't—"

"Then why did you tell me you were going to call the police from the car, Cord?" Her voice reached a new and higher level. "Why did you leave me to find Jackie's body—and how did you get back here without passing me in the hall?"

She felt cold—so *cold*. Even the warmth of his chest against hers and the reassuring strength of his embrace didn't seem to be enough to ward off the shivers that she could feel starting somewhere deep inside her. With an immense effort, she pulled her gaze from the empty hallway and met his suddenly comprehending features.

"It wasn't you, was it?"

"I guess it wasn't your day to die, Stewart." Cindy Lopez, wan and exhausted-looking, raked a weary hand through her hair. She looked over her shoulder at the open door to the Redmond apartment and shrugged tiredly. "Just Jackie's. At least she didn't suffer. It happened quickly enough."

"We're all through in there, Detective." An older man, stocky and gray-haired, whom Julia vaguely recognized as one of the department's crime scene technicians, came out, carrying a metal case under one arm and stripping a pair of thin latex gloves from his hands. "Everything that place could tell us we got. But don't expect a miracle—our boy was no amateur." He nodded briefly at Julia and grimaced at Cord.

"Just like old times, Hunter. The technology keeps getting better, but the criminals keep getting smarter."

"You got that right," Cord said tightly. "But she was definitely killed on the sofa, Greg?"

"Killed on the sofa, by someone she probably knew—no signs of prior agitation or struggle," the older man said briefly. "Then for some twisted reason he dragged her out of the apartment and stashed her in that utility cupboard there."

"Because he saw me arrive—the living room window looks down onto the street. It was quiet enough that he would have heard me driving up and parking just outside." Julia forced a steadiness she didn't feel into her voice. "Which means whoever he was, he knows me, because he knew I would only be there to see Jackie."

"That makes sense." Lopez fished in her pockets distractedly, took out a stick of gum and popped it into her mouth. She chewed thoughtfully. "He sees you arrive and he has to assume that if you don't get an answer at Redmond's door you might get suspicious. He can't simply leave because he'll almost certainly run into you as you're coming in, and you either know him or would remember what he looks like."

"Why the hell didn't I see that utility closet earlier this evening?" Cord's eyes were dark with anger, but it was directed at himself. "How could I have missed it?"

"The first time we came to see Jackie, she already had the door open when we were only halfway down the hall, and it was blocking our view." Julia let out a breath. "I didn't realize there was anything there, either."

"He puts Redmond's body in the cupboard and he runs down

the hall, takes the light out of the wall fixture and smashes it,'' Lopez said. "By then you're probably on your way up the first flight of stairs so he runs back and hides with the body. But he leaves the apartment door open—why? He had to know that would alert you.''

"I was the rabbit. He was the fox," Julia said flatly. Lopez and Greg looked at her uncomprehendingly, but Cord's eyes met hers.

"It was an ambush," he said softly. "He wanted you in that apartment where there was less chance of being interrupted.''

"What the hell's this fox and rabbit business?'' Lopez asked with a touch of annoyance.

"It's a Seneca thing," Cord and Julia said at the same time. They looked at each other, and at his quick grin she was startled into an answering smile.

"You two rehearse that or what?'' Lopez said sourly. "Just what I need, a comedy routine when I'm trying to quit smoking, solve a triple homicide and get home sometime tonight to get a couple of hours sleep before heading back to work.'' She glared at them, and then her features softened. "I guess this time the rabbit got away.''

"He had to have been there the whole time." Julia's brief good humor ebbed as she remembered her cautious approach along the darkened hallway. "I sensed someone watching me, but when Cord appeared I assumed it was his presence I'd somehow been aware of. I should have realized," she said suddenly, her eyes darkening.

"Realized what?" Cord took in her even more pronounced pallor and moved unobtrusively closer to her side. "Did you pick up on something?"

"Nothing that would help us in tracking him down." She shook her head, her brows knitted as if she had a headache. "No, it's stupid. It's probably just hindsight, anyway.''

"You got an impression of evil, didn't you?" It was Greg who spoke, his mouth a grim line. "I got it, too, the whole time I was in that apartment. My great-grandmother had second sight, and all I get is a feeling that I want to toss my cookies once in a while, but it adds up to the same thing. I've only felt it a few times in my career, but it always turns out to be right. They used to call you the Guardian Angel, I know—but tonight you had one watching over you.''

"Evil? Try supremely arrogant," Lopez said shortly. "He was playing a damn game in the dark, for God's sake. He could have just pushed you aside, he could have broken your neck like he'd broken Redmond's." She caught Cord's angry glance and shrugged defensively. "Hey, I'm only putting myself in his shoes, Hunter. But he didn't do any of those things. Instead he deliberately—"

"He posed as me." Cord's voice held cold fury. "While you were away from the door for those few seconds and I was inside he put Jackie's body on her own doorstep, and then he told you to go back, knowing that you'd discover it in the most grisly way possible." A muscle jumped in his jaw. "But he posed as *me*—well enough to fool you for the few seconds he needed. That's important."

"He knows you both," Lopez said slowly. "If Tascoe wasn't still at the station I'd—"

"Dean Tascoe?" Greg gave her a sharp glance, and Lopez frowned.

"Yeah. Chuck Hendrix and Tommy Dow are grilling him for me on his connection to Vince DiMarco. We thought he might know something about Paul and Sheila's murders—though it looks like that theory's a washout now, with Jackie's death."

"Did Chuck and Tommy offer to take over the interrogation?" Looking up, Julia saw Cord exchange a look with Greg, and in both men's faces there was tight frustration.

"Hendrix said since Paul was my partner I probably wouldn't be able to keep an objective distance while I was questioning Tascoe," Lopez said. "He was right—the guy rubs me the wrong way in the first place, and thinking he had anything to do with—"

"Dow used to be Tascoe's partner. Hendrix and Tascoe used to go drinking together," Greg cut in. "If I was a betting man I'd give you ten-to-one odds that Tascoe's interrogation didn't last any longer than it took for you to walk out of the room.

He'd have had plenty of time to come back here and kill his girlfriend before Julia showed up.''

Lopez stared at him almost accusingly. Then she grabbed her cell phone out of her coat pocket and started punching in a number. ''Dammit,'' she muttered, putting the receiver to her ear. ''*Dammit!* This freakin' old boys' network is the goddamn *limit!*'' She cradled the phone on her shoulder and pulled a pack of cigarettes and a lighter out of her pocket. Then she looked at Julia and put them back. ''If you can break free, Stewart, I guess I can,'' she growled. Her attention switched to the phone, and she spoke rapidly into it.

It looked like she'd become a role model, Julia thought resignedly as Lopez barked questions at the hapless desk sergeant on the other end of the line, and Cord and Greg, a few feet away, talked together for a moment, their voices low and their expressions serious. Some role model—right now she felt the craving stronger than she had in over a year. Greg was right— it *had* been evil she'd sensed tonight, and as soon as she got back to the motel she knew she would turn the shower on as hot as she could stand it and scrub at her arms where the shadow in the hallway had gripped her.

But it wouldn't be enough. There was something powerfully seductive in the thought of dulling the horrors of tonight completely, in seeking out, even if only for a few hours, total oblivion.

''You look bushed. We'll pick up your car tomorrow.'' Cord's hand was on her shoulder, his fingers nearly brushing her hair, and she looked up blankly.

''That's right, an APB for Dean Tascoe. Yeah, *that* Dean Tascoe, Jerry,'' Lopez snarled into the cell phone. ''And if anything gets fouled up, don't think I don't have the *cojones* to come down there and personally hang you out to dry.'' She raised a distracted hand at them as Cord gently propelled Julia down the hall. Beside her Greg resignedly set down his case and leaned wearily against the wall.

''Hunter—good seeing you again,'' he called after them. ''But we gotta stop meeting like this.'' He gave them a tired

grin and a thumbs-down sign, and beside her Julia saw the ghost
of a smile cross Cord's features.

"He's a good guy," he said as they passed the burro lady's
door, which was firmly closed. Sometime in the last hour she'd
seen the woman's daughter come to take her away for the night,
Julia remembered. The shoes that had stood on the mat outside
were gone. "He's right—we always seem to run into each other
on the bad ones. He worked the Bradley farmhouse, and he was
there when Donner's group got killed."

"He's one of the few who actually met with Donner in
prison, isn't he?" There was no real interest in Julia's question,
but she knew she needed to keep her mind occupied. As Cord
held the front door of the building open for her and they stepped
into the rain-fresh night air, he nodded curtly.

"We both did, but that was afterward. I didn't get anything
from him, of course. He claimed he'd had no knowledge of the
killings his people had carried out, and since he'd been in prison
the whole time we couldn't prove anything against him."

He passed a tired hand over his face and took a deep breath.
"Okay. Now that we're alone I want to hear what the hell you
were thinking of, coming here by yourself tonight."

They'd crossed the street to the Bronco, and he unlocked the
passenger side door and waited while she got in. A moment
later he slid into the driver's seat, but he didn't attempt to start
the ignition. "You nearly got killed."

"I know." Julia stared straight ahead at the windshield. "I
know I nearly got killed, and I know what I did was irresponsible. It won't happen again. Can we go now?"

She heard his sharply indrawn breath. "What the hell's the
matter with you, Julia? For crying out loud—I died a thousand
deaths when I came down that damned hallway in the dark and
thought that something had happened to you! And when I realized that he'd been there all the time—"

"I *know,* Cord!" She turned to face him, her features drawn.
"I just can't *talk* about it right now—I can't talk about *anything*
right now. I—I've got to make a phone call," she said distractedly.

"It's nearly two in the morning." His voice was incredulous. "Who's awake at this hour?"

"No one's awake!" she snapped, losing the last of her control. "I'll be waking someone up—but they'll understand, Cord, because that's just the way it *works* sometimes. They'll understand, and they'll stay on the phone or maybe meet me for a coffee somewhere. I'd do the same for anyone else in the group—but tonight it's me who needs the lifeline!"

"You want to talk to someone from AA." The anger drained from his face. His hands tightened on the steering wheel, and he looked suddenly uncertain. "I guess it's no good offering myself as a listener, is it?"

"To hold my hand while I feel sorry for myself for a couple of hours?" she muttered, looking down at her lap. "Believe me, you don't want to see me like that."

"No. *You* don't want me to see you like that," Cord said quietly. "But I was always a blind man where you were concerned, Julia."

She didn't realize she was crying until the first fat drop fell onto her clenched hands, and by then it was already too late. She sat there silently, the tears falling from eyes that she kept squeezed shut, her shoulders held rigid against the tremors that felt like they were shaking her apart inside, and suddenly Cord's arms were around her, his hand pulling her head into the hollow of his shoulder, his voice a soothing, wordless murmur against her hair. He held her tightly, rocking her, and she inhaled the scent of his skin through her tears.

"I *missed* you, Cord. I missed you so *much!*"

The words burst from her throat with a desperate life of their own. She'd had no intention of telling him, but dear God, she couldn't take one more minute of this *pain.* She raised her head and looked at him, her eyes drowned.

"You were my refuge and—and you were gone," she said in a whisper. "I want you *back.*"

She stared at him almost fearfully—the strong cheekbones, the straight mouth, his unreadable gaze…and then suddenly it was as if the universe—no, her *life*—slipped half a degree sideways and clicked into the position it was meant to be in.

"Didn't you know?" Cord asked softly. "You've been safe in my heart all the time."

Chapter 11

"*But* why did the maiden leap from way up there?" Davey looked up at the cliff skeptically. "She must have known she was going to die."

"She wanted to die." Tossing her long black braid over her shoulder, Cord's mom shielded her eyes from the glare of the afternoon sun and tipped her head back, staring at the sheer drop to the deep blue lake. "She'd lost the only man she'd ever loved, and she couldn't live without him. But it's only a legend, you guys. My great-grandfather probably made it up years ago to bring the tourists in." She smiled at the three of them—Davey looking unconvinced, a wide-eyed and silent Julia and her own son, who was still thoughtfully assessing the cliff the locals called Maiden's Leap.

"I'd do it," Cord said slowly. "Except I wouldn't do it to kill myself. I'd do it to save the maiden."

"Would you do it to save me, Cord?" Five-year-old Julia's nose had a scattering of summer freckles on it, and her sandy fingers were wrapped around the stems of some wilting cornflowers and daisies. She looked uncertainly at her big brother's

*older friend, and he grinned at her. He dropped a tanned hand
to her hair, ruffling it affectionately.*

"Sure, honey. I'd do it in a heartbeat...."

Julia came out of the dream slowly, drifting back to consciousness as if she was gently being washed ashore by a warm
wave. Her lashes fanned peacefully on her cheeks, she pointed
her toes and stretched her legs luxuriously, still wrapped in the
peaceful sense of well-being the dream had engendered in her.
It had been a perfect summer's day, and Cord had said he would
jump off Maiden's Leap to save her....

She'd lost him, but now he was back.

The events of the previous twenty-four hours returned as she
came fully awake and opened her eyes. She was wearing a short
blue sleep shirt, one of her purchases from yesterday, and across
the slight curve of her breasts revealed by the lacy scoop neckline lay Cord's arm, keeping her close. Even at rest a hard swell
of muscle was visible beneath the coppery skin.

They'd come back here last night, and he'd never left her
side. He'd held her as she'd talked, occasionally smoothing the
damp hair from her forehead with one strong hand, and she'd
poured it all out—the wrenching pain she'd felt every time
she'd heard of a child she hadn't been there to save, the case
files in piles on her desk that she'd known had been too much
for one person to handle, the terrible sense of inadequacy that
had begun to overwhelm her long before the time she'd confronted Hall and his daughter on the ledge. She'd told him
everything.

Well, no—not quite, Julia thought with a flicker of guilty
honesty. She hadn't told him that she'd thought she'd been
pregnant—and she hadn't told him how devastating that ulti-
mately erroneous belief had been. She wasn't going to tell him.

There was no reason to. Things had changed—*she'd*
changed.

She'd taken on the responsibility for Lizbet's safety. A year
ago that responsibility would have crushed her with fear, but
not now. The dangers were still out there—they always had
been and they always would be—but she could keep them away

from the child she'd sworn to protect, and nothing would happen to Lizbet as long as she did everything *right*.

She squeezed her eyes shut, drawing in a deep, steadying breath. She was back in Cord's arms, and nothing was going to come between them ever again. He was the other half of her soul, and one day they would make a child together.

"Bad dream?" His voice, husky with sleep, came from somewhere over her left shoulder, and she relaxed against his solid warmth.

"No." She slanted her gaze at him and felt him stir behind her. "I was dreaming about the day your mom took us to Maiden's Leap, and you said you'd jump off it to save me."

"Jeez, what *could* I say?" There was a wicked gleam in the one dark eye she could see. The other was covered with a tangle of blue-black hair. "You were perfectly capable of sitting that fat little butt right down on the sand and pitching a tantrum if I'd given you any other answer."

"My butt was never fat. And I didn't throw tantrums, Cord— I was a perfect child." How long had it been since she'd indulged in something as innocuous as teasing? Julia wondered tremulously. It just felt so *good*, lying here with Cord and talking nonsense.

"Okay, then—chubby. You were a chubby little five-year-old, and you may have been perfect with everyone else, but with me you could be a hellion," he insisted. "And it only got worse as you got older, honey. It's a darn good thing I like bad girls."

"Me?" Startled, she twisted around in his arms to face him. "Me, a *bad* girl? Please, Cord—I'm the original Little Miss Conservative. I always worried I was too *dull* for—"

"You're flashing me, honey. See, that's what I mean—good girls never accidentally on purpose fall out of their tops."

His tone was disapproving, but as Julia looked down in confused consternation one large tanned hand slipped adroitly around the now exposed swell of her breast. "Baby dolls with lace trim," he said with appreciative interest. "What are the panties like?"

He was still teasing her, but the timbre of his voice had taken on a lower, more seductive note, and his thumb was idly circling her nipple as if at any moment he might decide to stop. It was still teasing, Julia thought as a flush of heat suffused her. But the word had taken on a whole new connotation.

"You know what the panties are like, Detective Hunter." She could feel herself blushing. "You saw them last night."

"But last night wasn't the right time, honey," he said softly. "Last night you just needed me to hold you. Now you need something else."

"Maybe." Her teasing might be a little rusty, Julia thought, but she was pretty sure she still remembered how to raise Cord Hunter's temperature. She looked at him through her lashes, and with one finger she traced a hesitant line down the side of his neck to his collarbone. The dark eyes watching her widened slightly, and she saw him catch his breath. "And maybe right now you need something that I can give you. What do you want, Cord?"

"I want to make you mine all over again."

Under the sheets he brought his leg up and over hers, half-covering her with his body, and cupping the curve of her rump with his free hand, he effortlessly scooped her closer to him. He held her there, gazing into her eyes. She could feel him stroking her inner thigh, his hand slipping in and out of the lacy elasticized panty, and she knew he could feel her moistness. She felt like she was *melting* inside, Julia thought weakly. How could the man bring her to such a state with a single touch?

"I try real hard to be a sensitive guy, honey." His breathing had deepened and slowed, too, and there was a flush of darker color ridging the hard cheekbones. "But there's part of me that's just about as basic as a big old gray he-wolf, and that's never going to change. I want to be in you again. What do you think those dreams I had of you when I was in California were all about, anyway?"

"Birds?" She bit her lip and looked at him, and a slow grin lifted a corner of his mouth.

"Once. But in all the rest it was only my imagination that took flight." He shrugged wryly. "Hell, I thought when I turned twenty I would have left that kind of thing behind, but I guess I'm not as adult as I thought I was.''

He bent his head, and so swiftly that she only had time to gasp, he licked the hollow between her breasts. Both his hands slid up to gently grip her shoulders. "So now you know what I want. Except I'm not taking it until I get the word from you, Julia. There's history between us."

"Past history." She touched the small crescent-shaped scar on his cheek and then pressed a light kiss to it, her lips lingering on his skin. "I should have handled things differently two years ago. I built a wall around myself, and I ended up shutting out the one person I needed more than anyone. But I want you in my life, Cord—and I don't want any more walls between us." She paused and met his eyes. "I need you in me again, too— just as much as you do."

He gave her a frankly dubious look. "Oh, I sincerely doubt that, sweetheart." His tone was dry. "You have no damn idea how badly I want you."

"So make those dreams come true, Cord." A little laugh bubbled up inside of her. "I've got a pretty good idea of how they all ended, but there must have been a few interesting variations leading up to the inevitable. Show me."

He held her gaze for a second, and then he smiled at her— a slow, bad-boy smile. He hadn't been kidding, Julia thought with a touch of nervousness. There was a *big* streak of wolf in the man—bigger than he'd ever revealed to her before.

"Okay, you're on." His voice was deceptively soft. "But you've got to understand that these were dreams, so naturally whatever I wanted, all I had to do was think about it and then you were doing it. They were *my* dreams, after all," he added unapologetically.

"I think I get it. You were the king of the world and I was your adoring slave. Is that about right?" She tipped her head to one side, frowning thoughtfully.

"Sometimes an adoring concubine. Sometimes a dancing girl. But you get the picture—my every wish was your command. I think that's actually pretty standard for that kind of dream." He shot her an assessing glance, and his hands moved from her shoulders to her lace-trimmed neckline. "So do you think you can handle it?"

"I think so." Looking at him, she felt suddenly breathless. She shouldn't be, she thought shakily. She'd made love with Cord Hunter countless times in the past—he'd been the only man she ever *had* made love with—and even though they'd been apart, their coming together might be expected to be a quietly loving renewal of their physical bond.

But she'd forgotten how it had really been between them in bed. No—she hadn't forgotten, Julia corrected herself—she hadn't *allowed* herself to remember. Her nights without him had been hard enough to bear without torturing herself with desires he wasn't there to satisfy.

But he was here now. And he wanted to play.

"The baby dolls are good, but you're all covered up again. That's bad. You would never do that in my dreams."

Impatiently he raked back the strand of hair that had fallen over his eye and sighed. Then both his hands moved slowly down to cup her breasts, pushing aside the stretchy elasticized neckline of her top until it was low enough to reveal her completely, and immediately Julia felt a liquid heat run through her. Somehow she felt more exposed than if he'd removed her clothing, she thought faintly, barely able to look at his hands and what they were doing.

"You missed your cue." His voice was husky. "This is where you say, 'Oh, Cord, what are you doing?'"

"Oh, Cord…what *are* you doing to me?" Julia breathed. His palms, slightly calloused, lifted her just high enough so that the lacy elastic slipped underneath her breasts and stayed there.

"You're improvising. It threw me off there for a minute, but I like it," he said, his thumbs circling her nipples. "As for what I'm doing, I'm looking at your breasts. In a minute I'll be kissing them, but right now I just want to look. They're…" He caught his lower lip between his teeth and met her gaze. "They're just perfect. And they still fit exactly in my hands."

True to his word, he lowered his head until she felt the tip of his tongue flicking along the underside of one breast, tracing its curve from the outermost edge to the hollow of her cleavage,

his hands still pushing the tiny frill of lace on her top out of
the way. His mouth moved to her other breast, but this time he
took her nipple between his lips and circled it with his tongue.
She could feel it tightening to a peak, and she bent her head
back, arching her body toward him as erotic images she hadn't
thought she was capable of imagining tumbled through her
mind.

"See, I always wanted to lick you all over, honey." His voice
was velvet. A strand of his hair brushed against her skin as he
lifted his head, and Julia heard herself give a little moan of pure
pleasure. She opened her eyes and saw the drugged desire in
his. "You taste like heat, and I'm going to cool you down."

The sheet that had covered them slid off the side of the bed
as he raised himself, an arm braced on either side of her, and
straddled her. All he had on were one of his pairs of white
shorts, the waistband an almost startling contrast against his
tanned, washboard stomach, and in them he looked like a fighter
who'd just stepped out of the ring. His shoulders were broad,
and his biceps were more pronounced than she remembered
them.

He paused, looking down at her. "Baby, you're beautiful,"
he said softly. "I like to see your hair in your face and your
lips open like that. And you're blushing all over."

"I'm not blushing, Cord." As soon as she said it she felt the
color rise to her face. "I'm hot, and I thought you were going
to cool me down."

She was *tempting* him, she thought with a little start. Maybe
there was some bad girl in her, after all.

"Put your arms above your head and hold on to the bedstead,
honey." He bent to her, and his tongue darted in between her
parted lips, leaving them moist and wanting more. "By the
way—the panties are cute. Those ruffles make you look like a
birthday present."

What he did next took her completely by surprise. Moving
down on the bed, he lifted her foot, cradling it in his hands.
"Pretty feet, too," he said. "One rainy Saturday I want to paint
your toenails bright scarlet. Then we'll go out to dinner and
you can wear your most conservative black dress and black

heels, and only I'll know what a hussy you are under that prim exterior.''

He kissed the tip of her baby toe. ''Scarlet, or maybe shocking pink.'' His teeth nipped it lightly, his eyes watching her. ''Or maybe fuchsia.'' His tongue slipped between her baby toe and the next one. ''I'll get you an ankle bracelet and you can spend all one Sunday walking around the house wearing it and nothing else.''

He was grinning wickedly at her, and his hair had fallen across his brow again. Julia's foot was arched high in his hands, her toes curling into his palm every time his mouth touched her.

''I'm very sensitive there, Cord,'' she gasped. He licked the outside curve of her arch, and then she felt him moving to her ankle.

''I know your sensitive spots.'' He took the back of her ankle into his mouth and licked his way up her calf. ''I'm concentrating on them. You always shied away when I touched the back of your knee—but not in my dreams. And not now, honey. This time you have to ride it out.''

Like a kitten rasping at satin, he found the hollow at the back of her partially bent knee and lapped at it with slow, steady strokes. Julia found herself gripping the bed behind her, and her teeth sank into her bottom lip to keep herself from crying out. Her leg was raised and held by Cord, his knee was firmly pressed between her open thighs, and she could feel a groundswell of aching need rise within her. It was almost too much to bear, she thought, turning her face to the pillow as his tongue moved higher, edging toward the softness of her inner thigh. It *was* too much to bear.

Her hands lost their grasp and she reached out blindly for him, sinking her fingers into that silky, blue-black hair.

''Oh, Cord, no,'' she breathed. Her voice sounded like it was coming from far away, and she could hardly hear herself. ''No, I can't—I can't hold *on* any longer.''

He didn't answer her, but through the veil of her lashes she saw him close his eyes. His mouth left a wet and heated trail against the delicate skin of her thigh, and then she felt his tongue flick under the lace edge of the panties she was still wearing.

It was as though he was placing a tiny searing brand on her, and she felt her hips moving rhythmically toward him, his tongue sliding under the lace and out again as she moved. He was near enough to her that she could reach the waistband of his shorts and, hardly knowing what she was doing, she shoved impatiently at them, pushing them down to his hips. He didn't stop lapping at her, but with one hand finished the job she'd been unable to complete, drawing first one leanly muscled leg and then the other out of the shorts.

She wanted to *see* him, Julia thought hazily. He'd looked his fill on her, and she wanted the same. She wanted to see him and touch him and drive him crazy the way he was doing to her. And she would, she promised herself. She *would,* as soon as she—

"Oh, *please...*" The incoherent plea escaped from her lips in a sigh. His teeth, a gleam of white against his skin, had gently grasped the flimsy material of the baby dolls, and his eyes were a gleam of black as he slanted an upward glance at her face. He gave a little tug at the scrap of lace and cotton, and she felt it slip down over her hips.

"Please stop?" he said huskily. "Or please go on? Down there it felt like please go on, baby."

"Please—please go on."

Her words were slurred. It was *such* an effort to make sense when all of her senses were so close to satiation, she thought. And then rational thought disappeared totally as Cord's hands slipped under her derriere, scooping her easily up from the bed. Her legs parted just wide enough for him to move in between them, her knees bent at his shoulders, and the fragile lacy panties moved down to her hips.

He didn't bother to remove them. She could feel his thick, spiky lashes, like miniature paintbrushes, flick against the very top of her thigh, but that sensation was overwhelmed immediately as his tongue slowly massaged her through the thin cotton. He had to know what he was doing to her, Julia thought faintly. He *had* to know—and yet he still kept teasing her, kissing her, *touching* her. He was made of stone, or he'd learned some esoteric Zen-like control techniques out in California, or he—

He nipped her thigh delicately, and a shudder ran through him. His arms were sheened with sweat, and the hair falling into his eyes looked damp. He raised his head, and the eyes that met hers were glazed and unfocused.

"You taste so sweet, honey. But I've got to be in you now." His voice was a hoarse rasp, as if he was at the limit of his endurance. He settled her on the bed, but before he could bend over her she stopped him with a touch.

"I want to feel *you*, Cord." Her fingers ran lightly up the length of him and then to the thatch of dark hair. She slipped her palm between his legs and saw the tremor that ran through him. His neck muscles were tight, his jaw clenched.

"You're playing with fire," he said between his teeth. "I can only take so much, Julia."

"So let's finish what we started, Cord," she said softly, her gaze fixed on his. "Let's take it as far as we can go…together."

And *this* she had never been able to forget. That he was just barely holding himself back was evident in his tense posture, the muscles that stood out like ropes in his arms, but he was her Cord, and he had always remembered, no matter how erotic their love play became, that she'd belonged to his heart first, long before his body had come to know her. His hands framed her face—those hands that she'd seen handle a shovel, fire a gun and cradle a tiny, red-haired baby while she and his two best friends looked on—and he kissed her closed eyes, first one and then the other.

"I love you, honey," he breathed. "Always did…"

She opened her eyes and he was there, so close she could see that those black eyes were really a true dark brown, could see the tiny speck of green in his right iris, like the reflection of a perfect summer's day. She touched his face with the tips of her fingers.

"Always will, Cord," she whispered.

For a moment they looked at each other, as if the current that forever flowed between them was renewing and recharging so that if they somehow became separated for any length of time in the future they would have it to draw on, no matter how far apart they might be. Then a corner of his mouth lifted.

"Okay—here's how the dream always ended. You say, '*Now*, Cord.'"

"Now, Cord," she breathed.

"And I say, 'Yeah, now, honey,' and move in closer," he said faintly, lowering his torso, his weight supported by his elbows, one hand slipping around to the back of her head.

"Then I say, 'Cord, you forgot to take my panties off,'" Julia purred, and saw him blink. Even at that moment she could discern the flash of humor behind that dark gaze, but he shook his head.

"And you say, 'Cord, you can always get me another pair.' It's obvious you didn't memorize the script, honey."

"Cord—" He reached down impatiently, and she heard the scrap of cotton and lace rip, felt him pulling that one last, totally inadequate barrier between them away. "You can get me another pair," she finished.

"I knew you'd say that."

He smiled, that slow smile that had never failed to make her heart turn over, and then she was opening herself to him and he was moving into her, gently and slowly, but despite his care her breath caught in her throat. He was filling her—he was *more* than filling her, she thought with a flash of panic—but no, he was inside her now and everything fit just right.

"So tight, baby," he gasped. "Like—like a velvet glove."

The brushfires that he had lit earlier were running together, meeting and fueling this ultimate conflagration that she could feel racing along her nerve endings. He was deep inside her and then he was withdrawing, and then he was inside her again, his movements as powerfully smooth as the rise and fall of waves upon a beach. She felt herself straining to meet him, to take him into herself, her nails digging into the hardness of his shoulders and her breath coming in short, harsh gasps from her swollen lips. She closed her eyes and saw sunlight, saw water, the brilliant blue of the sky over the lake, and then she opened them and saw his lashes fanning his cheekbones, his neck arched back as if he was looking for mercy and finding none.

"Please, Cord," she gasped.

"*Now,* Julia," he breathed.

She felt as if she was falling through water, plunging straight down through liquid crystal, and she could almost *see* the myriad of piercingly exquisite explosions as her consciousness fragmented. They burst in her mind like fragile globes, like a swirl of underwater bubbles, and for a dreamy moment she realized she'd stopped breathing and she wondered hazily if she was drowning. *No,* she thought—no, it wasn't like drowning at all, because she *could* breathe, she'd only exchanged one element for another, more vivid one.

The world no longer existed. It was as if the second hand of the universe had quivered and stopped. *Crushed pearls,* Julia thought as she felt Cord inside her. *It's as if I'm being filled with crushed pearls.*

And then she felt herself rushing upward again, her consciousness returning in a shattered mosaic of green and gold, her eyes open and wet as she sped to the surface of the water and saw him there above her, his eyes still closed, one last convulsive shudder running through him.

He drew in a ragged, shallow breath, but his eyes stayed closed, his lashes wet with the same sweat that slicked his chest and his braced arms. His lips were parted.

Slowly—almost reluctantly—he opened his eyes and met her unfocused gaze. He sighed and closed them again, and then he lowered himself gently, their bodies still joined, his weight a solid warmth to one side of her.

"*Always* did, Julia." His voice was hoarse. "Always will."

Chapter 12

"At least it's not a funeral. Two in three days would have been just too much, even if we didn't know the woman well."

It was two days later. Cord swung the Bronco into a graveled parking lot and squinted dubiously at the white wooden building beside it. "It's obviously some kind of impromptu memorial service."

"This place certainly doesn't look like any church I've ever seen." Glancing across the street at a boarded-up discount appliance outlet and an auto-glass repair business, Julia gave a slight frown. "The whole setup seems odd—especially with the daughter appearing out of the blue all of a sudden and arranging a memorial for a mother she couldn't even be bothered to contact for the last year or so."

"Which is why we're here." He turned off the ignition and set the parking brake, his mouth grim. "I'd like to find out a little more about the mysterious Susan Redmond myself. I don't like loose ends."

"Neither do I, and I could have *sworn* she was somehow being used to threaten her mother." Remembering the photos in the apartment where Jackie Redmond had lost her life so brutally, Julia felt a pang of compassion for the dead woman.

They got out of the vehicle and headed across the gravel toward the dilapidated building. The sun was bright, but there was an unseasonably brisk breeze whipping up little eddies of dust along the adjoining sidewalk. A piece of newspaper scudded like tumbleweed across their path and then flattened against the cinder block foundation of the building.

"Any new leads on Tascoe's whereabouts yet?" Her brows drew together as she recalled her encounter two nights ago with the ex-cop and the nightmarish ending to that evening at the apartment.

"He's gone to ground somewhere." One arm around her shoulders, the other hand shoved deep in his pants pocket, Cord smiled humorlessly. "Hendrix and Dow are damned lucky they still have their pensions, so I doubt whether any of his other old buddies on the force will be sticking their necks out for him, but he's tough and smart. Lopez has her work cut out for her, searching for him."

"But he'll be caught eventually. He's the prime suspect in three murders now, after all."

She looked up at him, and despite the setting and the situation, felt a sliver of pure happiness pierce her heart. Yesterday, aside from a necessarily brief meeting with a harried Lopez, they'd managed to put the case out of their minds for a few hours and had gone out to visit Lizbet. Mary had told them she'd overheard her talking in her room to an adoring King the night before, and that she'd started joining in the twins' games—silently still, but with more enthusiasm than she'd shown previously. They'd taken the little girl for a walk down to the lake, and riding on Cord's shoulders, she'd stared with wide-eyed interest at the gaily colored sailboats on the water. Julia's heart had turned over, watching her, and a trace of the old terror had momentarily dimmed the perfection of the day.

She'd fought it back. Lizbet was safe with the Whitefields, and there was a whole police force on the lookout for the man wanted for questioning in the deaths of her parents. The thought should have reassured her more than it did, except for one thing.

"I still think they're looking for the wrong man, Cord." She glanced at him, a stubbornly unconvinced expression on her features. "Lopez is completely disregarding the way Paul was killed, and right from the start I haven't been able to shake the feeling that somehow that's the whole key to the killer's—"

She stopped suddenly, her body rigid and her mind racing. *Sheila shot, Paul pierced through the chest and two to go—*

"It's *payback* time," she whispered slowly. "*That's* what it is."

He met her gaze with sharp intensity. "Payback for what?" he asked urgently. "And who's collecting it?"

"I don't know enough about your old cases to tell you that, but Paul and Sheila's deaths have to be a *reenactment* of something," she said shakily, her words tumbling out in a rush. "Even Lopez thought the stabbing was symbolic, except she thought that DiMarco was paying Paul back for striking at the heart of his organization. But that's not it—"

She passed an unsteady hand across her brow and then shook her head in frustration. "No. Just when I think I have it, it's gone. It *reminds* me of something—of a case you worked on in the past, I'm sure of it. But that's as far as I've gotten."

Ahead of them a group of soberly dressed people approached the white building and went in. Cord kept his eyes on Julia.

"A copycat killer, imitating past homicides that we worked on?" His face was grim. "God, I hope you're wrong. The killer could be just about any crackpot out there hoping to make a name for himself."

"But the killer, whoever he is, has a reason for these murders. Or he *thinks* he does," Julia said slowly. "Remember the call-girl killings, Cord? Didn't the father of one of the women killed accuse you and Paul of not giving the case enough priority?"

"Crystal Aiken's father. She was the second victim—garroted in a hotel room." He nodded, his mouth set in a tight line. "Sometimes I still find myself going over that case, wondering what we missed and why, after murdering four girls, the killer just seemed to disappear off the face of the earth. But Aiken went to the media and said that we obviously didn't care about the deaths of a few hookers." He winced. "Unfortunately he'd heard Tascoe refer to the victims that way—he was working the case, too, and exhibiting his usual flair for diplomacy."

"Crystal was garroted." Julia's eyes were dark with horror, but she went on. "I know one of the other women was shot, but how did the others die? Was one of them stabbed?"

"Whoever the killer was, he never used the same method twice," Cord affirmed. "And Tanya Baker was killed with an ice pick, though not to the heart. But it's similar enough to be worth investigating Aiken's current whereabouts and state of mind."

"And if he checks out clean, we're still left with yet another connection to Tascoe." She gnawed at her thumbnail worriedly until he took her hand firmly in his. She looked at him and gave a shamefaced little smile. "I know. But it *bothers* me, Cord. He obviously really cared for Jackie, and her death doesn't seem to fit the pattern."

"I don't buy Tascoe's guilt as completely as Lopez does, either, but if he's innocent, why did he run?" His strong fingers still wrapped around hers, he looked toward the building. "We'd better get in there. They'll be starting the service any minute."

They'd reached the sidewalk, and she stared with frank skepticism at the run-down storefront. The huge window was whitewashed over, making it impossible to see inside, but it wasn't hard to guess that until recently its purpose had been more in line with the other dying or defunct businesses in the area.

"It wouldn't surprise me if we've got the wrong place entirely and we walk in on a liquidation blowout sale instead of a memorial to Jackie Redmond," she muttered. Beside her, Cord grinned involuntarily, and then his smile faded.

"Of course, if your theory's right, it isn't necessarily the callgirl murders that our killer is copycatting," he said, rubbing his jaw in frustration. "There were other unsolved murders—hell, there were plenty of *solved* cases that some nutcase might want to emulate. Probably the best way to narrow down the field of possibilities would be to run a computer check and start with those that involved both shooting and—"

"*Solved* cases?" Julia stumbled on the first step to the entrance, and only his quick reaction kept her from falling. Her face was pale as she clutched his supporting arm, and when she spoke her voice was husky with urgency. "Cord—how did the Bradleys die in that farmhouse?"

"It doesn't fit." His reply was curtly dismissive, but then he caught himself. "You don't need to know the details, Julia— God knows I wish I could erase them from my memory. But trust me, there's no connection between the way Paul and Sheila were murdered and what happened at—" He stopped, his gaze shadowed. "Besides, except for the core investigative team, no one else knew enough about those killings to reenact them. Even the media showed some reticence that time."

"No one else—except for the killers themselves," Julia said softly. "What if there was a member of the Donner family who got away undiscovered?"

"Donner himself is the only one of his merry little band still living, unless a fellow inmate's managed to get to him in the prison yard in the last couple of years," Cord said flatly. "Yeah, he knew just how the Bradleys and the other victims died—I was always convinced he'd planned the whole thing before he got caught and imprisoned for that department store bombing, though he swore up and down his 'family' hadn't been carrying out his instructions when they went on their last spree without him."

His shoulders shifted slightly under his suit jacket, as if his body was too tense even to manage a shrug. "But again, the deaths weren't similar at all. And even if they had been, Donner's locked up for life."

Gary Donner and his followers were the one subject that he couldn't handle with even a pretence of composure, Julia thought as they mounted the last few steps. He'd always berated himself for not somehow being able to prevent those last deaths at the farmhouse, never thinking to give himself credit for discovering the Donner family's hideout as soon as he had. He and Paul had gone without sleep for weeks, obsessively following down every lead on the killers, no matter how elusive or faint, and they'd undoubtedly saved future victims from the Donner band.

She shivered. Donner's followers' dedication to their evil mission had been so complete that they'd chosen death rather than surrendering to the authorities when they'd finally been found. Cord's reaction was understandable.

"I recognize a few people from the department, but I'd never have pegged someone like *him* as one of Jackie's close acquaintances." Cord's voice by her ear was low, but his meaning was clear.

The building had to have been a store at one time, Julia thought as they halted a few feet inside the entrance. It still was nothing more than a large open space, although right now there were a few dozen oddly assorted people standing around, many of them looking as confused as she felt. She followed Cord's glance and saw who he'd been talking about—a painfully thin young man, almost a boy, with a pair of crudely drawn tattoos on the backs of his hands and an old scar snaking up the side of his neck and disappearing into his close-cropped blond hair.

"Maybe he's a friend of her daughter's," she said doubtfully. "He looks like a junkie—which could be a tip-off as to the kind of company Susan Redmond's been keeping since she left home."

"Maybe not." Cord's gaze narrowed. "That kid looks like he knew the mean streets pretty well at one time, but his clothes aren't what you'd expect for someone who's still out there hustling and scoring. Neatly pressed chinos and a clean shirt? And that girl over there with the bleached blond hair—I'd bet my bottom dollar that a few weeks ago she was standing on a street corner somewhere, but she's not even wearing any makeup."

"You're right, Cord—*we're* probably the most disreputable-looking couple in the joint. What's going on here?"

Even as Julia voiced the question, a young woman detached herself from a nearby group and approached them, her hand extended. "I'm Susan Redmond." She was pale to the point of colorlessness. Her eyes were the only spark of life about her—light blue, nonetheless they seemed to blaze with an inner fire. "Did you know my mother well?" Her voice was subdued, but

Julia had the sudden conviction that she had only achieved that calmly uninflected tone through long effort.

"We worked with her at one time," Cord said smoothly, before Julia could respond. "The department's going to miss her. You said you were her daughter?" he added, his voice rising in polite surprise. His implication was unspoken, but a faint flush of color touched Susan Redmond's pale cheeks.

"We hadn't seen each other as much as I'd have liked to this last year or so. I regret that." Her small sad smile was confined to her lips, Julia noticed. Those pale blue eyes held no regret at all, and if anything burned even brighter. "But my work at the Center is so important that the few personal sacrifices I've had to make are really nothing in comparison. We're saving lives here."

"Suze, John says the sound system's working okay now." The boy with the tattoos had joined them. "Do you want me to go up to the front with you?"

"That's all right, Donny. Has he arrived yet?"

"He phoned. He said he and Mr. Marshall might be a little late, but he wants you to go ahead and start—and Suze, Mr. Marshall's agreed to buy that property for the Center."

The fire behind those blue eyes flared and was immediately banked again. "Good news." Susan turned to Julia and Cord, her normally restrained manner firmly in place. "I've planned to say a few words, so if you'll excuse me? Afterward some of the members will be talking about the changes the Center's made to their lives, and we'll be collecting donations for a new outreach program we're setting up in my mother's name. I hope you'll stay."

"We wouldn't miss it," Cord said blandly. As Redmond turned and made her way through the throng to the front of the room, he exchanged a silent glance with Julia and then looked at Donny.

"The Center's expanding?" he ventured casually.

"Suze is handling all the details It's going to be the second facility for the Friendship Center, and eventually there'll be two more for advanced members," the young man said enthusiastically.

"Susan said the Friendship Center saves lives." There was a note of skepticism in Cord's voice, and Julia glanced sharply at him. "That sounds like a pretty tall order for a place no one's even heard of."

"Someday everyone will know about the Friendship Center. And Suze is right—they *do* save lives here." Donny reddened as he directed a pugnacious stare at Cord, and Julia tried to defuse the situation.

"How? Does the Center offer some kind of drug rehab program?"

He shrugged, suddenly at a loss. "That's part of it, but it's more than that. Father says he gives them a new focus. He says their biggest problem is that their lives are empty, and the Friendship Center fills that emptiness."

Father—so the center was affiliated with some kind of organized religion, Julia thought, feeling a little less uneasy. It obviously was headed by a priest who didn't confine his preaching to the pulpit, but had gone out into the community to effect a change in these young people's lives.

Still, the man's influence over Susan Redmond hadn't been entirely beneficial—he'd separated her from her mother, and despite this off-kilter memorial that was being staged in honor of Jackie Redmond, it was too late for Susan to heal the breach in their relationship. A phone call when she'd been alive would have meant far more to her mother than any saccharine platitudes the girl could utter now.

"Take a look at this. They're passing these out." Handing her something, Cord darted a look at their young companion, but Donny's attention was fixed on the slim woman at the front of the room. As Susan, her voice hesitantly soft, said a few preliminary words of thanks for the crowd's attendance, Julia looked at what Cord had given her.

At first glance it seemed innocuous enough, if inappropriate for the occasion. Printed in slightly smeared ink on a single sheet of poor-quality paper that had been folded into three to create a rudimentary brochure, its cover bore the title Friendship Center, followed by the banal phrase, "A Family for Those

Who Are Alone." Opening it up, Julia quickly scanned the
densely printed paragraphs inside.

"...for those who are looking for a direction in their
lives...new purpose and strength...your voice will be
heard...only those who persevere will win..."

It was a garbled mishmash of words and phrases followed
by amateurish sketches on the last page of the three new proposed centers and a blatant appeal for contributions to make
them a reality. Looking quickly at the guests around her who
had received brochures, Julia realized that they were just as
taken aback as she was. An older woman a few feet away whom
she recognized as one of the police department's dispatchers
and a co-worker of Jackie's looked slightly outraged as she
stuffed the paper into her purse.

"This has nothing to do with Redmond at all. It's a damned
fund-raiser for this Friendship Center her daughter's involved
with," Cord whispered in her ear. "They'll probably start passing the hat any minute now."

"My mother, as many of you here know, worked for the
very authorities who are supposed to bring law and order to our
streets."

Susan's subdued voice, amplified by the sound system that
Donny had been so concerned about, was gaining a strength
that had nothing to do with the speakers dotted around the
room, and looking up, Julia saw that the pale face was marked
with two hectic spots of color high on her cheeks, and the blue
eyes seemed almost piercingly bright. She listened as the girl
continued. Cord moved closer, and she was suddenly thankful
for his solid bulk beside her.

"I say 'supposed to,' because at the end my mother's faith
in that system must have been shattered." The clear voice went
on. "But our cities are filled with others whose faith in the
traditional solutions has been betrayed—and too many of them
are young people, crying out for help and finding none. That's
why the Friendship Center was started—to reach out and help
those that the system has failed. Some of them are here today."
She inclined her head to a waiting couple—one of them the girl
with the bleached hair. "Jason and Darla's lives have been

turned around by the Center. After what they have to say, I'm sure that you'll feel privileged to make a donation in memory of my mother to help us carry on the invaluable work we do here.''

"They *are* passing the hat,'' Julia said heatedly as Susan handed over the microphone to the first of the Center's protégés and Donny left their side to meet her. "I can't believe this could have anything to do with a regular church.''

"It's a con job.'' The older woman Julia had noticed a moment ago turned to them. "I came here to pay my respects to an old friend, not to buy a bottle of snake oil from her daughter. Jackie was a very private person—she'd be horrified to know what a travesty this turned out to be.'' She thrust out a firm hand. "Ann Johnson—remember me? I retired a few months ago. Detective Hunter, isn't it? And bless my soul—you've got the famous Guardian Angel with you.''

Her voice was gruffly friendly. A shapeless black hat was crammed over her forehead, but it didn't obscure the alert intelligence in the snapping brown eyes below it.

"Hold on a minute.'' Cord closed his eyes, frowning. "Kind of a husky, throaty quality…'' He opened his eyes and grinned. "Okay, so *you're* Ann. You were always a sexy voice over my radio—I don't think we ever met face-to-face.''

The woman chuckled, her face pink. Inwardly Julia groaned, but she couldn't help smiling. Cord Hunter was a great big flirt, she thought, and no woman, young or old, was immune to his charm. Or maybe it would be more accurate to say that he'd noted the woman's distress at what she'd termed this con job and was trying to cheer her up.

"Oh, dear—I should have preserved the illusion,'' Ann Johnson said. She turned to Julia, her craggy features softening. "You of all people must have found that nasty little dig at the department unwarranted. I've got a neighbor who says a prayer for you every single day of her life. Her little granddaughter was one of the hostages in that convenience store holdup that went wrong, and you talked the girlfriend of the gunman into bringing Chandra out just before the situation got totally out of control.''

During those two solitary years at the lake house, Julia thought, she'd been haunted by ghosts. But now it seemed that there was a whole host of shadowy children out there—children she would never meet again, most of whom she'd never even hear about. They were the children who would go on to live happy, healthy lives, who would themselves make a difference in the lives of those around them. Her throat tightened, and before she could manage a response she felt a hearty hand upon her shoulder.

"Well, if it isn't little Julia Stewart—my God, the last time I saw you I believe you still were wearing braces!"

The man confronting her didn't seem to fit in either of the two vastly different groups that had attended Jackie Redmond's supposed memorial service—he definitely had never known the life that Donny had escaped from, but he equally wasn't part of Jackie's circle of friends and co-workers. His suit had been expertly tailored to hide a well-fed paunch, and his manner was smoothly self-assured. Beneath the snowy linen of one shirt cuff glinted the dull gold of a Rolex watch.

"How's your father? I hear he had bypass surgery a while back, but knowing Willard, I'm sure he was back at the office in record time. I've been intending to give him a call, see if he'd like to provide some much-needed backing to the Center here." There was a faint dusting of talc on the fleshy jaw, and at his last words Julia placed him.

"It's Mr. Marshall, isn't it? Tom Marshall?" Automatically she took the hand he was extending, concealing her shocked dismay at the news that her father had been ill. "Yes, it has been a while."

She disengaged her hand from his clasp and half-turned, intending to introduce Cord and Ann Johnson to her father's former business partner, but before she could get a word out he went on as if their presence was of no consequence to him. Out of the corner of her eye she saw Cord frown slightly.

"You know, that bypass operation might well have served as a wake-up call for Willard," Marshall said, fixing a ponderously serious expression on his face. "Maybe he's ready to reach the same conclusion I did a few months ago—that it's time to give something back to the community by supporting a worthy cause like the Center. Have you met the fellow who's behind all this?''

"No, we—'' Cord started, but Marshall was in full spate, and he didn't even glance at him.

"My God—now *there's* a story these people should hear," he said with an intensity Julia guessed he usually reserved for discussing the possibility of a ten-for-one return on an investment. "Wrongly accused of a crime he didn't commit, fought for years to get his name cleared, and at the end of the day does he hold a grudge? No—he turns around and dedicates his life to helping others get back on track. The man's a damn saint. I want you to meet him, Julia, so when I hit Willard up for a contribution I've got his little girl already in my corner.''

His avuncular attitude was grating on her nerves, and the constant references to a supposed closeness with her father that she knew didn't exist were all the more painful since he'd mentioned Willard Stewart's health problem. She'd had to learn of it from a near stranger, Julia thought tiredly. It was a prime example of the distance between them that had existed for as long as she could remember.

"I don't have any influence over my father's business dealings,'' she said. "And I know he already gives generously to a number of charities that he feels are worthwhile, Tom. I'm afraid—''

She felt rather than saw Cord's sudden stillness beside her, and breaking off in mid-sentence, she turned to him, puzzled.

"Cord, what is it?'' she began, but one look at his face silenced her.

The bones stood out starkly under his skin, and his eyes, fixed on something or someone behind her, were so dark that the pupils were barely discernible from the irises around them. A moment ago, like her, he'd been politely concealing bored irritation at Marshall's gushingly enthusiastic monologue, but now that veneer of civilized forbearance had been stripped away.

On one of the back roads by the lake there'd been an auto-wrecking yard before the summer residents had petitioned the town to change a bylaw and have the place relocated, Julia remembered. The owner had kept a huge mongrel—part mastiff, part Doberman—permanently chained up beside the shack that had served as his office, and every time a prospective customer had driven into the yard the dog had lunged at them till it seemed certain that the heavy chain holding him back would surely break.

Cord's expression was as full of barely leashed hatred as that long-ago junkyard dog's had been.

"And as our generous benefactor has just agreed to back us on the retreat facility we've planned, we're already halfway toward reaching our final goal of a proposed group of four friendship centers, each serving our young people at a different point in their paths toward becoming constructive members of their new family."

The pleasant and earnest voice was audible even over the conversation around them, but Julia barely glanced over her shoulder at the nondescript and casually dressed man addressing a group of people a few feet away. Her eyes darted back to Cord worriedly.

"What is it—"

"Dear God!" Ann Johnson's exclamation was a breathlessly shocked prayer. "Hunter, isn't that—"

"But we still need to raise funds for the third and fourth facilities, and every contribution, no matter how small, is appreciated. So be generous, folks. Remember—"

Turning again, Julia saw the pleasant-voiced man with the thinning brown hair make an expansive gesture with his hands, and then, as if he sensed her presence, he met her eyes with a smile.

Nondescript? How had she ever come to *that* conclusion? she thought, suddenly confused. His gaze was powerfully compelling, as if with a glance he knew a person's most secret fears, most hidden desires. She tried to turn away, but somehow she couldn't seem to wrench herself from that mesmerizing stare.

"—two down," the pleasant voice continued.

"*Gary Donner!*" Cord's voice was a harshly explosive whisper.

The brown-haired man looked across the few feet separating them, straight into Julia's horrified eyes.

"*And two to go,*" Donner said to her, and her alone.

Chapter 13

"God dammit, Hunter—in case you haven't noticed I've had a lot more to worry about than bringing you up to speed on the current status of the local perps," Lopez snapped. Striding ahead of them, she pushed open a door that was clearly marked Emergency Exit Only and stalked outside, a cigarette already between her lips and her lighter in her hand.

They'd come straight from the memorial service to the precinct, but judging from Lopez's attitude, Julia sensed she and Cord had arrived at a bad time. The woman continued impatiently.

"We still haven't located Tascoe, when we tried to contact DiMarco last night for further questioning he'd disappeared into thin air, and the damn press is all over me every time I step out the front door. Erica's gone to visit her sister and she took the cat, so even when I *do* get home for a couple of hours each night the place is so freakin' empty that I end up watching reruns of *Starsky and Hutch* and falling asleep in front of the television."

She raked her hand through a swath of glossy hair and glared at the cigarette in her hand. "On top of that I've started smoking again, so forgive me if I don't get real excited about you discovering that Gary Donner is now running some kind of shady charitable organization."

"It's not that I'm worried about," Cord said tightly, falling silent as the door to the back parking lot opened once more and a weary-looking man in jeans and a tweed jacket joined them.

"Thought I'd find you here." The newcomer flicked a professionally encompassing glance at Cord, nodded at Julia and then focused his attention on Lopez. "The last of the lab results are in."

"And?" Leaning against the brick wall behind her as if she hardly had the energy to stand, Lopez didn't sound hopeful.

"And *nada*." He rubbed a hand across one side of his face. "Well, not quite. Jenny says she found microscopic traces of some kind of shell caught in the carpet fiber. She's trying to identify them."

"Traces of shell casings?" Lopez frowned.

"No, *shells*. You know—like in seashells on the seashore," the man said with a tired grin. He turned suddenly to Cord. "Hey, it's Hunter, right? I thought the face was familiar, but I'm so bushed I probably wouldn't recognize my own mother. Julia, tell him I'm usually a pretty polite guy when I'm not suffering from sleep deficit." He stuck out his hand. "Phil Stamp. I'm Lopez's new partner. I hear you think you've got a lead?"

She was the one who wasn't all there, Julia thought. She'd worked with Phil for about six months a few years ago, when he'd asked to be transferred to the Child Protection Unit. He'd been good at the job, but in the end he'd told her he was transferring out again.

"It's the stress, Julia," he'd confessed helplessly to her when he'd told her. "I've worked Vice and I'm going to try to get back into Homicide, but when the victims are always kids, day in and day out, it starts to get to you. I've started to dream about them, and my wife says I'm becoming paranoid about our two little tykes. I don't know how you take it."

He was a decent guy, and competent, she thought. But then,

he had a pretty high standard to live up to in replacing Paul as Lopez's partner.

"It's not a lead." Lopez took a disgusted last drag off her cigarette and pitched it onto the asphalt parking lot, sighing. "Hunter here just found out that his own personal Lex Luthor isn't safely tucked away in prison like he thought he was, and he expects me to drop everything and—"

The woman was exhausted and overworked and obviously stressed to the limit, Julia thought, her head jerking up. But *nobody* was allowed to talk about Cord that way.

"Shut up and *listen* to the man, Lopez!" she ordered, taking a swift step toward the dark-haired woman, her hands clenched at her sides. "Donner's not a con man, he's a *killer,* whether he got a new trial and an apology from the governor or not— and there's a damn good chance he's running circles around you and laughing at all of us."

"I thought you were a powder puff, sweetheart." Lopez's angry eyes were fixed on Julia, her lips slightly curled. "I thought that's why you got out of the job—because you couldn't take the heat. Why don't you run along and let us get on with investigating the death of my partner?"

"*You're* the one who's cracking, Cindy."

Before anyone could stop her Julia's hand shot out and grabbed the other woman's jacket lapel, pulling her away from the wall she'd been leaning against and bringing her face to within inches of her own. She heard Phil's indrawn breath and saw Cord take a step forward.

"Honey, back off," he began.

"I can't and I *won't,*" she said, her unwavering gaze on Cindy Lopez's shocked face. "You've got to listen to someone, Lopez, and it might as well be me, because you're right—I *did* fall apart. And right now I feel like I'm watching myself two years ago, because you're making all the same mistakes, building the same destructive walls around yourself as I did. Paul's death wasn't your fault, *understand?*"

She let go of Lopez's lapel as suddenly as she'd grabbed it, her hands falling to her sides. "You're heading for the same fall I took, Cindy. Believe me, it's a long way down, and an even longer climb back up again. But it doesn't have to be that way. You sent Erica away, didn't you?''

''We got into a stupid argument. I said it'd probably be easier on both of us if she left for a while,'' Lopez muttered grudgingly. ''But what the hell has—''

''She's your support system, and you need all the support you can get while you're on this case. Ask her to come back,'' Julia said firmly. ''And while you're at it, take the chip off your shoulder when it comes to dealing with Cord and me. We're on your side, dammit—Cord was Paul's partner, too.''

''And if he still had been, Paul would be alive today, for God's sake!'' Lopez burst out unexpectedly, her tough facade shattering. ''How the hell am I supposed to live with the knowledge that I wasn't there for my partner when he needed me? I let him down, goddammit—*I let my partner down!*''

''You didn't let anyone down, Cin.'' Phil's voice was roughly compassionate. ''For crying out loud, no one could have foreseen what happened to Paul and his wife.''

''You can stop paying now,'' Julia said quietly. Lopez looked up, her eyes sheened with unshed tears.

''What—what do you mean?'' There was an edge of fearful apprehension in her question, and her chin jutted out pugnaciously. ''What are you talking about?''

''Your cousin Tina. The one who died of an overdose,'' Julia said. ''That's what drives you, isn't it? Guilt. You think you should have been able to save her, but you didn't, and you've been blaming yourself ever since. Every case you take on is an attempt to atone for the death you feel responsible for, and you won't allow yourself to be less than perfect, or to ask anyone's help.''

''What happened to Tina is none of your business, Stewart.'' The warm olive skin looked ashen, and Lopez took refuge in a halfhearted aggressiveness. ''So maybe I do feel guilty that I was too busy with my own life to see what was happening to—''

''Get *over* it,'' Julia said flatly. ''Get over it before it destroys you. You're a good cop, but you're useless if you're so crippled with misplaced guilt that you can't handle the job. Get over it, and fast—*sweetheart.*''

For a moment the brown eyes stared at her disbelievingly. Phil cleared his throat uncomfortably, and Cord stood, unmoving, beside Julia as if in silent solidarity. Then a dry sound came from Lopez's throat.

''Hell, was I wrong about you, Stewart.'' The dry sound was a rusty little laugh that held more than a hint of tears. ''The lady ain't no powder puff, Hunter, is she?''

''She ain't,'' he replied blandly. ''In fact, sometimes she even scares *me.*''

''Yeah, but I thought I was a whole lot tougher than you, Hunter,'' the dark-haired detective said with a touch of her old wryness. Her eyes met Julia's, and her expression sobered. ''I'll think about what you said, Stewart. And I guess I'm going to have to run a check on Donner on your say-so, too, right?''

''We think he killed Paul and Sheila,'' Cord said. ''So yeah, I'd appreciate any information you can get on the bastard, pronto.''

His words had the same affect as if he'd dropped a ticking time bomb at their feet. Phil Stamp was the first to recover.

''Run that one by us again?'' he said thinly.

''He came up to us at that farce of a memorial service for Jackie Redmond. He's got her daughter wrapped around his little finger, and we think he was somehow using her against Jackie to get information about the department and Paul.'' Cord drew a deep breath. ''Julia's theory is that he plans to duplicate a series of homicides from the past as a way of proving that a whole police force is no match for him.''

''He already dragged the department's reputation through the mud once,'' Stamp said, his face grim. ''Since you didn't know he was out of prison, then you wouldn't know how he swung the deal. Seems all along he had a rock-solid alibi for the department store bombing that he was serving time for. Donner pulled it out like a rabbit from a hat at his second trial.''

''Plus the eyewitness who fingered him for the bombing recanted,'' Lopez said disgustedly. ''We were caught with our pants down, and I mean around our damned ankles.''

"So his alibi's lying and the recanting witness was threatened." Cord sounded disbelieving. "How new is that scenario?"

"It's not. What's new is that in the end we believed them," Stamp answered. "It was hard not to, especially when the real bomber came forth and confessed."

"What?" Julia stared at the two detectives. "And you bought it? Come on—Donner's jerking everybody around here!"

"No, you're wrong." Cord's gaze darkened. He spoke slowly, as if he was thinking aloud. "He was jerking everyone around the *first* time. He framed himself for that bombing."

"I don't get it." Lopez raked her hair back, her brows drawn together in a frown. "Why the hell would he do that? No one willingly hands himself a life sentence, Hunter, unless…" Her voice trailed off and her eyes widened.

"Unless prison itself was his alibi for the crimes he was really planning." Stamp looked up suddenly. "That's it, isn't it? He masterminded the serial killings beforehand, and then sent his obedient 'family' to carry them out, but in the meantime he had himself incarcerated so that no one could ever prove he had anything to do with the murders."

"That's the way I read it," Cord said tightly. "And God help me, I think I know the way Donner's mind works better than anyone. He never had to worry about being in for life anyway. He had a get-out-of-jail-free card ready and waiting for him anytime he decided to use it."

She'd known the man was pure evil when Cord had been working the Donner case originally, Julia thought fearfully. But now she'd encountered him herself—twice, because she was sure it had been Donner she'd run into in the hallway the night of Jackie's murder. That had been bad enough. But what was worse was the feeling she'd experienced at the memorial service, when his eyes had met hers.

Because then he'd been trying to get inside her very *mind*. And for a moment he'd come close to succeeding.

"There's one other person who knows Donner inside and out," Lopez said suddenly. She grimaced. "I never thought I'd hear myself saying this, but we could use Tascoe's help on this case."

"Except that he's vanished from the face of the earth," Phil said. "But yeah, when we searched his place we found clippings, photos, interviews with people who knew Donner. Dean's been studying him for months. Maybe he's figuring on writing the unauthorized biography of the bastard."

"Or maybe he was hoping to nail him all by himself. He was pulled off the Donner case the first time," Cord said. "He was well aware that Donner was a free man again, and at some point he must have found out from Jackie that she was being pressured to pass on information to him."

"So what do we do, put a 'Come home, Dean, all is forgiven' notice in the newspaper classifieds?" Lopez looked frustrated. "What you're telling me is that finding Tascoe is even more important than ever, except this time when we haul him in we handle him with kid gloves and ask him pretty please to help us."

"What I'd really like is for you to bring Donner in for questioning, find out where he was the night of Paul and Sheila's murders." Cord didn't look hopeful. "But that's not going to happen, is it?"

"I want that as much as you do, Hunter." Lopez shrugged. "But you know we don't have the grounds to do that, and as far as the media are concerned, he's already been railroaded into a wrongful conviction once by this department. My butt would be in a sling if word got out I was trying to pin something new on him without solid evidence—and in case you're thinking of a private Q and A session with Donner yourself, don't forget you're bound by the same procedural code as I am."

"I *know.*" Cord's mouth tightened. "Donner's counting on that. Maybe I should take a leaf from Tascoe's book and disregard procedure for once. He was a loose cannon, sure—but that's exactly what we need right now."

"I'll pretend I didn't hear that." Lopez shot him a look. "You know I'd have to arrest you if Donner complained of being harassed, Hunter."

"Well, if it's a loose cannon you need, I guess that just leaves me." Julia had been standing quietly, her brow furrowed in concentration, but now one corner of her mouth lifted in a crooked smile. "I'm the crazy who snapped on the job, hit the bottle and sank without a trace for two whole years. I'd say I'm qualified to take over Tascoe's role—and I've already got an inside track with Donner's backer, Marshall. He wants me to arrange a meeting with my father."

"Forget it." Cord's reply was automatic. "I don't even want you in the same room with that monster. We'll have to think of some other—"

"That's right—he *is* a monster," Julia said. Her smile had faded and her voice was low as she raised her eyes to his. "He's the original bogeyman come to life, and he wants Lizbet. He won't get her, Cord—I'm going to make sure of that."

Their gazes locked. Phil and Lopez might not have even been there, so complete was the silent communication that flowed like a live current from those angry obsidian eyes to the stubborn hazel ones, and then back again. Finally Cord spoke, his tone intense.

"I'm Lizbet's guardian too, Julia. It's *our* responsibility, not yours alone."

"Hunter's right." Lopez's voice was sharp. "For God's sake, Stewart, you just read me the riot act because *I* wouldn't ask for help, and now you're insisting that you're the only one who can take on Donner and keep Lizbet safe. Whose death are *you* trying to atone for?"

The hectic flush of color that had stained Julia's cheeks a moment ago drained completely away. She stared at Lopez, her face so white that it seemed almost bloodless.

"Nobody's!" she rasped. Her hands were balled into fists at her sides, and with an obvious effort she unclenched them. "It's not the same situation. All I'm saying is that I don't wear a badge anymore, and that gives me more latitude in dealing with Donner."

"You've got a point." Cord's quiet comment drew startled glances from both Julia and Lopez. Only Phil, after one quick look at the other man's impassive features, remained silent.

"Are you nuts, Hunter?" Lopez railed at him. "If Donner's as dangerous as you say he is, why the hell are you agreeing with her? Who knows what she could be walking into?"

"I'll be walking into a business meeting with the Friendship Center director and his prime backer," Julia retorted. "And though I don't need Cord's permission to do that, I'm glad he finally sees that—"

She broke off suddenly. Beside her Cord had flipped open the cover of his cell phone and was punching in a number. He brought it to his ear and looked inquiringly at her.

"Sorry—you were saying?"

"I was saying I appreciate the fact that—" Again she broke off, this time because he'd held up a courteous hand to stop her flow of words and had turned his attention to the phone.

She was more than a little taken aback by his actions, and obviously Lopez found his behavior unexpected, too. Out of the corner of her eye Julia saw Phil Stamp turn slightly away. He was smiling.

"That's right, effective immediately." Cord squinted at his wrist watch, angling the dial out of the direct sunlight. "It's oh-four hundred hours, Eastern Standard Time, and you're three hours behind us. The important thing is that I'm off the payroll as of now. It's official? Thanks, Mike. Yeah, you'll get the full story later, I promise."

He snapped the phone shut and slipped it into his suit pocket, his head bent. He looked up, his expression bland.

"Just a detail I had to take care of." He frowned. "Hell, I nearly forgot this. Hang on to it for me, will you, Phil? Who knows, I might want it back sometime."

The object he handed to a grinning Phil was his ID wallet. It fell open slightly as the other man took it, and in the sunlight Julia saw the bright gold gleam of Cord's detective badge.

He looked at her outraged expression, and all of a sudden the humor he'd displayed was gone, to be replaced with a deadly determination.

"Set up the meeting with Marshall and Donner," he said softly. "Tell them to expect two loose cannons."

* * *

"At least Lopez promised to put a couple of men on Donner's tail for the next few days. It's not much, but it's something," Cord said as he and Julia strode into the lobby of the downtown office complex where Julia's father worked. She didn't answer him, and he caught her by the arm before she could reach the bank of elevators.

"I know you're still pissed off at me, but like you told Lopez, get over it," he said in a low voice, glancing over his shoulder at the armed security guard manning a nearby bank of video monitors. "We're playing into Donner's hands if we don't present a united front at this meeting."

"Damn right I'm pissed off at you." Julia shook off his hand. "You ambushed me in front of Stamp and Lopez."

"Okay, I should have taken you aside and told you privately that I was handing in my badge." He sighed and thumbed the call button for an elevator. "But the other night when you fell asleep in my arms I lay there in the dark, holding you. I was bone-tired, but I couldn't fall asleep—I didn't *want* to fall asleep. I just lay there, with you safe in my arms, and I made a promise to myself."

"What was the promise?" The angry rigidity had left her, and when he reached out to touch her hair she felt herself sway slightly toward him, her eyes on his face.

"I vowed I'd never lose you again. So there was no way I was going to stand by today and watch you waltz off to a meeting with Gary Donner all by yourself, even if we don't know yet whether he was involved in this particular case." He gazed at her, his expression intent. "Maybe we're all wrong about him this time—but that doesn't alter the fact that he's dangerous, Julia. When I'm around him I can almost *smell* the evil coming off him."

"He smells like death." *And if I'm right, he's after Lizbet,* Julia thought, fear lancing through her. She controlled the tremor she could feel starting deep inside and reached for Cord's hand, pressing it to her cheek. "I wasn't really looking forward to confronting the man on my own. I'm glad you're going to be with me, Cord." She gave a small grimace. "My father's a different matter. I don't know why he insisted on sitting in on this—I told him it was just a ploy to get some time alone with Donner.''

''Maybe he's worried about you, the same as I am,'' Cord ventured. ''It would be natural—he's your father, after all.''

''Right. And it would have been natural for him to let me know that he'd had major surgery a few months ago.'' In front of them the elevator doors swished quietly open and Julia stepped in. ''But that's just it—there never has been that kind of bond between us. I don't think he's capable of loving another person.''

''Except for your brother, right?'' The elevator doors closed. ''You always said Davey was the only one he ever cared for.''

''He loved Davey, yes. Even as a child I knew that, and after Davey—'' Julia faltered. ''After he drowned I thought maybe if I could do all the things he'd done, and do them as well or even better than he had, my father would realize he still had a daughter, even if his son had been taken from him. But it didn't work. He was always so *distant*.'' She sighed, pushing her hair back and squaring her shoulders. ''I became a darn good high diver and a whiz at archery, at least.'' Her smile was half-hearted.

Cord pushed the button for their floor with one hand, his other arm pulling her close. ''Maybe he's scared to get close to you. Maybe he's afraid of losing you, too.''

She shook her head firmly. ''I wish I could believe you, but I can't. He's not afraid of losing me—for God's sake, months go by when we don't have any contact. And as for being afraid of me, that's just ridiculous.''

''Are you kidding? I thought you were going to deck poor Lopez this afternoon, honey. I'd never seen you like that.'' The elevator doors opened as Cord flashed her a quick and dirty grin. ''Just watching you got me all hot and bothered,'' he said in an undertone as they stepped into the reception area.

Julia felt instant desire spread through her. The man was *impossible,* she thought helplessly. He'd deliberately timed his provocative one-liner for this exact moment. She felt the receptionist's eyes on them as they approached and fixed a cool smile on her face.

"I'll talk to Lopez and see if we can arrange a mud-wrestling match for you next time," she said in her sexiest purr, but so low that only he could hear. His arm was still around her, and she casually let her hand slip around the back of his waist and then lower, in a suggestive little pat that was hidden from the woman at the desk in front of them. Cord's eyes glazed with sudden heat. "Watch it, you're about to trip over your tongue, big guy," she murmured, and then immediately schooled her voice to a professional briskness.

"I'm Julia Stewart. I believe my father's—" Before she could finish announcing herself she saw the tall, spare figure of Willard Stewart enter the reception area, and she turned to greet him.

"Julia, it's good to see you."

Taking her hands in his, he kissed her cheek lightly, and for a moment she could smell the aftershave he'd worn for years— a blend of limes and sharp spices.

She hadn't admitted it to herself, she realized, but she'd been afraid that his recent ill health would have left its effects on him. But Willard Stewart wouldn't let a little thing like bypass surgery get the better of him, she thought dryly. He looked like a cover from *Forbes* magazine, with his elegantly tailored English suit and his pale hair, silvered at the temples, brushed neatly back from a lightly tanned forehead.

"And Cordell—I hear you're out in California now." They shook hands. "How's your father?"

"He's fine." Cord's voice held genuine warmth. "I haven't had time to visit him on this trip, but I guess Julia's told you why."

"Yes, I heard about your friends. I only met them the one time when I ran into you four at that restaurant a few Christmases ago, but I was shocked at the news. Miss Yerby—" Stewart turned to the receptionist behind them "—could you have coffee brought into conference room two? And when the other parties arrive, please call and let me know."

He led the way down a thickly carpeted corridor and then

swung open a heavy teak door. "We can talk more privately in here," he said, letting Julia and Cord enter the room ahead of him. "I'd like to get a better idea of what you hope to accomplish with this meeting."

The room's furnishings had simple lines, but everything was in impeccable, if slightly austere, taste. Like the man who ran the company, Julia thought, sitting in the steel and black leather chair that Cord pulled out for her before taking his place at the long conference table. There was a discreet knock at the door and the receptionist entered, pushing a small cart with a coffee service on it. She set it on the table and then left.

"We think there's a good chance the man you're about to meet killed Paul and Sheila," Cord said without preamble. "If he did, he's also targeting their child."

Her father had his faults, Julia thought as Willard Stewart poured a stream of fragrant coffee into paper-thin china cups, but lack of nerve wasn't one of them. He listened intently, but with as little extraneous emotion as if he was being presented with a proposal for a new business venture, as Cord swiftly outlined the events of the last few days. Only once did he make the slightest noise, his cup clattering in his saucer as he set it down a trifle awkwardly on the polished tabletop.

"Please continue," he said with his usual chilly courtesy as Cord paused. "You say that the person who killed this Jackie woman actually passed himself off as you when Julia ran into him in the dark?"

"He was a whispered voice, that's all," Julia said, attempting to match his lack of emotion. "But the encounter was an arrogant move on his part. A split second longer, and I would have known there was something wrong."

"And he would have killed you with as little compunction as he'd just murdered the secretary," murmured her father. "I had hoped that when you left the police force—" He stopped, frowning. "But we haven't much time before the meeting. My apologies, Cordell."

Within a few minutes Cord had told him all they knew, including the possibility that they were on the trail of the wrong man entirely.

"Tascoe's still the most likely suspect, but as soon as I knew Donner was out of prison and had a connection, however tenuous, to the case, I got a real bad feeling. I know that's not hard evidence, but—"

"Hard evidence can be concocted," Willard Stewart said in his cool, dry voice. "Gut feelings have saved me from investing in many a company whose balance sheets are sterling, and those decisions usually prove to be wise ones."

"But this *isn't* a business deal, Father," Julia interrupted. "This man is dangerous. I'd feel better if you went along with my original plan—we'll tell Marshall and Donner that you were called away at the last minute and you'd like them to deal through me. I don't see why you have to get involved in this."

Pale gray eyes surveyed her with some surprise. After setting his coffee cup unhurriedly down, Willard Stewart flicked an invisible speck of lint from a spotless cuff.

"Because you're my daughter, of course, Julia."

She stared at him, but before she could come up with an adequate reply the phone on the desk rang once.

"They've arrived." Willard Stewart rose to his feet, but waved at them to remain seated. "No, I'll escort them in personally—Tom Marshall always did like having his ego stroked, as I remember."

"I wondered how you knew we'd arrived before your receptionist called," Julia said, trying to dispel the nervousness that suddenly assailed her. "I might have known you had a secret signal set up to alert you."

Her father strolled to the door, his posture as ramrod straight as it had always been. "Actually, I have a small video monitor by my desk so I can see who walks in even before Miss Yerby calls. The camera's mounted on the frame of the elevator, so all I really get is a back view of new arrivals." He glanced at the folded handkerchief in his breast pocket, straightened it infinitesimally and gave her a wintry smile. "Still, it provides me with some idea of what's going on."

"Was that his way of telling us he saw his daughter groping my butt?" Cord said into the silence that followed the other man's exit. "Remind me never to play poker with your daddy, honey."

"He's cool, all right," Julia muttered, her cheeks scarlet. "And stubborn, too—did you notice how he dodged my question about why he's insisting on sitting in on this meeting?"

"Is that how you heard it?" He gave her a curious glance. "I think he gave you a straight answer. You're his daughter, and to him that's reason enough. I would have preferred to keep this gathering as small as possible, too, but maybe having him here will help," he added. "Donner wants those four friendship centers so bad he can taste them. If he thinks they're within his grasp he'll be less cautious."

"Two down, two to go," Julia said. She caught his puzzled glance. "Donner said that at the memorial service. He's got his first two centers, and now he wants the last two. What does he intend to do with a bunch of street kids out in the middle of nowhere?"

A quick phone call to the county clerk had told them that the property Marshall had procured for the Friendship Center was a hundred acres of hilly bushland, well away from any main highways. A tiny hamlet twenty miles away was as near as civilization came to it.

"God knows, but—" Cord looked up as the door to the conference room swung open, and Julia followed his gaze to see her father courteously ushering in his old business partner and the director of the Friendship Center.

Cord was right, she thought as Gary Donner, again attired in casual pants and a shirt, crossed the threshold, smiling at some remark that Marshall had just made. The atmosphere of the room had thickened, as if his presence had added some toxic element to the air around them. But although Cord, slowly pushing back his chair and rising as the other men entered, had switched all his senses onto full alert, Tom Marshall and her father seemed unaware of the miasma that she found almost overpowering. Her father had obviously just put the same question to Gary Donner that she'd asked Cord only seconds ago.

"It *is* isolated, I agree." It was hard to reconcile that light, pleasant voice with everything she'd learned about the man,

Julia thought, her chest tightening as she watched him pause and turn to her father at the doorway. "But the isolation is necessary to completely break the destructive ties that bind these young people to their former ways of life."

"I thought the way you summed it up before was very descriptive," Marshall said ponderously, his brow furrowing. "How did you put it? You saw this as building a new support system for these kids?"

Donner smiled and finally seemed to realize that Cord and Julia were only a few feet away. He spread his hands in a gently encompassing gesture, including them in his answer.

"It's more than that. I like to think of what I'm doing as creating a whole new *family*."

Chapter 14

"I must admit, Tom, the cause seems worthwhile." Willard Stewart steepled his fingers thoughtfully and ran a practiced eye over the sheaf of papers in front of him. "Testimonials from civic leaders, letters of thanks from parents. Impressive."

Beside her father, Julia pretended an equal interest in the documentation that Donner had provided. The meeting had been going on for an hour, and still Cord hadn't steered the conversation around to Donner himself. Even as the thought crossed her mind he leaned forward, his arms on the polished surface of the table in front of him.

"Very praiseworthy. But all of us here know that there are certain questions to be asked of Mr. Donner before Mr. Stewart would feel comfortable making even the smallest contribution toward this cause."

Tom Marshall had been smiling. Now his face darkened. "My God, must this man forever be hounded over some trumped-up accusations that already have cost him years of his life?" The heavy jowls shook in outrage. "Willard, I expected to be dealing with you, not some agent of the very police force that wrongfully robbed Mr. Donner of his liberty—"

"Detective Hunter's concern is understandable," Donner interrupted quietly. "His dealings with me in the past have been under horrific circumstances, and it's only natural he would want to bring this out in the open. I imagine that every time he looks at me he finds himself back in the Bradley farmhouse—am I right, Detective?"

Directly across the table from Cord, Julia saw the darkness that shadowed his gaze, as if something had momentarily extinguished his soul. Then the dark eyes blinked and the firm mouth thinned.

"The Bradley farmhouse. The Wilkins apartment. The kitchen at the White Rose diner. Yes, Donner, you take me back."

"You're forgetting the parking garage where it all ended, Detective—the parking garage where the perpetrators of all those murders were killed themselves. I wasn't among them."

"No, you were safely tucked away in prison, for the one crime you didn't commit. That was a stroke of good luck—or was it good planning?" Cord asked.

He was keeping his voice even with an effort, Julia realized. Donner's reference to the Bradley farmhouse had been deliberate, and she suddenly wanted to shake his composure with the same tactics.

"At the end of the day we have to accept that there was never any evidence linking Mr. Donner to the outrages his former acquaintances committed," she said softly.

Donner looked at her, swiftly hiding his surprise, but before he could speak Marshall's hearty tones boomed out.

"Finally—the voice of reason. Of *course* there was never any evidence. The only crime Gary may have committed was in his choice of friends, but how was he to know they—"

"And they *were* your friends, weren't they, Donner?" Julia mused. "Despite everything you finally learned about them, you must have been devastated when you heard of their deaths."

"I was shocked, yes." He pulled a sheet of paper toward him needlessly, and then, as though realizing what he was doing, his hands stilled. "But I know that the authorities had no choice in the matter."

"Your own son was present, wasn't he? He would have been just a toddler then, and Diane Travis was looking after him for you."

She felt as if she was feeling her way in the dark, Julia thought. Something about this conversation rattled Donner, but she wasn't sure which of her barbs were finding their mark.

"Again, reckless disregard on the part of the authorities." Marshall pursed his lips. "Young Steven came close to being killed when Travis tried to escape."

"But we didn't know there was a child in that car." Cord's voice was harsh. "His mother had custody of Steven after your divorce, and if Travis hadn't kidnapped him a few days earlier he would never have been in the crash that killed her. Was that kidnapping on your instructions, too?"

"My son had been *stolen* from me!" Donner retorted, his self-possession finally cracking. "I got to see him every second Saturday—*my* son, and I wasn't allowed to raise him!"

"But he didn't die, Mr. Donner." Willard Stewart's uninflected tones cut through the charged atmosphere. "You should be grateful for that."

"No, he didn't die."

The brief spasm of emotion that had marred the bland ordinary features smoothed into composure again. His eyes weren't blue, as she'd thought, Julia noticed with a start. They were a clear brilliant green, and—

She gave herself a mental shake. She was more agitated than she was admitting to herself, she thought in confusion. Donner's eyes were as nondescript as the rest of him—an ordinary and slightly muddy gray.

And right now they were focused on her father.

"He didn't die, thank God. But I'm still fighting to regain visiting rights with him." Donner sighed. "Of course, your loss was much more tragic and final. The death of a child can tear a family apart with feelings of guilt and pain, I'm sure."

She felt the blood drain from her face. *How had he known?* Tom Marshall wouldn't have told him that the man they were meeting had once had a son who had drowned, because Marshall didn't know about Davey. Her father's reserve was unassailable on personal matters.

Which meant that Gary Donner had deliberately set out to uncover everything he could about her and her family.

"You are referring to my son, I imagine." If Willard Stewart's voice had been chilly before, now it was pack ice. His spare, stiff-backed figure seemed to freeze into motionlessness, and even his gaze was unblinking as he stared across his conference table at Gary Donner. "Please refrain from doing so ever again."

He slid back his chair and gave a slight nod. "I would like some time to consider my decision, Mr. Donner. I'm not one to rush into things, as Mr. Marshall can tell you. Tom, you'll be hearing from me one way or another within the week."

He rose, and unwillingly his two guests got to their feet also. Cord remained seated, his arms folded across his chest and his eyes watching Donner's every move. Julia didn't dare to attempt to stand. It was all she could do to fight back the nausea that assailed her, and her legs felt like they weren't attached to the rest of her body.

The first time she'd met Donner she'd had the unsettling feeling that he knew everything about her. He *did,* she thought with bright fear. He knew everything—how Davey had died, how her family had been torn apart. He even knew about the terrible, crippling *guilt* that had—

"I'll save you the phone call, Willard." Marshall's plump features were so tight that his mouth looked like a rosebud. His tone was caustic. "You don't intend to support the center." He clapped a meaty hand on Donner's shoulder, his voice rising. "You've been taken in by the smears and innuendos that have dogged this innocent man for—"

He broke off, his words ending in a strange, whistling breath, and Julia looked up. She was the only one in a position to see what had caused Marshall's sudden gasp, she realized immediately. The man's normally ruddy face was the color of chalk, his eyes were unfocused with pain, and the thumb of the hand that had been resting heavily on Donner's shoulder was bent back to his wrist. Donner smiled and removed Marshall's hand from his shoulder, patting it almost affectionately as he did so.

"Now, Tom, I don't need a champion," he remonstrated pleasantly. "Mr. Stewart, I'll respect your decision, whatever it is. All I ask is that you judge me on my actions, not on rumor."

"That's all any of us can ask," Willard Stewart said remotely. "During our lifetime, Mr. Donner—and beyond it. I'll see you out, gentlemen."

As the teak door closed behind the trio Cord's confused gaze turned to Julia. "What the hell happened at the end there?" he rasped. "One moment that pompous fool was telling us what a saint his poor, misunderstood protégé was and the next—"

"And the next moment he realized he was holding hands with the devil," Julia finished for him. "I think Donner broke Marshall's thumb right in front of three witnesses, and what we saw was the balance of power taking a hundred-and-eighty-degree turn in that little partnership." Her legs still felt shaky, but with Donner's departure the nausea had subsided. "Cord, he played us *all* during that meeting—even my father. We didn't even ask him where he was the night of Paul and Sheila's murders."

"We didn't have to." He shoved a stiff square of parchment, one of the documents that Donner had left for her father's perusal, across the table at her. "It's an outstanding citizen commendation from the Chamber of Commerce, presented to Donner personally at their annual awards dinner. Check the date."

She knew what she was going to find even before she looked at the document. She raised her eyes to his.

"We'll have to confirm this, Cord. He may not have actually been there to receive—"

"He was there." His tone was bleak. "Everything else about the man is all wrong, but Donner's alibis *always* check out."

The cramped, utilitarian room was beginning to seem like home, Julia thought drearily as she tossed her shoulder bag on the motel dresser and massaged her temples wearily. Behind her Cord's expression bore the same evidence of exhausted futility, but as their eyes met in the mirror he attempted a smile, and his strong fingers lightly massaged the tight muscles at the back of her neck.

"Good thing I handed in my badge before they took it away from me," he said wryly. "I've obviously lost it where Donner's concerned."

"Because you're not convinced he didn't kill Paul and Sheila?"

Closing her eyes, she felt the sure touch of his fingers seeking and relieving knots in muscles she hadn't even known she had. She let herself lean back against him, filled with a sudden fierce thankfulness that, whatever the outcome, their interview with Donner was over and done with.

On the way from her father's office they'd stopped at the local television station, and an obliging technician had rooted out the video footage of the Chamber of Commerce awards banquet. He'd fast-forwarded it until Cord had told him to stop, and the two of them had watched in silence as Gary Donner, for once attired in a neat suit and conservative tie, had shaken hands with a beaming businessman, collected his commendation with graceful thanks and had said a few brief words about the Friendship Center before leaving the stage.

Cord had been right, Julia had told herself hopelessly. Donner's alibis *always* checked out.

"Because I'm not convinced that he didn't have a hand in every unsolved crime that's occurred within a hundred-mile radius over the last ten or fifteen years," he replied unwillingly. "I can't seem to think rationally where he's concerned. My God, Julia—what if I've been wrong all along? What if he really *was* unaware of the killings his 'family' carried out?"

His hands stilled on her shoulders, and opening her eyes she saw the doubt that crossed his features. She turned to him.

"Don't forget what he did to Marshall at the end of our meeting. And that reference to creating a new 'family'—we can't dismiss that. He's hiding something, I *know* it. So do you."

"He's a violent man, I'll grant you that," Cord sighed. "But all the reference to his new family shows is that he knows exactly how to push my buttons. He threw that in to get me off balance, just like he threw in the Bradley farmhouse, and just like he brought up the subject of Davey. None of that proves he's guilty of the crimes we're trying to pin on him.''

"But *how* did he know about Davey? What's even more important is *why* does he know something so private about me?''

"That bothered me, too, honey, but it wouldn't have been impossible for him to find out about it.'' He took her hands in both of his. "He plays with people's minds. That's how he operates.''

"And it's worked.'' She searched his face fearfully. "I don't know *who* to suspect anymore.''

"We're left with Tascoe. When I talked with Stamp he said they're closing in on him—they found the boardinghouse where he was staying up until yesterday.''

"If Tascoe really did kill Paul and Sheila, then he's got to be totally unhinged.'' Her eyes clouded. "And for God's sake—we still don't have any proof that he was involved with DiMarco's drug operation.''

"DiMarco told us that Dean was looking to sell information,'' he reminded her. "I know he's not the best source we could hope for, but why would he finger Tascoe if there wasn't something to his story?''

"Because Tascoe was a threat to him?'' she ventured. "Don't you think it's odd that Dean Tascoe's name keeps coming up in relation to cases and suspects that the department's been investigating, Cord? It's like he's been a shadowy one-man police force.''

"You mentioned that once before.'' The dark eyes narrowed thoughtfully. "Vigilante policing, to show the powers that be he deserves to be given his old job back?''

"I'm reaching, aren't I?'' She gave him a small smile and sat down on the bed, her shoulders slumping tiredly. "I told you, Cord—investigation never was my speciality. I always worked on instinct and impressions, but now I can't even trust those anymore.''

"You're strung out, and so am I, honey.'' Sitting down beside her, he framed her troubled face with his hands and leaned forward until the tips of their noses touched. "Remember porcupine kisses?" He smiled. "You asked me once if they kissed, and I told you yes, but—"

"But *very* carefully." Julia rubbed the tip of her nose against his and laughed softly. "I remember. I remember everything we've ever done together."

"Refresh my memory on what we did last night, honey." He frowned exaggeratedly. "You know, I'm a few years older than you are, and this'll probably start happening more and more—me forgetting things, you having to remind me. That's really the only reason I let you hang around—that and because I like looking at that cute butt of yours."

"That's why I let *you* hang around *me*." She widened her eyes in mock surprise. "The nice buns factor. But this memory thing has me worried—are you absolutely sure you don't remember this?"

As she spoke, she brought her mouth to his. Her tongue darted quickly inside his parted lips and then out again. Cord sighed.

"Hell, it's worse than I thought. What else did we do?"

"Well, I bit the back of your neck, like this." Undoing the first few buttons of his shirt, she pushed open the neckline until the hard ridge of his collarbone was exposed. Raising herself slightly, she nipped him gently on the sensitive nape of his neck. "Nothing?" she breathed. "It doesn't ring a bell?"

He shook his head tensely. "Nope." His eyes were half-closed, and she could feel his biceps harden, as if he was keeping a rigid control over his reactions. "Not a darn thing, honey," he said tightly.

"As a last resort, I guess we *could* do it all over again." She gave him a dubious look. "But there's really no guarantee your memory won't blank out on you again, is there?"

"Oh, I don't know." He turned his head to meet her gaze, and a corner of his mouth lifted teasingly. "It just depends how memorable we make it."

Their lovemaking the night before had had a raw urgency about it that had brought her to fever pitch again and again, but this time, by unspoken agreement, they came together in a languorous, almost dream-like coupling. It was as if they were two halves of a whole, Julia thought hazily at one point, when Cord's legs were entwined with hers and their fingers were laced together. Nothing could separate them now. Nothing would ever come between them again. They would marry and grow old together, he and she, and their world would be perfect and complete as long as they had each other.

He'll want children. You know he'll want children—will you be able to make a family with him?

Even the small voice in her head was only a momentary distraction, and as the two of them urged each other slowly toward an ultimate height, she forgot everything but the way Cord was making her feel, the touch of his hands, the heat of his mouth....

"You don't know what it does to me to hear you crying out my name," Cord said softly a few hours later as they lay together in the darkening room. "Sometimes when I'm walking around in the daytime, or talking to someone, or driving, the memory of how you look just before you call out flashes into my mind, and I just about die, honey."

She traced the line of his mouth with a soft finger. "I know. It happens to me, too, Cord."

He stared at her for a long moment, and in the dusky shadows she saw him smile. "Let's make it legal."

His voice was still charged and husky with sex, but the look in those eyes so close to hers was serious and waiting. Julia felt foolishly as if she was about to cry.

"I—I'd like that, Cord." Her lips curved tremulously, and then the tears were spilling over, even as a little embarrassed laugh escaped her. His arms were around her immediately, holding her close to his heart.

"Is this a good sign or a bad sign?" he said shakily, his gaze bright. "Because if I'd known I was going to make you cry, I would have just asked you to be my mistress for the next fifty years." He tipped her chin up and kissed the corner of her mouth.

"I don't want to be your mistress, Cord. I want us to get married and have a family one day," she whispered, her voice uneven. "And this time it'll be different. Maybe that's partly why I was so terrified when I found out I was preg—"

She bit the word off, but she knew even as she did that she'd left it too late. He stared at her, his expression a mixture of confusion and disbelief.

"You were pregnant?" he said in a voice that didn't sound like his. "You were pregnant, and I never knew?"

He drew slightly away from her, but for some reason it felt like he'd opened an unbridgeable gap between them. "What happened to the *baby?* You didn't—oh dear God, you didn't have an—"

"No!" His eyes were so *dark,* Julia thought fearfully. "Of course I didn't—it was a false alarm. The test result was wrong, except I didn't know for a few weeks, and I—"

"For a few *weeks?* For a few weeks you thought we were going to have a baby, and you didn't think that was something I should *know?* In God's name, why? Why wouldn't you tell me something so important?"

Sitting up, he snapped on the bedside lamp, and in the sudden light his features were drawn. "Were you deciding what to do about our child? Did you even have any intention of letting me in on the decision?"

"I don't know!" She sat up, clutching the sheet to her breasts. "You don't understand, Cord—I was out of my mind with *fear* when I found out. I just kept hoping I'd wake up and find out it wasn't *true.*"

Her voice had risen unevenly, and her eyes, only moments ago spilling over with tears of happiness, were anguished and so dry they felt as if they were burning.

"You see, I never could have kept our child safe—never. *Never!*" she whispered harshly, shaking her head in frantic denial. "I would have *failed* both of you one day—I knew I would. It would just have been a matter of time before I let my guard down, or I slipped up somehow, or I—or I—"

"Did you sneak down to the Sunfish and put the life belts in like I told you, Julia? You sure?"

Her expression was haunted, her voice almost inaudible. "I would have *lost* our child. I would have tried to do everything right, and it wouldn't have been good enough! I would have been responsible for losing the child I loved, and *nothing* I ever did would be able to atone for that, not if I spent the rest of my life trying to make it right again, not if I made sure I was *perfect,* that I never let anyone down ever again, that I—that I—"

Her eyes squeezed shut and just as immediately flew open as Cord gripped her arms and gave her a little shake. "You were five years *old,* goddammit!" he said hoarsely, his face almost touching hers. "You were a child *yourself!*"

"I—" Julia met the brilliant black gaze fearfully. "I don't understand," she whispered. "What are you talking about?"

"Davey's death," Cord said flatly. "Davey's death, and the fact that you survived. You've never been able to forgive yourself for either of those things, have you?"

She tried to pull away, but his grip was unbreakable. "The only child you betrayed was *yourself.* The only child you didn't save was that frightened little girl who's been screaming out her pain and her fear somewhere deep inside you all these years—the little girl you won't forgive. You always felt *she* should have been the one to die, didn't you?"

"That's crazy," she said automatically. "That's not true. You *know* it's not—"

"It is true, and I've known it for years. I just had no idea it went so deep." His voice lost its edge. "You could see it in Lopez—the crippling guilt, the pain. Why can't you see it in yourself?"

"Because it's not true, dammit!" Finally jerking her arms from him, Julia's eyes blazed. "And this has nothing to do with how I reacted two years ago, anyway. I was stressed—the job had overwhelmed me—"

"You don't *want* to admit that you blame that little five-year-old girl, do you?" he asked slowly. "Because if you ever did admit it, you'd have to forgive her—and that you'll never do."

He gazed at her, and at first she couldn't identify the expression on his face. Then she recognized it for what it was, and suddenly an icy hand seemed to be wrapping itself around her heart.

There was no anger in those dark eyes anymore. They were filled with regret, and very slowly he reached out and pushed her hair from her temples with a touch so light she could hardly feel it.

"*I* loved her," he said softly. "And I loved the woman who took her place. All I ever wanted was to love you and to make you happy, Julia—you, and the little girl you'd once been. But I ended up almost tearing you apart, and that's why I left the first time."

She opened her mouth as if to speak, although what she intended to say she didn't know. All of a sudden it was vitally important to say something—anything—to interrupt him. But he anticipated her, laying a gentle finger on her lips.

"I didn't know what I was doing wrong, but I knew I was destroying you. I walked away from you, even though leaving almost destroyed *me*. The only thing that kept me going was the hope that one day you'd want me back." He smiled, but his eyes were bright with pain. "I let myself hope that, because I knew what we had was indestructible, no matter what happened in our lives. And I was right—it *is* indestructible."

Her hand reached tremblingly to his and she let out a shaky breath. "I thought you were telling me you were *leaving* me," she said, her voice faltering. "Oh, Cord—I thought you didn't *want* me anymore."

"I'll want you till the day I die, honey. My last thought on this earth will be of you, and the last thing I see when I close my eyes that final time will be your face," he said huskily. "And you love me...but you can't love yourself. You won't forgive that little girl, and you won't let her go in peace—not while I'm still in your life, anyway."

He brought her fingertips to his mouth and pressed a kiss against them. "That's why this time when I walk away it'll be for good."

The ice around her heart was numbingly cold, and it felt like it was sluggishly spreading through her veins, forcing its way through her limbs. If she made even the slightest movement she would crack, she thought distantly. She had to be very, very careful, because she was about to break in two.

The boom came around and attacked him, Cord! Davey fell in the water, and he's not wearing a life jacket like he's supposed to, and it's all my fault, Cord—it's my fault! I made him die, Cord!

She wanted to close her eyes to shut out the memory, but she knew that would be dangerous. Maybe in a while she would start to thaw out a little—enough to go through the motions, at least. But the ice would still be inside her.

"Your dad told me he's got a business trip coming up in the next few days," Cord said softly. "I think you should go with him, honey. I'd feel better if I knew you were safe while Tascoe's still—"

The phone on the bedside table rang, and its shrill sound hit Julia with the force of a hammer, shattering the numb stillness that had encased her.

"I'm not going anywhere!" Her voice sounded rusty even to herself. "Lizbet's still in danger, and I have to keep her safe. You'll see, Cord—I'll *prove* to you I can do it!"

"You don't have to prove anything to—" he began, but she overrode him as the phone rang again.

"But I've *got* to! You think you have to leave because I'll fall apart again, or because I can't handle it, or—"

"No—that's *you* talking. You think you have to prove yourself, you think you have to be perfect for me or anyone else to love you, even a little, but—"

Again the phone shrilled, and with a muttered oath Cord grabbed the receiver. "Hunter," he said curtly. "Who the hell is—" He bit back the rest of his sentence. Watching him, Julia saw his hand tighten around the phone. "How did it happen?" he snapped, but before he could have received an answer he spoke again, his voice sharp. "Forget it—just tell me when they lost him." He swore again, with more earthiness than she'd ever heard from him. "Okay, Stamp, I appreciate you letting us know. Yeah, I hope so. I'll keep you posted."

He cut the connection, and immediately started dialing a number. "The officers who were tailing Donner lost him about an hour ago.'' He ground the words out. ''Just in case, I want Mary and Frank and the kids to leave the house right away. Frank's got a brother in town—they can stay with him for the night.''

Julia slid from the bed, handed Cord his jeans and pulled her own on, her movements swiftly controlled. She felt a slight sense of wonder that she was functioning so efficiently when her world had just been torn apart. But emotion was a luxury she couldn't afford, she thought. Part of her had never stopped being a cop, and that was the part that was taking over right now.

After they knew Lizbet was safe she could fall to pieces, she told herself tightly. Not before.

She slipped her arms into a shoulder holster and picked up the .45 that Cord had insisted she get after Jackie's Redmond's death. ''I thought you weren't taking him seriously as a suspect anymore.''

''I know. But Stamp says losing his tail was a deliberate move on Donner's part. That's got me—'' He switched his attention to the instrument in his hand and spoke urgently into the receiver. ''Mary—''

He stopped before he'd gotten a more than a word out and Julia heard a muffled metallic voice coming from the phone he held to his ear. The next moment Cord was slamming the receiver down and grabbing for his gun.

''It's a damn *recording*,'' he said grimly, pulling his sweatshirt over his head then opening the dresser drawer where he kept his spare ammunition. ''The Whitefield phone's out of service.''

Chapter 15

Cord had snatched Julia's car keys as he'd run out the door, and now as they sped down the highway he glanced at her. "You got a screwdriver or something in the glove box?" he asked distractedly.

"I think so." Tensely Julia watched the taillights of the car ahead of them magically change from tiny, far-off pinpoints to glowing cherry discs and then flash by on the right-hand side in a blur of hot red as Cord passed the vehicle. She let out her breath. "It's a miniature one. Will it do?"

"Yeah, it'll do. Pry off the plastic cover of the dome light and unscrew the bulb. When we get off the highway I'll stop and smash the brake lights. At least the paint job on this thing's a lot less conspicuous than the Bronco."

"You think he's there already." Her tone was flat as she jammed the blade of the screwdriver under the plastic dome above her head and popped it off. "Why didn't you tell Phil to send backup?"

"For the same reason I chose a dark blue vehicle over a white one—if Donner's there, I don't want to alert him to our presence. I won't have this turning into a standoff situation like it did with his suicidal 'family.' ''

Their exit came rushing up, and he took it. "And no, I'm not sure he's there already. I'm not sure of anything where he's concerned, but I don't like the fact that two experienced police officers told Phil Stamp that the bastard did a deliberate end run around them and lost them. Besides, for Donner's alibi to be watertight I'll have to know that he was in his seat at least an hour before he got that award.''

He applied the brakes, and in the bright beam of their headlights Julia saw a cloud of gritty dust fly up as they hit the graveled shoulder of the road. Cord turned to her, his face grim.

"I figure there was a wide enough window of opportunity for him to have killed Paul and Sheila and then driven hell-for-leather across town, just in time to take his place at the banquet and go up to collect his award. If that's the way it was, it explains why he couldn't waste any more precious minutes looking for Lizbet at the house—he had it timed down to the second.''

He got out of the car, and she clenched her hands tightly in her lap as she watched him in the cold white light cast by the Ford's high beams. He picked up a medium-size rock at the side of the road and hefted it appraisingly in his hand before striding to the back of the car. She gave an involuntary start as he slammed the rock into the passenger-side taillight with such force that the idling vehicle rocked with the impact, but she was ready for the next one, and as he rejoined her and pulled onto the road again she spoke, her voice even and controlled.

"How do you want to handle this?''

"We'll back in from the road and I'll cut the engine just before we get to the red maple by the side of the driveway. The phone line runs in right about there.'' He frowned. "If someone cut it deliberately that's where they'd do it, and if that's the case then we'll know immediately what we're dealing with.''

She was struck by a sudden thought. "Cord—what are we going to do about King? Mary lets him out at night to patrol the property. He'll raise the alarm before he realizes it's us.''

Ahead of them a big buck rabbit shot across the road, briefly illuminated in the headlights' glare, and Cord swerved slightly, missing the animal by inches. He looked at her.

"Honey, if it's Donner, he would have taken out King before he even tampered with the phone," he said gently.

"Of course." Julia bit down on her lip, hoping the physical pain would counteract the lancing sorrow that had just shot through her. Of *course* Donner would have killed King, she thought numbly. He was after a child—an animal would be merely an annoyance, to be dispatched as emotionlessly as if he was swatting a mosquito. The big German shepherd whose loyalty and unconditional love had served her so truly and so well since the day Cord had placed the squirming little puppy with big feet and a huge red bow around his neck into her arms would have been the first threat that Donner would have eliminated.

"Let's assume the worst-case scenario," she said hoarsely. "Say the phone line's been cut—what then?"

"The important thing is getting to Lizbet and the twins. Donner's a city boy—if Mary's two can slip into the woods behind the house they're home free, and if she's still unharmed she'll try to get them there," Cord said. "Frank keeps a shotgun in the house, but Donner would probably guess that there was a weapon of some sort on the premises. He'd have made sure Frank never got a chance to use it."

The first time she'd met Frank Whitefield, a few days ago, Julia had been struck by how much the tall, lanky man reminded her of Cord's father. He'd had the same gentle humor, the same patience with his children and the little girl he and his wife had taken in. And as Jackson Hunter had been a Vietnam vet, Frank had seen military service during Desert Storm. There was a chance he might have delayed Donner from getting to Mary and the children long enough for them to escape, Julia thought. But the price would have been high.

"I'd better douse the lights."

As Cord spoke, the brightly lit road ahead of them was plunged into blackness, and he lessened their speed a little. A second later Julia's eyes began to adjust to the lack of artificial light, and she saw that the moon was nearly full, a shaved round of ancient gold in the heavens.

"A hunter's moon." Already Cord had lowered his voice, but there was a sudden fierceness in his words. "That's good. I'm in a hunting mood tonight," he added, almost to himself.

It was a side of him she'd only seen once before, and then it had frightened her, because she hadn't been able to relate to the Cord who'd come back from the Bradley farmhouse, his eyes dark with the horrors he'd witnessed and his energies completely focused on tracking down the killers who'd perpetrated them. Now the implacable anger in him struck a faint answering chord in her.

"Leave the keys in the ignition. If the twins and Mary get to the woods they'll be safe, but city boy or not, Donner won't stop looking for Lizbet—not this time. Whoever finds her first, their main priority is getting her safely away." She looked at him. "That means you leave me behind if you have to, Cord."

He gave a grudging nod. "She's our first concern, agreed. But I don't intend to leave her or you behind."

She'd have to be satisfied with that, she told herself as they slowed for the half-hidden laneway that led to the house. Just when she thought he must have missed it in the dark, he braked, then put the Ford into reverse.

When his father had lived here, the lane had been a neatly trimmed avenue of greenery, but now the arching, spiny branches of barberry and the whip-like stems of the overgrown mock orange bushes had taken on a wild unruliness, and she jumped as a springy limb from a flowering currant brushed against her through her opened window.

"This is far enough." Cord looked at her as he killed the engine. "I'll have to climb the pole to check on the phone line."

He opened the car door noiselessly, and she followed suit, but as she stepped out she realized that he'd already melted into the darkness. The telephone pole was a stone's throw away, and casting her eyes in its direction she saw him, a shadowy figure near its base, starting to climb it.

The house was still out of sight, but out here sound carried,

she thought edgily. She should have been able to hear some
evidence that just a few hundred yards away was a family settling down for the evening, but the silence was total. She slid
her Ruger from her shoulder holster and snapped the safety off,
slowly scanning the shadowy landscape for any movement and
keeping low to the ground, her knees bent, to minimize her
silhouette. Out of the corner of her eye she saw Cord climbing
down the pole, and her foot nudged something solid.

In a blur of motion she pivoted toward it, her heart in her
mouth and her finger tensing instinctively on the trigger of the
gun, but even as she did a cloud passed over the moon, and for
a moment all she could see was a denser shape of black against
the ground.

Then the moon sailed serenely out from behind the cloud,
and she suddenly knew what she'd found.

"King!"

Snapping the safety on and holstering her gun, she dropped
to her knees beside the big German shepherd, groping blindly
for him in the dark. Her fingers felt fur, already damp and cool
with the night dew, and then the cold, ropy thickness of blood
beginning to congeal.

"The line's been—aw, hell, Julia." Cord was there, hunker-
ing down beside her, and he reached quickly for her. "God
damn him. God *damn* him," he repeated under his breath, his
curse sounding like a deliberate request to the Almighty rather
than a casual obscenity.

"Oh, King—oh, my *brave* boy," she whispered unevenly,
her trembling hand ineffectually trying to smooth down the stiff,
matted fur. She felt Cord's hand on her hair, offering silent
comfort. He said nothing, and she knew that he, too, was trying
to hold back the pain.

Her vision wavered. A moment, perfect and frozen in her
memory, came suddenly into her mind—King as a puppy, sitting side by side with Lizbet at that long-ago third birthday
party, patiently bearing the little girl's sticky hugs and grinning
foolishly under the hat she'd put on him.

That strong heart had been loyal to the end, she thought,
anguished. He'd given his life for the child he'd loved. With a

delicate finger she touched the velvety muzzle that she'd stroked so often in the past.

"Like a gentleman, boy."

Softly echoing the words she'd rewarded him with so often during his life, Julia stroked him as if at any minute that big tail would beat in pleasure at her praise, and those brown eyes would open and gaze in unquestioning adoration at her. "You died like a gentleman," she whispered, the tears thick in her throat. "Good boy. *Such* a good dog."

Her fingers brushed against something unfamiliar and, knuckling the tears from her eyes almost angrily, she peered closer. Strong white fangs, partially visible under a bared top lip, caught the moonlight. Between them was a scrap of heavy material, and she gently pulled the fabric from his teeth.

It was a piece of denim, raggedly ripped. King had gotten one lunge in before Donner had killed him, she thought with a rush of primitive satisfaction. Cord took the scrap from her and examined it.

"He must have encountered the bastard as he finished cutting the line," he said in an undertone. There was a raw edge to his voice, and he cleared his throat and went on. "We'll bury him under that pine he used to like to lie under, honey. He'll sleep well there."

"I—I'd like that." She fought back the wrenching sense of loss that washed over her, and giving the cold muzzle one last, loving stroke, rose stiffly to her feet.

"We should keep going." He got to his feet, too, and inclined his head to hers, keeping his voice low. "You okay?"

She wasn't okay. Right now she felt like nothing was ever going to be okay again. King was dead. As wrenching as that fact was by itself, it had other, even more ominous implications.

The big dog had been the first line of defence around Lizbet. That line had been breached. Julia felt panic rising under her rib cage like a fear-crazed bird.

"I shouldn't have left her with anyone else," she muttered under her breath. "I should have kept her by my side—I *never* should have let her out of my sight."

"That just wasn't possible—not while we were trying to find

out who killed her parents. You know that as well as I do."
His voice hardened. "Stay focused. We've got a job to do."

His brusqueness brought her to her senses, and she forced
the panic away. Looking at King's still body, she felt something
shift in her mind, as if an extra pathway of synapses that had
previously been blocked had just opened up.

Deep inside her, a spark of cold, bright anger flared, wavered
and then steadied to a brilliant and terrible flame.

Cord glanced at her. She nodded decisively, and then the two
of them were moving silently through the shadows, their progress cautiously swift. Cord knew this property like the back
of his hand, but she knew it, too, she thought. As a little girl
she'd spent more time here than she had at her own house, and
the shadowy shapes of bushes and rocks that surrounded them,
far from seeming threatening and alien, were familiar and beloved landmarks on the misty but never-forgotten map of her
childhood.

To her left she noted the jagged stalks of last year's clump
of feverfew, the daisy-like flower Jane Hunter had dried and
used in a recipe for insect repellent that she'd learned from her
mother. Over there on her right was the large round shadow of
the snowball bush, and farther on she thought she could see the
moonlight gleaming on the spikes of monkshood that Cord's
father had once warned her never to touch. The purple flowers
did look like hoods, she remembered, but the plant was also
called wolfsbane, since it was so deadly poisonous that the ex-
tract from its roots had been used to kill predators. Native
American tribes had tipped their arrows with that same juice,
and death to an enemy struck by one of those arrows was swift
and certain.

Cord was beside her, and she flicked a sideways glance at
him, almost immediately shrinking into the shadow of an iron-
wood tree, her hand touching his arm in warning. He froze and
inclined his head to hers.

"Just over there by that lilac." Her mouth was beside his
ear, and a short strand of his hair brushed her lips. "The shadows seem more solid. I think there's someone there."

He darted a quick look in the direction she'd indicated and

then nodded wordlessly, motioning for her to stay. Reluctantly she sank deeper into the darkness. He bent down, and at first she thought he was picking something up off the ground, but as he straightened she saw the pinprick of moonlight, immediately hidden, on the blade in his hand.

She felt no revulsion at the sight of the knife. It was the most noiseless of weapons, she thought coldly. If there was any possibility that Donner had one of his new "family" here with him standing lookout, a shot would immediately galvanize him into murderous action. She couldn't see Cord at all, and she realized he would have circled the area to come around from the back. Whoever was waiting for them a few feet away would be taken by complete surprise. Staying to the shadows, she edged closer.

She was just in time to see Cord's broad-shouldered silhouette surge from the darkness and merge with the shadowy figure she'd been watching. She heard a low grunt of pain, and then saw the gleam of light on the flat of the blade that Cord was holding to the man's throat, but by then she'd covered the last of the dew-soaked grass between her and the two struggling figures.

Not struggling, she corrected herself. The man's head had been pulled up and to the left by Cord's powerful grip, and he had frozen at the first touch of cold steel on the exposed side of his neck. The stranger was a fraction of an inch away from sudden death, and he knew it.

"Who are you working for?" Cord's softly whispered question held barely controlled fury. "Tell me *now,* goddammit, or you're a dead man."

The other man's face was away from her, his head bent so cruelly back that his attempt at responding was a mere croak, but something about him seemed suddenly familiar to Julia. Cord lowered his head enough for him to speak, and she suppressed a gasp.

"Tascoe!"

The discredited ex-cop shot an incredulous glance at her, then froze again as Cord tightened his grip.

"See if he's armed."

Remembering Cord's ankle sheath, she started at Tascoe's

feet and instantly discovered the small but deadly .38, obviously kept there as a backup weapon. Patting each meaty leg to his thighs with a grimace, she found nothing else until she flipped back the light windbreaker the man was wearing and relieved him of his shouldered police-issue .45.

"He's clean now," she told Cord curtly, her eyes never leaving the other man's face.

The arm around Tascoe's neck was released so abruptly that the man staggered, his hands going immediately to his windpipe.

"You—you damn near crushed my larynx, Chief." He raised his head and glared at Cord. "Where the hell did *you* come from?"

"We'll ask the questions, Tascoe." Cord bent swiftly and sheathed the knife he'd been holding. After pulling his pant leg over the weapon again, he straightened to his full height, his attitude still tensely watchful. "Down at the station," he added grimly.

The heavy features clouded with confusion, and then Tascoe gave a low laugh. "You got the wrong man, Chief. I'm on your side here."

"It doesn't look that way to me. There's a dead dog over there by a cut telephone line, and you're creeping around in the dark armed to the teeth." Cord ground the words out. "Come on, we're taking you to Lopez."

"He's wearing polyester," Julia said slowly, looking at the awful pants Tascoe had on. "Whoever King bit was wearing jeans." She drew a shallow breath and holstered her gun as she confronted the ex-cop. "What's going on here, Tascoe?"

"I told you—I'm on your side." Wincing and rubbing the arm that Cord had reluctantly released, Tascoe looked at him. "Give me back my weapons, Chief, because I'm going to need them. Gary Donner's in the house—I followed him here."

His confirmation of their worst fears hit Julia like a blow to the heart, and she felt the blood draining from her face.

"I've had my eye on that murdering bastard ever since he walked out of his second trial a free man," Tascoe said, his beefy features tight with hatred. "But I only found out he'd been using Jackie to get information the night you came to her apartment. I went looking for him the minute Hendrix and Dow let me go, but she must have been—'' He swallowed heavily, his eyes squeezing shut briefly before he continued, his voice hoarse with pain. ''He must have killed her almost as soon as we all left that night. I knew Lopez would haul me in again, so—''

''What the hell were you thinking?'' Julia asked, her face inches from his. ''There's a *child* in that house—Paul and Sheila's little girl! If you hadn't been so set on playing Lone Ranger we might have had Donner in custody by now.''

She stopped suddenly, her hand going to her throat. ''Oh, my *God*,'' she whispered, her eyes wide with horror. ''You knew he killed Paul and Sheila, didn't you? You *knew* it—because you were following him the night he went to their house!''

''I followed him there, yeah,'' Tascoe muttered, not meeting her accusing gaze. ''But my first thought was that Durant wasn't as lily-white as he pretended to be—I figured Donner was in on something with him.''

''You're scum,'' Cord said tightly. ''You were a dirty cop, so you figured Paul was, too. While you were waiting for Donner outside he was murdering my best friends. If I hadn't shown up he would have added a child to his victims. I should have killed you a few minutes ago, Tascoe.''

''Maybe you should have, Chief.'' The other man raised his head and shrugged wearily. ''I haven't been able to live with myself since that night. If I'd only known he was starting already...'' His voice trailed off, and he passed a meaty hand across his brow. ''But all I knew was that he was in the house for about half an hour. Then he came out again like a bat out of hell, got into his car and took off so damn fast I nearly lost him.''

''He had to make the awards banquet,'' Julia said emotionlessly. ''We're wasting time here. Cord, give him back his guns. We've got to get to Lizbet before Donner harms her.''

''He's not planning on killing the kid, for crying out loud.'' Tascoe looked surprised. ''I thought you'd figured it out, too.''

"Figured what out?" Cord snapped. "If you've got some inside information about what Donner's plans are, Tascoe, spill it. He's trying to duplicate a series of murders from the past, right?"

"Maybe that's the way he sees it." Tascoe nodded slowly. "But it's really all about revenge. He's duplicating the deaths of his 'family' in their last standoff with the police. And Lizbet's Steven—he won't kill her. He's just going to make sure you never see her again."

"My son had been stolen from me!"

Donner's uncharacteristic outburst during the meeting in her father's office resounded in Julia's mind with the force of a thunderclap. "He wants to kidnap her—to raise her as his own, just the way he thinks Steven was taken and turned against him," she breathed.

"That's right." Tascoe grunted. "When you showed up just now I thought you'd put the pieces together, like I did. Sheila was shot like the Wilcox woman."

"Isabel Wilcox came out of the parking garage where they'd been cornered, pulled a gun and took down the two nearest officers before she was killed herself," Cord said shortly. "But how does Paul's death fit in?"

"That freaky psycho Wallace, remember?" Tascoe said. "He thought he could leap from the roof of the parking garage to the next building and escape. Bad way to go, even for someone like him."

"I don't understand—" Julia began, but Cord cut her off.

"There was a fence down below, with iron railings." He didn't elaborate, and he didn't have to. Her eyes darkened in sick comprehension, and then he went on, addressing Tascoe. "We can catch up on the rest of the history lesson later. What I need to know now is what's going on in that house."

"The husband's unconscious," Tascoe said. "I arrived about ten minutes after Donner did, parked my car in a bunch of bushes and came from there on foot. The first thing I saw was the dog." He shot Julia a look. "I got in sight of the house just in time to see Donner dragging a body around the house to that little hatchway thing that opens up in the ground, whatever the hell that is.''

"The entrance to the root cellar,'' Cord said. "But Donner wouldn't bother locking Frank away if he was dead already.''

"I think he's trying to keep to the script he wrote for himself.'' Tascoe scowled. "It's not queasiness that's keeping him from turning this into a bloodbath, it's that he wants everything to mirror what happened to his family as close as possible. But the woman tied up in the house doesn't know that.''

"Mary,'' Julia supplied, her lips tight. "Where in the house is she?''

"In the kitchen. He locked the two older kids in some kind of pantry—I only got a quick look through the window,'' he explained. "But the woman's tied to a chair, and the little girl's asleep on her lap—either that or she's been drugged to keep her quiet,'' he said doubtfully. "And Donner's just sitting there, as if he's waiting for something. I knew when I saw the kids I couldn't risk trying to take him down myself. I was on my way back to use my car phone to call that dipstick Phil Stamp and his little firecracker partner to tell them to get over here,'' he ended grudgingly.

"That's exactly what we don't want,'' Cord said sharply. "If Donner decides to go out in a blaze of gunfire innocent people are going to die. Besides, we've got no guarantee that he's not about to leave with Lizbet any second now. Tascoe, get your guns and follow us. I've got a plan.''

As the three of them crept closer to the deceptively quiet house, Julia found herself growing tenser by the second. Cord outlined his proposal briefly. He would enter the house by a back upstairs window, he told them—there was a maple tree whose limbs came close enough for him to get into the bedroom that had been his as a boy. Julia and Tascoe were to stay at the front of the house.

"Where's Donner's vehicle?'' he asked, frowning.

"Beats me, Chief,'' Tascoe answered with a shrug.

They were at the last stand of shrubs before the lawn started, and Cord gave her a quick look. "We have to assume that if he gets suspicious he's going to make a run for it with Lizbet,'' he told her. "I want you and Tascoe to watch the porch in case he does, and by then I'll be coming at him from behind. Don't let him get her to his car."

"We'll make damn sure he doesn't."

Tascoe straightened, and for a moment Julia could see the man he must have been years ago. The *cop* he must have been, she thought, taking in the grim determination in his stance, the implacable set of his mouth. The meaty hand was holding a gun, and she hadn't even seen him reach for it.

"You watch your back too, Chie—" The big ex-cop met Cord's resigned gaze. *"Hunter,"* he corrected himself softly. He clapped him on the shoulder. "Watch your back, Hunter, and we'll take care of this end of things."

"I should be the one entering the house." Julia put her hand on Cord's arm urgently. "I'm lighter than you, and I—"

"I've gone in and out of that window a hundred times in the past," he said flatly. "Plus I know every damn creaking floorboard on the way down to the kitchen. I'm going and that's final." His glittering black gaze met her stubborn hazel one, and his expression lost some of its hardness. "You've known me all your life, Julia. You didn't really think I'd agree, did you?"

"No. Because you were the only one I could never win an argument against," she whispered heatedly. "But we're going to be right there, Cord, and if anything even *looks* like it's about to happen, I'm going in."

"Agreed." He cupped her chin lightly. "Stubborn as hell. That's one of the things I loved you for all these years, honey."

A corner of his mouth lifted in a grin that seemed almost regretful, and then he turned and melted into the shadows, heading toward the back of the house.

"Ain't love grand," Tascoe sighed theatrically beside her. "You two have been all over each other for as long as I've known you. Why haven't you gotten hitched yet?"

"That's none of your business," Julia retorted, flicking him a look of pure dislike, her earlier and more positive appraisal of the man vanishing. "Come on, it's time we got into position,'' she snapped, expecting him to balk at her peremptory tone.

But he didn't. Despite the man's problems with authority—especially *female* authority, she thought dryly—he was enough of a professional to put his personal feelings aside and creep silently to the house with her. Maybe she could learn something from Dean Tascoe, she told herself brutally.

Underlying her fears for Lizbet, her shock and sorrow at finding King and the adrenaline-induced edginess she was feeling, was a dull, numbing pain. He'd decided to leave her. This time it would be no use telling herself that if she turned around quickly enough she would find him standing there, waiting for her. This time he wouldn't be back, and she couldn't blame him. But maybe she could change his mind.

''We can't afford any mistakes, Tascoe,'' she said in an undertone. ''*None*—do you understand? We're going to get that little girl out, and this whole operation is going to go down *perfectly,* get it?''

They were only feet from the kitchen window, and he shrugged. ''Perfect only happens in the movies. A million things could go wrong, but as long as we—''

''*No!*'' She grabbed the front of his windbreaker. ''I can't afford to *fail* her! She's coming out, Cord's coming out, and if I have to take Donner down by *myself* that's the way it's going to happen! You better get that straight right now, Tascoe.''

''I guess I do understand,'' he said slowly. His big hand gently pried her fingers loose from his windbreaker, but for a moment he held them, his eyes for once losing their mocking blue glint. ''You need to prove something—to yourself or him or the world, I don't know. But I know what failure's like, and I know what it's like to want to erase it. Yeah, the kid's coming out safe, Hunter's coming out safe, and we'll take Donner down, Stewart.'' He grinned suddenly, the blue eyes hardening again. ''Or freakin' die tryin', right?''

There'd been a reason men like Dow and Hendrix had put their careers on the line for this uncouth, out-of-shape loose cannon, Julia thought unwillingly. Whether his badge had been taken away from him or not, he would never stop being a cop. It was all he knew.

"Or die trying, Tascoe." She flashed him a quick smile, suddenly glad that he was there with her. "Can you see what's happening inside?"

The window was high enough off the ground that he had to boost himself up a few inches to look in. When he dropped to the ground he was frowning. "He's still just sitting there, but now he's got the kid. Even if Hunter surprises him, he won't be able to risk taking a shot at the bastard."

"He knows someone's here. He's using Lizbet as a shield and as soon as Cord shows himself Donner'll gun him down, knowing he won't risk harming her," Julia said harshly. "The man's like a feral dog—he can *smell* danger. What are we going to do?"

"We can't just stand here and watch your boyfriend get killed, that's for sure," Tascoe said with grim determination. "We've got to get that son of a bitch out into the open. Cover me, partner."

Even as he finished speaking he was walking boldly around to the front of the house, making no attempt to stay quiet, and the next moment, to Julia's shock, he was shouting at the top of his lungs.

"Donner, I know you're in there!" In a patch of moonlight just beyond the porch, the stocky, balding ex-cop stood his ground. "Come on out so I can send you to hell, you murdering scum!"

Almost immediately, and as coolly as if he was coming out for a breath of fresh air before turning in for the night, Donner pushed open the screen door and walked onto the porch. He was dressed in his usual casual manner, but there was a jagged rip in the knee of his jeans.

And he was holding a sleeping or unconscious Lizbet, Julia saw with cold horror. The tiny, heart-shaped face, white in the moonlight, was nestled into his shoulder. In his other hand was a gun.

"Dean Tascoe," the light, pleasant voice said. "Shouldn't

you be sitting on a bar stool somewhere, drowning your sorrows? I hear you've recently suffered a bereavement.''

"That's why I'm here, Donner." Tascoe glared at the other man. "I know you killed Jackie. Put the kid down and face me like a man."

Julia crept silently to the side of the porch. Donner was only about four feet away from her, but he might as well have been in the next county, she thought despairingly. There was no way she could vault onto the porch, over the wooden railing and snatch Lizbet from him before he knew what was happening. But surely at any moment Cord would come through the door behind him—

"This isn't going to work out quite the way you planned it, Tascoe." There was real amusement in his voice. "*I* would have tried to get in by that upstairs window, so I figured Hunter would choose that way to enter—but as soon as he got over the sill the leghold trap I set there earlier would have slammed shut on him. It'll take two strong men and a pry bar to open it, I'm told, and even at that his bone has to have been broken."

Julia bent over in the concealing shrubbery, willing the bile that had risen to her throat to subside but unable to free herself of the horrific image his words had conjured up. She'd seen leghold traps—in the garden shed at the lake house an old one had hung on the wall, rusty and disused for years. Cord's father had found it in the woods behind the house and had removed it grimly, but even dismantled and harmless, the cruel steel teeth had looked like the instruments of torture they were.

Cord was upstairs right now, his leg crushed between one of those evil things, she thought. He wouldn't be able to release himself—Donner was right about that, it was impossible for one man to force open those cruel jaws. Even if Cord managed to pry it open slightly, the chances of it springing back and breaking his leg a second time were high.

It was down to her and Tascoe—two ex-cops, two ex-alcoholics, two failures.

"Two *ex-failures*," she whispered to herself slowly. "Two ex-failures who've come to the end of the line."

"Like I said—not quite the way you planned it, Tascoe,"

Donner continued. "You weren't part of my plan, either, but I'm willing to improvise. Throw your guns down on the ground—both of them." Again he chuckled, low and amused. "I know you always carry that little barroom equalizer on your ankle. I make it a habit to research my enemies."

"I don't think so, Donner." Tascoe shook his head. "I'm not fool enough to go up against you unarmed."

"I think you are." Donner shifted slightly, and Julia bit down on her lip to keep from crying out as she saw the muzzle of his gun brush lightly against the strawberry-blond head nestled on his shoulder. "It's you or the child, Tascoe. What's it going to be?"

But already Dean Tascoe was bending to his ankle. With a grunt he straightened, and the next moment both his weapons went sailing through the bright moonlight, landing by the porch.

"Now I'll face you like a man, Tascoe. And in a minute I'll watch you die like a dog," Donner said, and this time when he spoke Julia knew she was hearing the man behind the pleasantly bland mask that he usually wore.

She froze as Donner half turned, but he didn't even look in the direction of the shrubbery that concealed her. Instead he put Lizbet gently down in one of the wicker porch chairs. It creaked slightly as the little girl stirred and then curled up in its cushions.

She had to be drugged, Julia thought. Aside from everything else, the child had to see a doctor as soon as possible, to make sure that whatever Donner had given her would wear off safely. If she was ever going to get the child away from him, now was the time.

"Now, Julia—get her out of here!"

With a roar of rage, Tascoe rushed Donner as he descended the last step from the porch, taking the other man by surprise. Had he had a chance to grab one of his guns? Julia wondered, but even as the thought was racing through her mind she'd sprung into action, leaping lightly over the porch railing and scooping up the tiny figure of the sleeping child.

Swinging her leg over the railing, Lizbet held tightly in her arms, Julia started in alarm as she heard the first shot, then the second and the third. Jerking her glance to the two struggling figures on the lawn in front of the house, she saw Dean Tascoe—ex-cop, ex-alcoholic, ex-failure—slam backward from the force of the bullets ripping into him.

"Still two to go," Gary Donner said, swinging his smiling gaze around to Julia as if he'd never had any doubt she was there.

The next moment another shot rang out, even as the echoes from the previous ones were still dying away, and his free hand went immediately to his shoulder as his gun fell from his grip.

"You!" he said disbelievingly.

"Get Lizbet to the car and get out of here, honey," rasped Cord. He was in the doorway, and looking down Julia saw that he was standing in a pool of blood. He was clutching the door frame, his features contorted in pain.

"Get her out of here—*now!*" he said again, the words coming from him with an effort. Julia gave him one last agonized look and dropped to the ground running.

The little girl weighed next to nothing, but by the time they reached the car Julia's heart was pounding. How long could Cord hold out? she wondered frantically, placing the unconscious child next to her and buckling the seat belt around the tiny body with shaking fingers. She turned the keys in the ignition and the engine rumbled to life, but from the direction of the house came another, more ominous sound.

She'd heard a shot. There were two possibilities, she told herself light-headedly—either Donner had grabbed his gun or Cord had prevented him by taking him down. But she couldn't count on the latter, and she couldn't dwell on the paralyzing horror of the former.

She had to get Lizbet to safety—and she had to get backup for Cord. The nearest town was Mason's Corners, and if she could only reach it and get to a phone in time—

"I've *got* to," she muttered grimly under her breath as the Ford bucked over a rise in the laneway and came down hard. "Or die trying."

Dean Tascoe was dead. There was no way he had survived that fusillade of bullets, she thought with sharp sorrow as the

lane rushed by on either side of her, branches from the overgrown trees and bushes snapping wildly against the sides of the
car. The turnoff onto the main road came up too fast, and she
hit the brakes, wrenching the steering wheel hard and not
breathing again until the Ford stopped fishtailing and she re-
gained control.

Tascoe had died a cop. It was all he'd ever wanted, and in
the end he'd gotten his honor back. He'd deliberately thrown
his life away to buy her a few moments of precious time, and
it was up to her not to let him have died in vain—and to make
sure that Cord's agonizing ordeal hadn't been for nothing. Her
foot pressed down on the accelerator, and she kept her gaze on
the road ahead, but all she could see was those dark eyes,
clouded with pain, and the spreading pool of blood from his
shattered leg.

No ordinary man could have done it. But Cord Hunter wasn't
an ordinary man, and that was where Donner had miscalculated.
Everything else had gone according to his plan—Tascoe's impression that the man had been waiting for something was half
right, Julia told herself. Gary Donner had been waiting for
someone—he'd known Cord would have been alerted by the
police that he'd shaken off the men tailing him, and he'd known
the first place they'd look for him would be where Lizbet was.

He'd second-guessed them all along, she thought with a spurt
of fear. He'd known *exactly* how they'd react, and he'd been
in control right from the start.

Was it possible he'd anticipated her fleeing with Lizbet, too?

She was letting her imagination run away with her, she told
herself angrily. The man might act like evil incarnate, but he
didn't have supernatural powers. He'd made a few lucky
guesses, that was all, and besides, she was only about five miles
away from civilization and safety—if she remembered correctly,
the turnoff to town would be coming up in a few minutes—

The steering wheel was wrenched from her hands, and then
she was losing control, the Ford skidding sideways in a sickening slide across the unstable graveled surface of the road.

She'd been *rammed!* Julia thought in shock as she desperately fought to get the car stabilized. Someone had shot out of

that last half-hidden laneway and rammed the back end of her car!

Then she stopped thinking and threw herself across the little girl on the seat beside her as the Ford's back tire blew and she felt the car starting to roll completely over.

Chapter 16

"**S**he's conscious. She even had some crushed ice a while ago."

Julia didn't know who Cord was talking to. She didn't care who he was talking to, and she didn't want *him* there, either, but telling him to go away would take more energy than she was capable of.

She just wanted to be left alone. If she didn't say anything, sooner or later everyone would go away.

Maybe that's how Lizbet had felt, she thought dully. Maybe the little girl had just wanted to be left alone all by herself, but instead she'd been dragged into more danger.

Donner had her. Donner would never be caught now.

"Yeah, the leg's fractured in two places, but with the cast and the crutches I can get around well enough." Cord was speaking again, in an undertone. Julia wondered briefly if it was Lopez he was addressing. "I blame myself. I should have known he would have had it all planned out."

"You came close to stopping him."

Willard Stewart's dry tones were uncharacteristically sympathetic, and she was so startled she almost opened her eyes.

What was her father doing here at the hospital? Earlier she'd heard a nurse saying that she'd only suffered a mild concussion, plus assorted cuts and bruises, so it wasn't as if she was in critical condition. What had possessed her father to drop everything and come to her bedside?

"Close isn't good enough," Cord was saying bitterly. "When he ran I fired, and if my damn leg hadn't given way just at that moment—"

"You did all you could, and so did that other detective—Tascoe, I think you said his name was?" Her father's voice was firm, and she heard Cord sigh.

"Dean Tascoe. And he lost his badge years ago—I was the one who blew the whistle on him. But he redeemed himself at the end." He took a deep breath. "He died in the line of duty. I'm going to make sure it's written up that way."

"A brave man. I'm grateful he gave his life to keep my daughter safe."

He could have been reading a stock report, there was so little emotion in his voice, Julia thought. Why did he stay? Why didn't they both just *go?*

"Detective Lopez told me that Donner is reenacting the deaths of the people who carried out those murders for him years ago."

Her father gave a little cough, and Julia heard the clink of a water pitcher against a glass. She knew exactly what she'd see if she opened her eyes—Willard Stewart, as immaculately turned out as ever, sipping at a glass of water as if he was addressing a board of directors meeting instead of speculating on the twisted reasons of a serial killer.

"That's why he took off in his car—he had it hidden out of sight, and he took a short cut. Everything had been planned toward that end—meeting Julia at that particular spot. In his mind he obviously was duplicating the crash that killed Diane Travis and robbed him of his son."

"That's odd." Her father sounded as if he was frowning. "He's stayed as close to his psychotic script as possible so far—didn't the Travis woman actually die in the explosion after the crash?"

"Yeah, they got Steven out just before the car blew. But I doubt Donner's splitting hairs now that he's got Lizbet." There was the clatter of something metallic and light, and Julia realized that Cord had risen to his feet and gathered his crutches. "Can you stay for a while? I'd like to check with Lopez and Stamp to see if there's any news about the search."

"Surely. She's my daughter, Hunter—I intend to stay as long as she needs me."

She understood now. Julia heard Cord making his way to the door, then the brief swell of busy hospital sounds as he opened it and left her alone with her father. Duty and obligation. Willard Steward would shirk neither. He would sit here with her till doomsday if need be, because she was his daughter, he was her father, and that was his obligation. She opened her eyes and met his.

"I thought you might be awake," he said calmly. "How do you feel?"

The dry, uninflected voice was Willard Stewart's, Julia thought in shock, but the man sitting beside her was someone she'd never seen before. Either that, or the blow to her head was making her hallucinate.

Unshaven—she'd *never* seen him unshaven—and with his normally smoothly brushed hair untidily out of place, he wasn't wearing the suit she'd imagined, but an old flannel shirt that she thought she remembered from decades ago. It was buttoned unevenly, and one side of his collar was flipped up to rasp against the silvery stubble on his chin. He had on a disreputable pair of stained chinos, and now she did remember—he'd worn them only when he'd been out on the water or working on the boat during those long-ago summers at the lake. He shifted slightly, and she saw with something akin to horror that Willard Stewart was wearing slippers jammed onto his bony bare feet.

He'd come out of his house and had appeared in public like *this?*

"Excuse my attire." He gave her a wintry smile. "I received the call that you'd been hurt sometime around three this morning. I came straight here."

He leaned over as she hoisted herself up against the stiff

hospital pillows and handed her a paper cup. It was filled with ice chips, Julia saw, and she took a few into her mouth gratefully.

"I heard you talking with Cord a few minutes ago. How—how does he look?" she asked, the image of her last sight of him filling her mind—the blood, the pain etched on his face, his hoarse voice shouting at her to take Lizbet and get her to safety—

"Like a man who was caught in a leghold trap. And you look like a woman who survived an accident that by rights you shouldn't have walked away from." A shadow crossed her father's patrician features. "The police tell me that all of Donner's acquaintances are being questioned, and his Friendship Center converts are being watched in case he shows up with the child. They'll find her, Julia."

"I don't think so, Father. I think we've lost her for good." She stared stonily ahead, avoiding her father's alert gaze and feeling the old emotions rising inside her. "Correction—*I* lost her. Cord and Dean Tascoe did all they could. Even King gave his life for her. I never should have taken on the responsibility of keeping her safe."

"That's foolish—" Willard Stewart began, but his daughter cut him off.

"Foolish, Father? I *saw* Donner come up to the car last night—did you know that?"

She raised the cup of ice to her cracked lips, but instead of reaching her mouth the chips fell onto the bedcover. She set the cup on the table beside her with a shaking hand.

"I lost consciousness when the car rolled the second time. I wasn't belted in, and I remember hitting my head against the glove box, but when I came to Lizbet was unhurt and that was all that mattered." She scooped the spilled chips of ice into her hand unseeingly, her eyes fixed on her father. "For a second I couldn't remember how the accident had happened, and when the passenger side door opened my first thought was that someone had come to help us."

"Don't relive it, Julia. You need to stay quiet—"

"But it was *Donner.*" She folded her fingers tightly over the ice in her palm. It was so cold it felt like it was burning her, and a detached part of her mind wondered if later she would find it had seared her skin. "It was Donner, and he was *smiling* at me—smiling as if he knew there was nothing I could do to stop him. I was wearing my gun, and I tried to get to it, but I couldn't move—"

"For God's sake, your *shoulder* was dislocated—"

"—and there was blood running into my eyes and onto Lizbet's T-shirt, Father, and I tried to hold onto her but he just lifted her out and *took* her. I—I *lost* her. She's gone for good— and *I* let it happen!"

And the boom came over and attacked him, Cord! Julia squeezed her eyes shut, fighting to control the panic that was ballooning inside her.

"I'm going to ring for a nurse." The dry voice sounded slightly alarmed. "This can't be good for you, Julia. You can't blame yourself for the machinations of a madman."

Too late she remembered how uncomfortable displays of emotion always made him feel. He was uncomfortable now, she saw. Under the light tan his face was pale, and the cool gray eyes held a hint of uneasiness.

Always in the past she had kept well inside the invisible but inviolate boundary that confined their relationship. Julia knew that she should make an effort to adhere to the rules that had governed them both all their lives, but suddenly she didn't care anymore.

"I'm not *ill*, Father. I don't need a nurse." She pushed her hair back with a trembling hand and realized that the ice she'd been holding had melted away to nothing. "I was responsible for keeping that child from harm and I *failed* her! Maybe reliving the moment that Donner took her from me is futile, but I can't help myself—I'll relive it for the rest of my life!"

Her voice had risen to a tremulous shrillness, and Willard Stewart laid an urgent hand on her arm, but she shook it off with agitated force. "I should have gotten to my *gun*, I should have guessed he would be *waiting* for us—dear God, I should have *died* before I let her go! *I* should have died!"

The wall around her emotions that had protected her all her

life wavered, crumbled and then came crashing down, letting the pain pour in with full force. Julia felt herself screaming inside, and she knew that at any moment those screams would become audible.

—and the rope rolled over her fingers and she started screaming and screaming—

"No!" Her father was on the bed beside her, his gray eyes stricken. "*No*, Julia—"

She looked at him blankly. "I should have *remembered,* Daddy! He told me to put the life jackets in, and I *forgot!* Davey drowned and it was all my fault and—and you *knew*, didn't you? You knew, and you never, never forgave me! *I* should have died, not *him!*"

For a moment their gazes locked. Her father's face was ashen with shock, and hers was drained of all color. His mouth moved soundlessly, as if for once the correct phrase had escaped him, or as if he had realized there was no correct phrase for the situation, and Julia suddenly blinked in confusion. She put a shaky hand to her forehead.

"Father, I—I'm sorry—"

"*What have I done?*" His voice was a raw, anguished whisper. "Dear God—you've blamed *yourself* for Davey's death all these years? *I* killed him, Julia—I took the life jackets out! It was *never* your fault!"

Over the hospital paging system a doctor was being called to emergency. Through the thin coverlet on the bed the melted ice had soaked her lap. Someone had brought her flowers already, Julia thought—cornflowers and daisies, like the ones that grew wild along the ditches at the lake house. She hadn't noticed them before.

"You—*you* took the life jacket out?" Her voice sounded like it belonged to someone else.

"I took it out the night before. I—I'd remembered seeing a rip in one of them, and I wanted to have it mended the next day." Her father's head was bowed, and his hands were clenched in his lap. "They were both in the Sunfish when I went looking for them late that night."

"Then I didn't—" Her fist went to her mouth. Her eyes were

wide and staring. "I *didn't* forget! I *must* have put them in the Sunfish, just like Davey told me to. It wasn't—it wasn't—"

"It wasn't your fault. My God, how could it have *ever* been, even if I hadn't been responsible for removing the damn thing. You were a child, Julia—a little girl! But I was Davey's father, and my son *drowned* because of my carelessness."

"You couldn't have known—"

"I saw the two of you go out in the Sunfish that morning!" Willard Stewart's head jerked up. His neck muscles were corded with tension, and his eyes blazed out of a face contorted with unbearable pain. "I saw you go out—and I forgot that I'd removed the life jacket! I was *annoyed* with him—annoyed that he'd taken the boat out with you in it without an adult present. I stood on the porch and I watched the two of you in the binoculars and I saw him fall *overboard,* Julia! I saw my son die— and I've lived with that guilt ever since."

"I thought you blamed me." Her tear-filled gaze searched his face. "I wanted to take his place, to do everything that he'd done so you would love me as much as you'd loved him. I was a better diver than he'd ever been, I took up archery because he'd been good at it—"

"I was proud of Davey—what man doesn't feel pride and love for the son who reminds him of himself? But *you*, Julia—" For the first time in his life, Willard Stewart reached out a tentative hand and touched his daughter's hair. "You I adored from the first moment I laid eyes on you."

His hand trembled on her hair, and his voice was low and urgent. "You were your mother all over again—but your mother before marriage to me tore her apart. You were so precious to me, and I knew I didn't deserve you. I knew you would never forgive me if you ever found out I was responsible for Davey's death—but believe me, if I'd had any inkling that you've carried that burden of guilt all these years…"

His words trailed off into silence, and Julia didn't speak. His hand dropped from her hair.

Cord had always told her she was more like her father than she knew. Now she could see it for herself, she thought. What she had taken for chilly reserve all her life had been the fear that had haunted her father for years—fear that if he ever revealed himself to the daughter he cared for so deeply, she would turn away from him forever. And so he had kept her at arm's length rather than risk seeing the rejection in her eyes he knew she would feel if he ever opened himself to her completely.

"You've told me now," she said softly.

"Yes." There was bitter self-recrimination in his tone. "I've told you now, because I see what hiding the truth has done to you all these years. You mustn't blame yourself for what happened with Lizbet, Julia—"

"Maybe you're right." Her gaze was steady. "But that doesn't change the fact that Donner has her. I'm going to get her back, Daddy."

He looked at her with sudden alarm. "No—leave it to the police. That monster nearly took your life once—"

"You of all people should understand." She reached for his hand, and his fingers tightened around hers. "You would have given your life to bring Davey back, wouldn't you? Not out of guilt, or to erase your own pain, but because you loved him. And I love that little girl, Daddy. She's counting on me—me and Cord."

"But you don't even know where Donner is," he protested. "He's dropped out of sight, Julia—how are you even going to find him?"

"How *are* you intending to find him?"

Cord stood in the doorway, and at the sight of him her heart missed a beat. She'd come close to losing him, Julia thought tremulously. He was all she'd ever wanted in the world, and she'd nearly lost him. She wouldn't risk it again.

"I'm not going to find him, Cord," she said evenly. "*We* are. I don't know how, but we're going to bring our little girl home."

His eyes met hers across the space that separated them, and then a corner of his mouth lifted in a slow smile that seemed to take in everything she'd left unspoken. Maybe it was going to be all right, she thought, her smile shaky. Ridiculously, she felt a fresh bout of tears come to her eyes, and she dashed them away, still holding his gaze.

"You're on, honey," Cord said softly. "Where do you want to start?"

"Has Lopez talked to Susan—" she began, but at that moment the phone beside the bed rang. Cord frowned, and her father raised an inquiring eyebrow.

"Do you want me to get it? It wouldn't be for me—I haven't let anyone know where I am." He started to reach for it as it rang a second time, but Julia stopped him.

"No!"

She knew who was calling her, she thought with cold certainty. She didn't know how she knew, but she did. She could sense him already. Cord met her eyes, and in his she saw the same knowledge.

The phone rang again, and she jerked it up so fast she almost dropped it.

"Hi, Julia. How's the head?"

The pleasantly casual tone, the solicitous concern and the realization that once more Donner had anticipated them robbed her of speech for the moment. She closed her eyes, fighting the nausea that swept over her at the sound of his voice. She heard her father's indrawn breath, and as she opened her eyes she saw Cord's expressionless features.

"I've got someone here I'm sure you'd like to talk to, but unfortunately she still hasn't said anything—not even to me. You know, getting the silent treatment from a five-year-old could get annoying after a while."

"Donner, get one thing straight." Julia gripped the phone's receiver so tightly that her knuckles whitened. "If you touch one hair—one *hair!*—of that child's head, I'll hunt you to the ends of the earth. I'll be the one that *you* have nightmares about—get it?"

Her voice throbbed with such intensity that for a moment the man on the other end of the line was silent. Then he spoke again, but this time there was an edge to his words.

"Something's changed," he said slowly. "You're not the woman you were yesterday, Julia."

"That's right, Donner." She fought to keep her tone even.

"Yesterday you got the better of me. That won't ever happen again."

"But I still have the child. I'd say the odds were definitely in my favor, wouldn't you?" She heard him exhale impatiently. "Let's cut to the chase, Julia. I guess you've finally figured out what this is all about, haven't you?"

"Two down and two to go. You lost the four members of your family years ago, and now you want revenge. Paul's dead, Sheila's dead, so that leaves Cord and me." Her voice hardened. "And Lizbet is Steven, who was taken away from you. But I'm not agreeing to any deal that includes her, Donner."

"I'm willing to lower my terms." The light voice took on a note of reasonableness. "It's Hunter I want. He was the driving force behind what happened to my people. The child is proving to be more of a liability than I'd figured on—God, every time I turn on the damn television I see a bad photo of myself staring out of the screen. I'll let you take her if you give me Hunter."

Julia's mind raced, and then she spoke, choosing her words with care. "Are you absolutely sure?"

"Of course I'm—" Donner broke off in mid-sentence, and she heard his indrawn breath. "He's with you now?"

"That's right."

"And you're offering yourself in his place." It wasn't a question, and for once she was grateful for the man's acuity.

"Losing you would be worse than losing his life," he continued slowly. "You see, I know all about the two of you and the way he's always loved you—it's the stuff legends are made of, isn't it?"

"Yes. But it cuts both ways, Donner," Julia said guardedly.

"I understand. Well, of course I *don't* understand that kind of selflessness, but I get what you're telling me—you'll trade your life for his and the child's. Call me a sentimental fool, but I accept." He gave a laugh of genuine amusement, and she closed her eyes in relief.

"Where do we meet you for the handover?" she asked, hoping he couldn't hear the tremor in her voice.

"You know what? Just because of all the trouble you two put me through last night, I'm going to let you sweat that one out yourselves. You've got two hours, Julia. Lizbet and I will be waiting for you.''

With a click the line went dead, and she stared at it disbelievingly.

"What did he say? Is he willing to deal with us?" Cord, balancing unsteadily on his crutches, was at her side.

"He's willing to give Lizbet up. He says she's become too much of a liability—I guess Lopez's manhunt has got him rattled," Julia said distantly. She looked at him, her eyes bleak. "Except we've only got two hours to meet with him—and he refused to tell me where he's hiding out.''

Chapter 17

Another of Donner's manipulative games, Julia thought frantically as she opened the passenger side door of her father's Lexus for Cord and waited while he threw his crutches into the back seat and maneuvered himself into the car's luxurious interior.

She ran around to the driver's side, clicking the button of the remote starter even before she opened the door, and the vehicle instantly purred to life. Maybe it only saved a second or two, she told herself, but with Donner's deadline seconds could prove valuable. She'd been grateful for the loan of her father's car, since her own was a write-off and Cord found it easier to climb in and out of than the Bronco.

"What the *hell* does he think he's playing at?" Cord exploded as they pulled away from the curb. "How in God's name are we supposed to guess where he is in a couple of hours!"

"He likes playing games," Julia said tightly. "But as far as he's concerned, he always plays fair. We have the key to his whereabouts—he just wants to see if we're smart enough to figure it out."

"It's not the Friendship Center or the property that Marshall bought for them." Cord stared out the windshield, his brows drawn together in a line. "Lopez checked them out thoroughly."

"We have to think the way he thinks." Julia gnawed at her thumbnail distractedly. "He's psychotic and he's evil. What else is he?"

"An arrogant son of a bitch," growled Cord.

"Exactly. That's the key to *him,* and that's part of the key to the puzzle. He's testing us because he'll only deal with a worthy opponent, but because he's Donner, even if we pass his test we're left feeling that he's been one step ahead of us all the time. He wants us to know that he knows more about us than we'll ever know about him."

She scowled. There was something she was missing, she thought—something that had struck her at the time but that she'd shoved aside.

Seashells at the seashore...

"Turn left here onto the freeway," Cord said suddenly, but she'd already jerked the steering wheel in that direction. She merged with the rest of the traffic on the on-ramp and then looked at him, their eyes meeting in understanding.

"The shells he ground into Jackie's carpet," she whispered.

"He's at the lake house," Cord agreed grimly. "He's showing us that he's even privy to confidential lab reports. I don't want you getting near him, Julia," he added with a worried frown.

"If he wants to deal with me, we're hardly in a position to argue with him," she said, keeping her eyes on the road. "Getting Lizbet back is the important thing."

"Getting you back was important," he said quietly. "You are back, aren't you?"

She glanced at him, her gaze steady. "I'm back. And nothing's ever going to take me away from you again."

"I wish you could have seen your father when he arrived at the hospital last night." He shook his head. "God, Julia—the man was out of his mind with worry. He really does love you."

"I know. We had a talk today—maybe the first real one

we've ever had," she said softly. "When this is all over I'll tell you about it."

"I'd like to hear it." His mouth curved wryly. "I'll tell you what—if Willard ever tries to pull his cool and frosty act again, we'll remind him of those bedroom slippers."

She was startled into laughter, but even as she looked at him her laughter died away. "I love you, Cord," she said with sudden fierceness. "No matter what I went through in the past, I *always* loved you. I *always* did."

"I love you, too, honey. I always will." His voice was soft, and it wrapped around her like velvet. "You fought your demons and won, didn't you?"

"Let's just say I found out they couldn't hurt me as much anymore." Flicking on her turn signal, she pulled onto the exit that led to the lake house.

"I still don't trust Donner. God, I wish I didn't feel so damned *helpless.*" Cord raked his hand through his hair and shifted his left leg uncomfortably. "I know he's got something up his sleeve—meekly handing Lizbet over and letting us walk out of there just isn't his style."

"He's not going to let us walk out of there. He's going to let you and her walk away." She didn't look at him. "I'm staying behind."

"I don't think so, honey." Now she did look at him, and his expression was as angry as she'd expected it to be. "I thought that's what we were just talking about, Julia—I thought you'd finally stopped blaming yourself—"

"I have," she said firmly. "This isn't about guilt or atonement, Cord. I don't plan on letting him kill me. But we have to get Lizbet out first, and then I'll—"

"You'll what? He'll make damn sure we're not armed, just the way he did with Tascoe last night. How the hell are you going to overpower someone like Gary Donner?"

"I don't *know!* But I think I've got a better chance of getting away from him than *you* do right now! Dammit, Cord—you can hardly get around!"

They'd come in from the other route that led to the lake house—subconsciously she hadn't wanted to pass the scene of last night's accident, Julia realized—and now they were on the road that led past Cord's old home. In a few minutes they would be at the lake house, and she had to make him realize that hers was the only possible alternative.

"Maybe so. But I still can't let you do it." His expression was set and stubborn.

"I've already agreed to the deal—" she began, but he cut her off.

"To *hell* with any deal that Donner thinks he has with you! It's *me* he wants—it's me he's always wanted. And it's me he's getting, Julia." His eyes were dark with pain. "How do you think I could ever survive losing you? How could I live with myself?"

"How am *I* supposed to survive, Cord?" Her vision blurred, and she almost missed the curving driveway onto the property. She smeared the heel of her hand angrily across her wet cheekbones. "You won't have a chance, and he'll *kill* you! How am I supposed to get through the rest of my life without you?" She pulled the car onto the grass verge just out of sight of the big old house and looked at him.

"I hope it doesn't come to that, honey." The anger had left his voice. "If there's any way you can get the cavalry back in time I know you'll do it. But if it doesn't work out that way—"

He saw the anguish that contorted her features, and suddenly his arms were around her, pulling her to him. "If it doesn't work out that way you know I'll never be far from you. What we have even Donner can't take away."

"I don't want a damned *eagle* on my windowsill at night!" she sobbed into his shirtfront. "I want *you!*"

She lifted her tearstained face to his and knew that she'd lost. He was the most tractable of men most of the time, she thought hopelessly. But when Cord Hunter made up his mind about something, even she couldn't persuade him to change it.

"You have me. I never belonged to anyone else but you," he said softly, and then his mouth was on hers and his arms were so tight around her that she could feel the heavy muscles in his arms tense. He wanted to take some part of her with him, she thought. He *knew* he wasn't coming back, and he didn't want to go into the darkness without the memory of her.

She strained against him, giving him the essence of herself, her hands desperately touching his face, his hair—and then he released her, his gaze lingering on hers as if he was saying goodbye already.

"We have to get up to the house," he said, pushing her hair from her eyes. "We'll leave your gun under the seat. The Whitefields' phone's been repaired already, and Mary and Frank are there with the kids."

He saw her look of surprise. "Frank fared about the same as you—just a slight concussion. He and Mary decided that the only way the children would get over what happened last night is if they kept things as normal as possible. They came back this morning."

"So I'll get Lizbet to them and phone Lopez to send a SWAT team out." Julia nodded. "Then I'll—"

"You'll wait for reinforcements. The gun's only for if something goes wrong and you need it to defend yourself," Cord said shortly. "I mean it, Julia—if Donner takes us both down, who's going to be left for Lizbet? She's already lost two parents."

He was right. There really was nothing left to say, she thought dazedly as she put the Lexus into gear again and heard the tires slowly crunching over the graveled drive. She kept the car at the lowest speed possible, not wanting to do anything that might alarm Donner inside the house, and when she got to the leafy glade just out of sight of the front door where she'd always parked her old Ford, she stopped.

"Gun under the seat," Cord said tersely as he got stiffly out. "I'll go in with mine so he doesn't get suspicious."

As they walked out of the shade into the sunshine she was struck by the incongruous beauty of the day. Summer had finally arrived, she thought dully, shielding her eyes against the glitter of the lake. There was a chance that after today she would always hate the season.

"So you figured it out." Gary Donner was standing on the flagstone path, his smile as welcoming as if he were their host for a weekend of boating and barbecues. "I knew you'd put two and two together and come up with the answer. Come on, let's talk over by the rock garden." He shook his head regretfully. "This must have been some place in its day, Julia. I guess your father let it run down, though, after Davey died?"

"I imagine it was painful for him to spend much time here after Davey drowned, yes," she agreed evenly. "However, that's past history, Gary. We're here for the child who's in jeopardy today."

He hadn't liked the fact that she'd used his first name, she saw with some surprise. That meant that he had vulnerable areas, too—and if he was vulnerable, he could make mistakes.

"We've changed the plan, Donner." Cord was a few feet behind them, and as he reached the rock garden it was obvious that the uneven terrain was making it hard for him to maneuver the unfamiliar crutches. "We've decided that—"

"You've decided that you're going to stay in exchange for the girl, not Julia."

Donner grinned, and the fact that he wasn't unattractive when he smiled sent a chill down Julia's spine. How many people had been taken in by that almost boyish countenance? For how many had that lighthearted grin, those twinkling green eyes, been the last things on earth that they'd seen?

"I had a feeling that was the way the cat was going to jump." He shrugged. "I'm easy. I'll kill you instead of her, Hunter."

His reaction was all wrong, she thought suspiciously. They'd expected to have to persuade him, but instead he was as unruffled as if—

She met his gaze and with a start saw that his eyes seemed almost as blue as the lake beyond. She looked again, and they were no color at all, and finally—*finally*—she knew what she was dealing with. He'd been watching her intently, and he tipped his head to one side quizzically.

"Such a serious look. I wonder what you think of me, Julia?"

"I think that sometime today you'll be going back to hell

where you belong, Gary," she answered him in as light a tone as he'd used. "Since you asked," she added.

"Somehow I can't see you sending me there," he said with a touch of anger in his voice. "Anyway, we're wasting time. Hunter, I'm sure you're armed. Get rid of your guns."

"I'm only wearing the one." With an effort, Cord unholstered his automatic and handed it to Donner. Julia stood silently by, wondering if this was yet another trap.

"I'll get little Lizzie, then." Donner winked at her. "You thought it was a double cross, didn't you? No, I'm a man of my word. Wait here—I'll only be a minute."

"As soon as he brings her, get her to the car and get out of here as fast as you can," Cord said in an undertone when Donner was out of sight. "He's always been a freaky bastard, but I don't know—there's something different about him today. He's planning something more, I know it."

"Maybe that's what he wants us to think," Julia said worriedly. "Cord, I can't leave you here with him."

"We've been through that," he said flatly. "Do what you can to get help, and then pray. Maybe that's really the only weapon we have against him now."

They both fell silent. As the minutes ticked by she felt her palms growing damp with nervousness.

"What the hell's *taking* him so long?" Cord exclaimed tensely, echoing her concern, but even as he spoke he was interrupted.

"She's still groggy, the little sweetheart, but I bet she's happy to be back with her Auntie Julia."

Julia's head jerked up. Coming down the flagstone path was Donner, and in his arms he held the fear-stiffened body of Lizbet. The child's eyes were blue and staring, and her hair looked lank and lifeless. Forgetting to be cautious, Julia ran to meet them, feeling as if her heart was about to crack in two.

"Lizbet!" Snatching the little girl from him, she peered intently into the pale, heart-shaped face, and then she held the tiny body to her tightly, her trembling hand smoothing the damp red hair. "Oh, *Lizbet,* baby."

Closing her eyes, she nestled her chin on the top of the silky head, inhaling the scent of little girl as if it was the most precious perfume in the world. Once upon a time she had known she could never have children of her own because she'd been afraid she wouldn't be strong enough to keep them safe, she thought, holding back the tears. Now she *did* have a child— Sheila's last, most loving legacy to her—and she knew that whatever strength was needed she would have to find.

"Don't be afraid anymore, pumpkin—we're going to take you home," she murmured into the little girl's hair. "We're going home, Lizbet."

"Let me see her." Cord was beside her, and as Julia loosened her grip on the little girl enough so that the wide blue eyes could meet his, he smiled, gently touching a strand of the strawberry red hair. "My two girls," he said softly. "My two sweethearts." A shadow passed behind his eyes, and he sighed. "Get her to the car and go, honey. I won't feel easy until I know you're both safely out of here."

"Oh—did I forget to tell you that *my* plan's been changed, too?" Donner shook his head ruefully. "Sorry about that, Hunter. Julia can go, but the little darling stays here with us. Put her down next to her Uncle Cord before you leave, Julia…and if you've got any bright ideas about taking off with her like you did last night, don't forget that I'm the only one here who's armed." He smiled. "I wouldn't be aiming at you, either. I'd take out the kid before you got halfway down the path."

"I was right. This was a double cross from the start, wasn't it?" Julia's arms hugged the small, limp body closer to her protectively. In defeated anguish she met Donner's mocking gaze over the top of Lizbet's head.

"Let them go, Donner." Cord's features were stone. "Whatever death you've got in mind for me I accept, only let Julia and Lizbet leave safely."

"You're going to die the way I want you to no matter what. But I would have thought even you would have doubts about entrusting a child's safety to the fallen Guardian Angel." Gary Donner grinned. "I mean, her track record lately certainly has shaken *my* confidence in her. No offense, Julia," he added, darting a bland look at her white face. "But let's face it—you had Lizbet last night and I got her away from you. I just wouldn't feel good about letting you look after her now, and I'm sure Cord must be wondering—"

"I never had any doubts. I still don't." Cord's eyes met hers as if the other man wasn't there. "There was only one little girl that you didn't take care of, honey, but I think even she's come home safely now, hasn't she?"

His gaze held hers for a heartbeat, but in that heartbeat were all the years they'd had together and the eternity that their souls would share, even if both their physical lives ended today. Julia felt the last of the bonds that tied her to the tragedy of the past slip away.

Cord trusted her with Lizbet's safety. And she trusted herself.

Goodbye, Davey, she thought with a rush of love. *Wish your little sister luck.*

"She came home safe and sound, Cord," she said quietly. "She's part of me again—and she and I are strong enough to take care of Lizbet."

"What the hell are you two talking about?" For the first time Donner's smooth voice had an edge to it, and Julia flicked him a contemptuous glance.

"You wouldn't understand if we told you," she said briefly. She switched her attention to Cord, taking in the almost unnoticeable tenseness in his posture and reading the signal in his eyes.

"Always have, Cord," she said in a whisper.

"Always will, honey," he answered softly, his gaze holding hers almost desperately.

"Put the damn kid down and just go," Donner snapped, raising his gun and leveling it at her. His finger tightened on the trigger threateningly. "Once again you screwed up big-time, Stewart, but this time you've lost everyone you care about—"

"*Now,* Julia—run!"

As the hoarse command tore from his throat, Cord threw himself in front of the other man, his crutches clattering to the ground. Julia just had time to see him knock Donner's aim sideways as the gun went off, its report shockingly loud, but as the two men fell to the ground she was already sprinting down the path, Lizbet held tightly in her arms.

It was all she could do not to look back, but she didn't dare. Racing around the corner of the house, the little girl's stiff body tense against hers, Julia felt as if her limbs were moving sluggishly through some thick, obstructive medium.

Donner was evil. He would kill Cord, and her only chance of saving him lay in speed. She had to get Lizbet to safety and then get back here as soon as she could, even if that meant breaking her promise to Cord and returning before help arrived. Even as she ran she was fumbling in her pocket for her keys, but as they came in sight of the car she dropped them. She bit back the curse that rose to her lips and gently set Lizbet on the ground as she picked them up.

"Come on, honey," she said with soft urgency, tugging at the little girl's hand. "We have to leave right away."

Lizbet stared at her, her blue eyes no longer vacant and clouded. She shook her head, the red hair swinging with the movement.

"Lizbet, we have to *go*," Julia urged. "Come on, I'll carry you." She bent to take the child into her arms once more.

"The bad man put something under that car, Auntie Julia." Julia froze, and Lizbet spoke again, her tone stubbornly serious. "I don't want to get in it. He wanted to hurt you."

She looked up at Julia, her small arms folded across her chest, and her grubby pink sneakers toed into the dirt. Beneath the stubbornness lurked fear.

"He—he put something underneath that car, pumpkin?" Her voice was so clear and so *sweet*, Julia thought wonderingly. It sounded like little bells—and it had rung out in time to save both their lives.

"He went right under. He was lying on his back on the grass, and then he came out and he was smiling. We shouldn't go in that car, Auntie Julia."

"You're right, we shouldn't. And we're not going to." She took the tiny hand in hers. "But we're going to trick the bad man, honey, so he thinks we did get in that car."

"Then will he let Uncle Cord go?" Lizbet sounded worried, and Julia's heart turned over.

"I don't think so. I think I'm going to have to come back for Uncle Cord, sweetie. Let's run into the woods a little, okay?"

Donner would be wondering why he hadn't heard an explosion yet, she realized, looking over her shoulder as she and Lizbet ran along the path that led to the Whitefields' house. She'd gone back and forth along that path so many times in the past that she'd probably worn it a few inches lower all by herself, she thought. Even now she could hear the sound of the Whitefield twins coming faintly from beyond the trees.

"This is far enough, honey." They were still in sight of the Lexus, and Julia pointed the remote at the car, hoping that she was still within its range. "Plug your ears, pumpkin."

She pressed the button, and the car started immediately. She could hear it from where they stood, the well-tuned engine ticking over like a Swiss watch—

A shocking *whump!* came from the Lexus, and instantly it was obscured from sight as a giant fireball enveloped it, reaching up to the lower branches of the pine she'd parked under. It was followed by a second, even louder explosion—the gas tank had just blown, Julia thought, stunned—and a fusillade of tiny sparks showered down from the sappy boughs of the pine. It reminded her of the crackle and pop of juniper branches on a bonfire, or—

A sound unlike anything she'd ever heard in her life came from the direction of the house—a hoarse cry so visceral it sounded like someone's soul was being torn from their body. Julia's grip on Lizbet tightened. Her blood felt like it had turned to ice in her veins.

Cord, she thought in anguish. He would have heard the explosion. He thought she was dead—he thought they were *both* dead!

And there was nothing she could do about it until she got Lizbet to safety, she told herself tightly. She was going to have to let him—and Donner—think they were dead for a little while longer.

"It smells like Christmas," Lizbet said softly, her blue eyes fixed on the sparks still floating up from the pine tree.

She obviously hadn't heard Cord call out, Julia thought thankfully, and holding Lizbet close, her heart suddenly filled with so much love for the fragile-looking little girl in her dirty sneakers and her torn T-shirt that she felt it would burst. Fragile she might seem, she thought, but she'd been bequeathed tough and sturdy genes. Lizbet was going to be all right—in fact, more than all right. She was going to be a handful one of these days. Julia could hardly wait.

But Donner might come along at any moment to check on his handiwork, she realized, her stomach clenching again, and her only weapon was a piece of twisted and melting metal somewhere in the inferno that had once been her father's Lexus. He'd never intended to let either of them go, and Willard Stewart had been right—he was keeping as close to the script of his psychotic plan as possible.

Diane Travis hadn't been killed in the crash, she'd been killed in the explosion that followed.

Sheila shot, Paul stabbed, I was to die in an explosion, and Cord—

The fourth and final member of Donner's family, and according to most accounts the most blindly devoted to his evil father figure, had been Rickie Dee Morris. And Rickie Dee had chosen a madman's death for himself.

He'd driven his vehicle off the top of the parking garage.

That was the death Donner had planned for Cord, Julia thought—which meant that she had more than enough time to get help, because there wasn't a building high enough for Donner's purposes within thirty miles. He was going to have to drive Cord to the location, and surely Lopez could set up roadblocks in time—

"There's Uncle Cord and the bad man," whispered Lizbet, her eyes wide.

Shrinking into the undergrowth around them and pulling the child close, Julia squinted past the still-burning Lexus to the house and saw with horror that Cord was attempting to run toward the blaze, Donner catching up to him easily. Even as she watched, the other man viciously swung something that looked at this distance to be the lever of a tire jack down on the base of Cord's skull.

Cord fell heavily to the ground, the aluminum crutches flashing in the sunlight as they fell with him. As efficiently as if he really was changing a tire, Donner tossed his makeshift weapon into the open trunk of the car that he must have just parked there, then bent to the body in the driveway.

"Auntie Julia, look at the bird!" Lizbet was tugging at her sleeve, but Julia didn't take her eyes from the terrible tableau she was witnessing.

"Not now, pumpkin," she murmured through dry lips. It was all she could do not to burst from cover and run, screaming imprecations at the soulless being she now knew Gary Donner to be. She bit down on her lower lip so hard she broke the skin, but she didn't even notice the taste of blood in her mouth. She watched helplessly as the man she loved was dragged like a carcass across the gravel and hoisted into the front passenger seat of the waiting vehicle by a surprisingly strong Donner.

"It's looking at us, Auntie Julia. It wants us to follow it," Lizbet said at her side, and once again Julia shushed her.

"Just a minute, sweetie. I want to see where the car goes."

If he turned right at the end of the driveway he would be bound for the freeway, and if left, he would be traveling through several small towns and hamlets before he got to a city of any size. He was already halfway to the road, and in a minute she would have the knowledge that might save Cord's life. Julia kept her eyes fixed on the intersection of the driveway and the road.

Nothing appeared. She could still hear the car, though the sound of its engine was getting fainter, and the dust cloud that had risen from the driveway was already beginning to settle, but of the vehicle itself there was no sign. Throwing caution aside, she rose to her feet and squinted disbelievingly through the obscuring foliage that blocked her view.

Before the driveway ended, there was a rutted track that meandered through the property and then skirted the lake. She could just make out the glint of sun on metal disappearing in that direction.

Had he taken a wrong turn? She dismissed the thought immediately, her mind racing. Gary Donner didn't make foolish mistakes. If he'd turned onto the lake track he'd done so for a reason, but what that reason was she couldn't imagine. The track petered out eventually into a dead end. In fact, it stopped at the top of the cliff overlooking the lake that the locals called—

"Dear God—he's heading for Maiden's Leap!" she breathed, her blood turning to ice. "He's going to send the car off the *cliff!*"

"He's trying to *tell* us something. Look!"

Her eyes still wide with horror, she turned distractedly to Lizbet, but as her gaze moved past the child she froze.

"That's the biggest bird I've ever seen in my life," the little girl said in awe. "What kind is he, Auntie Julia?"

"A—a golden eagle," Julia said in a hoarse whisper. "I've never seen one this far east, and I've never seen one so *huge.*"

The massive bird was perched on a nearby fallen tree, his talons gripping the bark securely. He had to be almost four feet long from the tip of that curved beak to the end of his tail, she thought incredulously, and then caught her breath as the bird rose and spread his wings as if he was stretching his muscles to ready himself for flight. The brown feathers shone like mahogany in the sun, and his wingspan was well over eight feet. The bird inclined his head at them, the golden wash over his neck that gave him his name catching the light and seeming to create a glow around him.

I felt sure that I really had become that eagle....

"Cord?" Her voice was so faint she wasn't even sure that she'd spoken aloud, but the golden head swiveled in her direction, and the golden eyes held hers. She was close enough to see the tiny speck of green in the right iris, like the reflection of a perfect summer's day.

"No, it *can't* be," she breathed, her hand to her throat.

She could hear the excited shouts of the Whitefield twins just beyond the woods, and then Mary's voice, calling for Frank.

They would have heard the explosion and seen the smoke. They would be coming to investigate—out here in the country neighbors looked out for each other. Lizbet would be safe with them.

The eagle rose in the small clearing and circled gracefully around their heads. He swooped down, landing only a few feet away from Lizbet.

"Does he want us to follow him?" the little girl said, her upturned face full of unafraid wonder. The eagle made an awkward little hop, bridging the gap between them, but even as Julia gasped and reached for Lizbet the child reached out and touched the bowed golden head. The bird made a soft skirling cry deep in his throat, and then turned and half-flew, half-hopped a few feet away from them.

Julia could hear the voices coming closer now, and she made up her mind. "I think he wants *you* to follow him, pumpkin. He's going to take you to Mary and Frank—can you hear them? The eagle is just here to make sure you're not afraid."

"I'm not afraid, Auntie Julia." Lizbet took a few steps forward, and as she approached the eagle hopped ahead, and then stopped as if he was waiting for her. "But aren't you coming with us?"

"I'll be with you later, sweetie. Let Mary and Frank know what happened, and tell them I've gone to find Uncle Cord, okay?"

But already Lizbet was running toward the massive bird, and as Julia watched she saw it fly farther into the woods and then land again.

Lizbet would be safe. Within seconds she would be with the Whitefields. Julia hesitated one last time and then turned toward the house.

She didn't have her gun anymore, she thought frantically, giving the Lexus a wide berth as she raced past it. She needed a weapon, but where was she going to find one? Her father had never been a hunter, and Cord's father had come back from Vietnam with an aversion to guns of any kind. She'd only once ever seen Jackson Hunter kill anything, and that had been out of necessity. A rabid dog had wandered onto the property and he'd gotten his old crossbow from the garden shed and—

Even as the memory flashed through her mind she was veering across the lawn to the once snug little building where Jackson Hunter had stored his tools and his garden equipment. She hadn't been in there for years, but she remembered where the crossbow had been kept—high in the beams of the shed, where curious children couldn't reach it.

He could have taken it with him, she thought despairingly, or it could have been rusted beyond use after all this time, or she wouldn't be able to operate the thing—

She shut off the train of thought coldly. She had a brief window of time in which to find a weapon—*any* weapon—cut across country and get to the cliff before Donner could finalize his terrible plan. He would have to stay to the track, which meant that she had at least ten more minutes before he reached Maiden's Leap, but by cutting through the woods at the other side of the house her journey could be made in less than half that time.

The shed was locked. She stared at the wooden door in disbelief, and then she turned and ran back a few paces. Digging the balls of her feet into the springy turf, she charged at the door, her shoulder slightly lowered and her arms crossed tightly at her chest, and just as she reached it she turned sideways, slamming into it with all the force she could muster.

The rusty lock burst from its screws and the door swung open, but she let her momentum carry her to the back of the shed. Her gaze lit on the sturdy workbench by the wall, and she hurried toward it, mentally judging the distance between it and the rafters. It would do, she thought rapidly, clambering up onto it. If the crossbow was there at all she should be able to see it.

Standing upright on the rock maple workbench, she rose to her tiptoes and peered into the gloomy recesses of the rafters that Cord's dad had covered with plywood. This was where he'd stored light, bulky items that he seldom used, like plastic sheeting and wire peony cages. Her reaching fingers scrabbled at a flat package wrapped with an oilcloth and felt the unmistakable shape of a crossbow stock.

"Thank you, God," Julia whispered, relief flooding through her.

She jumped down from the workbench, her precious parcel in her hands, and unwrapped it quickly on the lawn outside. It had been protected from the damp, at least, she thought, running a finger along the clean steel of the curved bow and narrowing her gaze on the woven steel of the string. She flipped back one last fold of the oilcloth and grabbed the bolt that in crossbows took the place of an arrow.

She'd never used one, but she'd seen them in action, and crossbow accuracy relied on the same set of skills as archery— a steady hand, keen sight and an ability to correctly judge the flight of the projectile. The weapon could be likened to an ordinary archer's bow mounted on the stock of a gun, Julia thought—except that it took a whole lot more strength to pull back a woven steel string. This one would probably weigh out at about a hundred and fifty pounds of pull before she could slip it over the metal pin that held it in readiness for the trigger to be released.

There was a pair of old leather gloves folded up with the oilcloth, and she took them, too, knowing that they might make the difference between success and failure. Strapping the crossbow onto her back and jamming the bolt and the gloves under the leather strap where it crossed her chest, she took a deep breath, but just as she was about to start running, she hesitated.

Growing by the entrance to the shed were the tall, slender stalks and deep blue lupin-like flowers of the plant Jackson Hunter had always called monkshood. For the space of a heartbeat Julia stared at them, her brows drawn together and a nebulous plan forming in her mind.

A minute later she was on the run, skimming lightly over the low hedge that marked the boundary of the lawn and pounding up the hill that led to the small woods before the cliffs.

She'd started running this spring with King, after too long a period of sedentary laziness, and now she was glad she had. The hill was blazingly hot under the late afternoon sun, and by the time she reached the shade of the trees her clothes were soaked with sweat. She plunged into the relative gloom of the woods and promptly tripped over a half-hidden tree root.

You're not going to make it. He's probably at the cliff already, and here you are lying with your face in a pile of old leaves. You've lost him—admit it.

"Or freakin' die *tryin',*" Julia grunted fiercely, getting painfully to her knees. "If Tascoe could give everything he had, then I can, *too.*"

She set off at the same pace as before, the crossbow banging heavily on her spine with every step and her gaze alert for any more of nature's booby traps. When she felt the ground begin to rise beneath her feet, she knew she was on the last leg of her life-or-death race. The woods covered the final steep hill that eventually turned into the open area at the cliffs.

Her breath was coming in labored rasps, and every muscle in her legs felt as if it was screaming, but even as she wondered how much longer she could go on without collapsing she saw the dappled sunlight ahead that marked the edge of the woods and the grassy clearing of Maiden's Leap, and she put on one last spurt of speed, finally staggering to a halt behind one of the last trees.

Her eyes were stinging with sweat, and she leaned against the tree gasping, wiping the back of her hand across her face. Her vision cleared, and all of a sudden the knife-like pain under her ribs had nothing to do with exertion.

Donner's car was about twenty feet away from the edge of the cliff. Its motor was racing, although the driver's side door was open, and she could see the metal glint of one of Cord's crutches jammed diagonally under the steering wheel. Its tip had to be somehow secured against the gas pedal, she thought, the blood draining from her face. She could just make out a still-unconscious Cord slumped in the passenger seat—but where was Donner? And why hadn't the car shot off the cliff already?

The answer to both those frantic questions was immediately apparent. On the far side of the car Gary Donner stood up. In his hands he held a length of tree limb, and from the way he was pulling on it, his face contorted with the effort, it was obvious he was using it as a lever to pry something away from in front of the rear tire.

Fumbling with the leather strap across her chest, Julia darted another quick look at the clearing. Now that she knew what to look for she could see it—a boulder jammed in front of the rear tire on the side of the car facing her. Donner was prying at its twin, and when he'd rolled it out of the way he'd start work on this one. He was using a tree limb instead of taking the risk of pushing the rock out with a foot because as soon as the second boulder rolled out of the way, there would be nothing to stop the car from shooting forward across the short strip of grass and then off Maiden's Leap into thin air.

But watching Gary Donner get run over by his own car wasn't what she was worried about. Watching the man she loved plunge to his death in the lake far below was.

"And that's why I'm here, Donner—to stop you before you can do it," Julia said in an undertone, pulling on the leather gloves and unclipping the carrying strap from the crossbow. Out of the corner of her eye she saw Donner's head jerk up, as if he'd heard her almost inaudible words, and she froze in fear.

There was no *way* the man could have heard her, especially with the engine of his car racing deafeningly right beside him. He had to be almost fifty yards away from her—it was *impossible* for any human to have hearing so keen. She held her breath, not letting it out until Donner, after one last wary look around, resumed his task.

At the end of the crossbow was a metal stirrup, and she inserted her sneaker-clad foot into it. Bending over, the butt end of the stock braced against her breastbone, she grasped the woven steel string of the bow and tried to pull it toward her and the metal pin at the end of the stock it was meant to slip over.

It didn't budge.

Grunting with effort, she tried again, and this time succeeded in pulling the steel string a few inches before her strength gave out. Looking up, she was just in time to see Donner fall backward as the rock on the far side of the car slipped free and rolled away.

He was going to *make* it. She was going to be standing here, still pulling on this damn string, at the moment the car with Cord in it plunged over Maiden's Leap.

This time when she strained against the woven steel bowstring she felt something pop in the muscles between her shoulder and her neck, but she ignored the searing pain that ripped through her and kept pulling. She had no choice, she thought hazily, clenching her jaw with the strain and feeling the steel biting through the thin leather of the gloves—if her foot slipped out of the stirrup now the weapon would recoil on her, the stock smashing into her breastbone with enough force to break it. The bowstring was only a few inches away from the metal pin, then an inch, and finally it was level with it, but she still had to pull it tighter to slip it securely over, and she had no more strength left.

"Or. Die. *Trying.*" Julia gasped, and on the last word the woven steel string slipped from her exhausted grasp—

—and neatly behind the metal pin that secured it.

Her whole body trembling, she slipped her foot from the stirrup and looked up. Donner was straining at the rock nearest her, and even as she watched she saw it move a little. In the front seat of the car she saw Cord's body lurch forward and then fall back against the seat from the sudden jerk.

She started to peel off the leather gloves, but then thought better of it. All that was left was to drop the bolt into the shallow groove that it sat in, just ahead of the metal pin, aim her sights on Donner and pull the trigger.

That would be all she would have left to do if Gary Donner had been anything other than what he was, she thought grimly. But he was the brain behind the Bradley farmhouse, the killer of her best friends and the one who stood poised to take from her the only man she'd ever loved. She had one last precaution to take.

"Monkshood, sometimes called wolfsbane, Julia—because its poison is so deadly people used to use it to kill predators. Never touch it, honey...."

Jane Hunter had warned her about the plant years ago. Now maybe the knowledge she'd passed on would help save her son's life.

The dark blue flower that she'd ripped out of the garden by the shed lay on the ground in front of her, its roots still earthy. Holding the bolt by one end, Julia crushed the other into the wolfsbane's roots, breaking the plant apart and exposing the white fleshy pith. She could see the juice of the roots spurting out, and in seconds the tip of the bolt was glistening with the most poisonous part of the plant. Keeping it well away from her, she dropped the bolt into the slot of the crossbow.

She'd prepared herself and her weapon as well as she could, she thought. Now all she could do was pray for a steady hand and a true aim.

Tossing the gloves aside, she raised the stock to her aching shoulder. The old crossbow had a primitive sight and, narrowing her gaze, she brought it in line with Donner's back. The weapon wasn't a gun, no matter how much it looked like part of one. In order for the bolt to kill Donner instantly she would have to hit his heart.

"And I'm pretty sure he doesn't even have one," she murmured, lodging the stock more securely against her shoulder. She took a deep breath, and then another, willing her heartbeat to slow, and her finger tightened on the trigger. Donner was heaving backward on the tree limb, but she forced herself to concentrate only on him and not on his progress.

She was ready.

"Donner!"

Even before she uttered the second syllable of his name his upper torso twisted around to face her, his arms and the lower part of his body still straining against the boulder, and at that exact moment she gently squeezed the trigger of the crossbow.

The bolt flew through the air. Donner's terrible eyes widened. The bolt lodged itself in his left breast.

And the boulder rolled free.

Chapter 18

"*No*, God! *Noo!*"

The scream was ripped from her throat with violent anguish, but her prayer went unanswered. Its engine whining, Donner's car shot forward at top speed toward the edge of the cliff and then over it, sailing into the sky for about twenty feet before it started to fall.

Julia was running, her heart feeling like it had ballooned in her chest and was about to burst, her mouth open in a silent rictus of shock as she watched the car's downward trajectory. *Cord* was in there! He was *falling*—the car was *falling*, with him *in* it! She couldn't *allow* it—not now! Not when she'd been so *close* to—

She stumbled and fell only feet from the lip of the cliff, and on her hands and knees she scrambled to the very edge.

In the bright sunshine it looked like a toy thrown by a petulant child. Nose downward from the heavier weight of the engine block, the car plunged into the beautiful blue waters of the lake far below and sank from view.

There had to be some mistake, she thought, her cracked and bleeding lips stretching into a smile. Because after everything the two of them had been through—after they'd lost each other and then painfully found their way back, after Tascoe's sacrifice, Cord's sacrifice, her efforts over the last half hour—

Well, of *course* it was a mistake! It was some kind of cosmic joke! And yes—she could see the irony, she could appreciate it, but now she was ready for it to end.

"You nearly did it, Julia."

She scrambled to her feet and whirled around. Donner was lying on the ground where the car had been, one arm supporting his weight as he lay there. The torn earth bore mute witness to the force with which the tires had spun the vehicle forward.

"You bring him back," she said with insane calm. *"You bring him back!"*

The silvery eyes looked at her in amusement. "That's beyond my capabilities. But I'm flattered you'd ask."

She stared at him, and as she did she saw with horror his hands move to the shaft of the bolt protruding from his chest. He gave it a tug and then frowned. He tugged again, and it slipped out a few inches. He paused and smiled at her.

"You really thought you could kill me, didn't you? I somehow had the impression you knew it was impossible." He shook his head, but despite his casual manner his skin was slick with sweat and his face had an unhealthy pallor.

"Who are you?" Julia whispered. *"What* are you, Donner?"

"Well, for starters, that's not my name." He pulled at the bolt with both hands, but his palms were covered in his own blood and his grip slipped. "And secondly, this isn't enough to stop me. You might want to start running, Julia."

"I don't think so." He looked worse than he had a moment ago, she thought. In fact, he looked *much* worse.

Donner let go of the bolt and touched his lips gingerly, as if they felt painful. He blinked at her and rubbed his eyes, leaving a smear of blood across his forehead.

"Whyn't you thinzo?" He looked disconcerted, and tried again, this time making an obvious effort to pronounce the words correctly. "Why…don't you…?"

He gave up, and stared at her with suddenly fearful eyes.

"Monkshood, known as wolfsbane," Julia quoted softly to

him. "It's poison, Donner, and it's in you. They used to use it to kill predators." She turned from him and started to walk toward the edge of the cliff, toeing off her sneakers as she did so.

"No!" Donner said thickly from behind her.

She glanced over her shoulder at him and started to pull her T-shirt over her head. His vision would be gone by now, she thought calmly. In a moment the organ her bolt might or might not have pierced would stop beating.

"I told you I'd send you back home today, Donner," she said, but even as she spoke she saw the bulging green eyes start from his head in one last convulsion, and then he fell back onto the dirt.

She'd done everything she'd set out to do—well, almost everything, she thought, smiling to herself. There was just one last task ahead of her, and God willing, she would be equal to it. She stepped out of her jeans and took a last two steps forward.

"Why did the maiden leap from the cliff?"

She knew the answer to that, Julia thought. She'd *always* known.

"Because she loved him so," she said out loud. Raising her arms high above her head and taking a deep breath, she dove off Maiden's Leap....

It was a perfect summer's day, and the air was cool wine pouring against her skin. No *wonder* Cord had wanted to be a bird, she thought, feeling laughter bubble up inside her. It was indescribable, it was miraculous, she was *flying!* Her feet were pointed so tightly together behind her that she felt as if they had been transformed into a tail, and her outstretched arms and flatly clasped hands cut the air like a knife.

And then she had entered another element, and the water closed over her like silk.

It was deep here, Julia thought, unafraid as she sped downward through the waters of the lake. It was deep and it was clear, but she couldn't look yet—she was still diving too fast. She felt the drag begin, slowing her down as she began to carefully shallow out her descent, and then she allowed herself to open her eyes.

Donner's red car was sitting upside down about ten feet ahead of her on the bottom of the lake. She swam toward it like a fish, knowing that everything in her life had come down to this and thankful that she was ready.

There was still air escaping from the trunk, but to her relief she saw that the passenger side window had been rolled down, which would make it easier to open the door. Her Cord was in there, she thought, swimming closer. He was unconscious, perhaps badly hurt, but he was there.

He wasn't unconscious, and except for his broken leg he wasn't badly hurt, but as she opened the door she saw that Donner hadn't taken any chances with him. His arms had been duct-taped in front of him to the strap of a seat belt, and he was desperately trying to pull something out of the top of the cast on his leg.

He looked up as she opened the passenger door, and despite the fact that he was obviously almost out of air he gave her a dreamy smile, his eyes unfocused. Then he motioned her away and bent to his task again.

He was a very stubborn man, Julia thought resignedly. He probably always would be. But she was a stubborn woman. She pushed his bound hands out of the way and reached into the space between the cast and his leg.

She found it immediately. Pulling the bone-handled knife from its sheath, she sawed frantically at the tape on his hands until it parted and he was free. She lifted his bad leg out of the car, held onto his hand, and then they were both shooting up toward the shimmering gold-green spangles high above their heads.

They broke the surface together, and all of a sudden her body was telling her just how starved of oxygen it had really been. She coughed and slipped underwater again for a moment, and then she bobbed up and coughed once more.

"Dear God, honey—is it really you?" Cord's voice cracked incredulously, and then he was right beside her, his pain-filled gaze on her as if he couldn't believe what he saw. His features were carved with grief. "I thought—I heard the explosion and

I thought—'' He reached out, his fingers brushing lightly against her wet hair, and she saw the wild joy leap in his eyes.

"I'm real," she said softly, her hand reaching up to hold his briefly. "I'm real, and Donner's dead. And I think you already know that Lizbet's safe."

He was treading water like she was, both of them gathering strength to swim those last twenty feet to land. One of the tiny blood vessels in his left eye had broken, but in the right one she could see the speck of green, like the reflection of a perfect summer's day.

"She made it to the Whitefields, honey." He swallowed a mouthful of water and choked, his eyes never leaving her face. "But how in God's name did you *get* here?"

He wouldn't believe her if she told him, Julia thought, looking into the dazzling blue of the sky to the cliff high above. Now that it was over, she could hardly believe it herself. Except that he was her Cord, and he believed in magic and legends. If anyone could believe her, he would. She touched his face wonderingly, and then his arm was around her and his mouth was on hers for a long, sweet moment.

She pulled away from him as they both started to go under again, and pointed into the sky.

"I flew." She smiled at him, her heart in her eyes. In his were all the years of love they'd had together, and all the years to come.

"I flew straight back into your arms," she added softly, and then they both struck out for shore.

Epilogue

Julia looked up as she heard Cord's brand-new SUV roll into the drive. He'd gone to town to get a blade for his circular saw, and of course Lizbet had gone with him, wearing the tiny tool belt he'd fashioned for her out of a scrap of leather when she'd appointed herself his number-one renovation helper. She smiled and wiped her hands on a dish towel. Jelly making was hot work, but the lake house smelled like the essence of summer. When the snow was on the ground again, months from now, opening up these jewel-like jars of raspberry preserves would be like having July back for a while.

She glanced at the clock. She still had time to make a pie for after dinner, she decided. Her father was coming, and she'd discovered that his once-tart exterior had held a surprisingly sweet tooth. But first things first—her husband and her gift of a daughter were home, and she wanted to sit with them on the porch for a while.

She had something to tell them both. Touching her still-flat stomach and smiling a secret little smile, she went to the screen door, then frowned. Kicked under the baseboard was one of King's favorite toys—a foolishly small and fluffy stuffed rabbit that he'd had since he'd been a pup. She picked it up, a brief sadness crossing her features, and then she froze.

From outside on the porch she could hear a noise that had once been part of her world here—the scrabbling sound of a dog's nails on wood. She heard Lizbet's excited and instantly muffled giggle and the soft voice of the man she loved saying something to their little girl.

"Is it on right, Uncle Cord? Can I let him go now?"

"Let him go, sweetie. He knows he's home," Cord replied, laughter in his voice.

Julia pushed the screen door open, and then the scrabbling noise became a big German shepherd running along the whole length of the porch toward her. He was wearing a huge red bow around his neck, she saw as she dropped to her knees and opened her arms wide—a huge red bow, just like the first time Cord had given him to her.

"King!" she cried, and at the sound of his name the dog ran to her arms, that heavy tail beating like a metronome and those deep brown eyes glowing with adoration. He was licking the tears from her face, but she didn't care, and she couldn't believe it.

"We couldn't tell you, Auntie Julia." Lizbet was hopping up and down excitedly, her tiny heart-shaped face shining with happiness. "Uncle Cord said it was touch and glow there for a while, so he made me promise not to tell you. But the vet says King's as good as new, except for the place where they shaved his fur off. It'll grow back in, don't worry."

"How—what—" Julia's voice broke, and she looked wonderingly at Cord, her face wet with tears of joy.

"One of the cops from the canine unit found him the night of your accident." He hunkered down beside her, pulling Lizbet close with one arm and pushing the hair out of Julia's eyes with a gentle hand. "The bullet creased his skull and gave him a massive concussion—he must have been comatose when we saw him, honey. When they told me there was a chance that surgery could save him, I asked them to do all they could, but they couldn't give me any promises." A shadow crossed his features. "Maybe I should have told you, but like Lizbet said, it was touch and glow there for a long time."

He grinned wryly, holding her eyes with his. "Forgive me?"

"Forgive—" She shook her head, laughing and crying at the same time, stroking King's velvety pricked ears. "Oh, Cord, sometimes you're just the *densest* of men! But I guess that's one of the reasons I love you so much."

King beat his tail on the porch, and Lizbet swung her gaze from one to the other of them expectantly. She gave an impatient hop.

"Well, *say* it!" she prompted with a giggle. "Say what you *always* say!"

Cord's dark gaze met Julia's hazel one over the head of the little girl. Julia smiled. She'd spring her surprise on them all at dinner, she thought happily, touching her stomach.

"Always have." She reached out and tucked a stray strand of strawberry-red hair behind one tiny ear, but her eyes stayed on his.

"Always will," Cord said softly...

...and in one dark eye Julia could see a speck of green, like the reflection of this perfect summer's day....

* * * * *

How To Marry A Monarch

Wanted: One Prince

But Princess Sophie Vlastos of Carpathia knew how
unlikely she was to find him in her home kingdom.
So she reinvented herself—as Lisa Stone.
Nanny extraordinaire. In Detroit. Detroit?

Now, instead of reporting to the queen, her boss was
Steven Koleski. Plumber. Part-time photographer.
Guardian of five beautiful children.

And handsome as any prince she'd ever seen…

Plain-Jane Princess.
The first book in Karen Templeton's
new miniseries, *How To Marry a Monarch.*
Coming in August 2001, only from
Silhouette Intimate Moments.

And coming in December 2001, look for
Honky-Tonk Cinderella, Prince Alek's story,
only from Silhouette Intimate Moments.

Available at your favorite retail outlet.

Silhouette®
Where love comes alive™

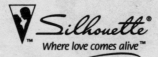

HARLEQUIN "SILHOUETTE MAKES YOU A STAR!" CONTEST 1308
OFFICIAL RULES
NO PURCHASE NECESSARY TO ENTER

1. To enter, follow directions published in the offer to which you are responding. Contest begins June 1, 2001, and ends on September 28, 2001. Entries must be postmarked by September 28, 2001, and received by October 5, 2001. Enter by hand-printing (or typing) on an 8 ½" x 11" piece of paper your name, address (including zip code), contest number/name and attaching a script containing <u>500 words</u> or less, <u>along with drawings, photographs or magazine cutouts, or combinations thereof</u> (i.e., collage) <u>on no larger than 9" x 12"</u> piece of paper, describing how the <u>Silhouette books make romance come alive for you.</u> Mail via first-class mail to: Harlequin "Silhouette Makes You a Star!" Contest 1308, (in the U.S.) P.O. Box 9069, Buffalo, NY 14269-9069, (in Canada) P.O. Box 637, Fort Erie, Ontario, Canada L2A 5X3. Limit one entry per person, household or organization.

2. Contests will be judged by a panel of members of the Harlequin editorial, marketing and public relations staff. Fifty percent of criteria will be judged against script and fifty percent will be judged against drawing, photographs and/or magazine cutouts. Judging criteria will be based on the following:

   - Sincerity—25%
   - Originality and Creativity—50%
   - Emotionally Compelling—25%

   In the event of a tie, duplicate prizes will be awarded. Decisions of the judges are final.

3. All entries become the property of Torstar Corp. and may be used for future promotional purposes. Entries will not be returned. No responsibility is assumed for lost, late, illegible, incomplete, inaccurate, nondelivered or misdirected mail.

4. Contest open only to residents of the U.S. <u>(except Puerto Rico)</u> and Canada who are 18 years of age or older, and is void wherever prohibited by law; all applicable laws and regulations apply. Any litigation within the Province of Quebec respecting the conduct or organization of a publicity contest may be submitted to the Régie des alcools, des courses et des jeux for a ruling. Any litigation respecting the awarding of a prize may be submitted to the Régie des alcools, des courses et des jeux only for the purpose of helping the parties reach a settlement. Employees and immediate family members of Torstar Corp. and D. L. Blair, Inc., their affiliates, subsidiaries and all other agencies, entities and persons connected with the use, marketing or conduct of this contest are not eligible to enter. Taxes on prizes are the sole responsibility of the winner. Acceptance of any prize offered constitutes permission to use winner's name, photograph or other likeness for the purposes of advertising, trade and promotion on behalf of Torstar Corp., its affiliates and subsidiaries without further compensation to the winner, unless prohibited by law.

5. Winner will be determined no later than November 30, 2001, and will be notified by mail. Winner will be required to sign and return an Affidavit of Eligibility/Release of Liability/Publicity Release form within 15 days after winner notification. Noncompliance within that time period may result in disqualification and an alternative winner may be selected. All travelers must execute a Release of Liability prior to ticketing and must possess required travel documents (e.g., passport, photo ID) where applicable. Trip must be booked by December 31, 2001, and completed within one year of notification. No substitution of prize permitted by winner. Torstar Corp. and D. L. Blair, Inc., their parents, affiliates and subsidiaries are not responsible for errors in printing of contest, entries and/or game pieces. In the event of printing or other errors that may result in unintended prize values or duplication of prizes, all affected game pieces or entries shall be null and void. **Purchase or acceptance of a product offer does not improve your chances of winning.**

6. Prizes: (1) Grand Prize—A 2-night/3-day trip for two (2) to New York City, including round-trip coach air transportation nearest winner's home and hotel accommodations (double occupancy) at The Plaza Hotel, a glamorous afternoon makeover at <u>a trendy New York spa</u>, $1,000 in U.S. spending money and an opportunity to <u>have a professional photo taken and appear in a Silhouette advertisement</u> (approximate retail value: $7,000). (10) Ten Runner-Up Prizes of gift packages (retail value $50 ea.). Prizes consist of only those items listed as part of the prize. Limit one prize per person. Prize is valued in U.S. currency.

7. For the name of the winner (available after December 31, 2001) send a self-addressed, stamped envelope to: Harlequin "Silhouette Makes You a Star!" Contest 1197 Winners, P.O. Box 4200 Blair, NE 68009-4200 or you may access the www.eHarlequin.com Web site through February 28, 2002.

Contest sponsored by Torstar Corp., P.O Box 9042, Buffalo, NY 14269-9042.

SRMYAS2

Silhouette® —

where love comes alive—online...

eHARLEQUIN.com

your romantic
books

♥ **Shop online!** Visit Shop eHarlequin and discover a wide selection of new releases and classic favorites at great discounted prices.

♥ **Read our daily and weekly Internet exclusive serials,** and participate in our interactive novel in the reading room.

♥ **Ever dreamed of being a writer?** Enter your chapter for a chance to become a featured author in our Writing Round Robin novel.

• • • • • • •

your
community

♥ **Have a Heart-to-Heart** with other members about the latest books and meet your favorite authors.

♥ **Discuss your romantic dilemma** in the Tales from the Heart message board.

your romantic
life

♥ **Check out our feature articles** on dating, flirting and other important romance topics and get your daily love dose with tips on how to keep the romance alive every day.

• • • • • • •

your romantic
escapes

♥ **Learn what the stars have in store for you** with our daily Passionscopes and weekly Erotiscopes.

♥ **Get the latest scoop** on your favorite royals in Royal Romance.

All this and more available at
www.eHarlequin.com
on Women.com Networks

SINTA1R